"Now do you remember me?"

Her arms empty, she tried blinking to drag herself back to the present. Elian swam into view. His azure eyes shot signals, signals that she couldn't decipher. *What does he want of me? Why can't we live for the moment? Just be in the here and now?* For an instant she thought of lying, but somehow she knew he would see through it, that it would only push him farther away. "I'm sorry."

He lifted his hands, then dropped them in frustration. He gazed at her, pleading. She couldn't help him. Bits of him seemed familiar—as though those features belonged to someone else she'd known a long time ago. Other bits, like his deep, gruff voice and his air of insolence, were strange and new. A fleeting sense of abandonment passed through her. Whoever he reminded her of had left her once before. She didn't want that loneliness again. She turned from him and put the key in the door. He caught her arm. "We'll meet again, Sydney."

She tried to match the hope in his voice. "Perhaps we will."

Praise for M. S. Spencer

"The two love stories are woven delightfully with one another…would love to see more by Spencer."
~*MR Reviews*
~*~
"This book…kept me on the edge of my seat, burning pages wanting to know how it turned out."
~*Rochelle's Reviews*
~*~
"I was completely drawn in. The characters were vivid and real. I found myself wanting to skip to the end to reassure myself it would all work out."
~*Gotromancereviews*
~*~
"What a great read!…I just loved Sydney, she was hilarious, full of life, adventurous, loving, protective, passionate, competitive."
~*SSLY*

Lapses of Memory

by

M. S. Spencer

This is a work of fiction. Names, characters, places, and incidents are either the product of the author's imagination or are used fictitiously, and any resemblance to actual persons living or dead, business establishments, events, or locales, is entirely coincidental.

Lapses of Memory

COPYRIGHT © 2017 by Meredith Ellsworth

All rights reserved. No part of this book may be used or reproduced in any manner whatsoever without written permission of the author or The Wild Rose Press, Inc. except in the case of brief quotations embodied in critical articles or reviews.
Contact Information: info@thewildrosepress.com

Cover Art by *RJ Morris*

The Wild Rose Press, Inc.
PO Box 708
Adams Basin, NY 14410-0708
Visit us at www.thewildrosepress.com

Publishing History
First Champagne Rose Edition, 2017
Print ISBN 978-1-5092-1292-7
Digital ISBN 978-1-5092-1293-4

Published in the United States of America

Dedication

To Michael R…
Remember

Chapter One

Alexandria, Virginia, Present Day

"I only remember bits and pieces you know—flashes and illuminated scenes. After all, I was only five years old."

"I'm amazed you remember anything, Mother. At that age, most children are oblivious to their surroundings."

The older woman shook her head. "Not me. I guess I was born to be a journalist. Nothing escaped my attention."

"And yet you're guilty of serial amnesia when it comes to Father."

The woman in the bed leaned back against the pillows, a blissful smile on her face. "Not entirely. I never forgot the set of Elian's jaw, or the way his forehead crinkled when he kissed me, or the cowlick."

"Perhaps," snorted her daughter. "But what about his hair color? His height? His weight?"

"Those things aren't important, Olivia. Somewhere in here"—the woman tapped her abdomen—"I knew him."

"Wandering through your digestive tract?"

"Possibly. Most of my encounters with him were associated with food."

"Not sex?"

1

"No, of course not. Well, not in the beginning." The woman's eyes glazed over.

"Mother!" Olivia settled back in her chair and pulled out her notebook. "You agreed to do this. You can't weasel out of it. All we need is a working title. *Sydney Bellek Meets Elian Davies*. Or should it be *Elian Davies versus Sydney Bellek*?"

"How about *Alien versus Predator*?"

"I believe that one's taken. I want your story."

"Sex scenes included?"

"Hey, you want this to be a best seller, don't you?"

"On what list?"

"Mother, you're doing it again. You're a writer. This should be easy. Just pretend it's fiction."

"That's your job." She rolled her eyes. "How on earth did two hard-bitten, hard-nosed journalists spawn a romance novelist?"

"Two wrongs make a right?"

Her mother grinned. "Okay. If I'm going to write the Great American Novel, I'd best start at the beginning. Let's see…as I pushed my way through the birth canal…"

"Mother!"

"I told you, no detail is ever too small."

"Except…"

"All right, all right." She took a sip from the shot glass at her bedside table. "Lemon vodka. You found it?"

Olivia poured her another tot. "Made it myself. I used the recipe you'd tucked into your *Joy of Cooking*."

"Ah yes. Boris gave it to me. He was such a dear. I told you about his wonderful Russian restaurant in Istanbul, didn't I?"

"The place modeled after the one in the Greta Garbo movie *Ninotchka*?"

"The other way around, dear. The other way around." She tossed the vodka off. "Yes, I'd only just arrived in Istanbul, and Tony took me for drinks and *zakuski*—that's Russian for *mezze*. Dear me, is there an English word for little dishes like that? *Hmm*. Anyway, it was called the Tsar's Kitchen—the restaurant, that is. A tiny warren of rooms up in Beyoğlu—"

"Mother!"

Sydney stopped, glass halfway to her lips. "What?"

Olivia indicated the notebook. "It's 1958. You're five years old. You're heading to Paris with your parents," she prompted.

"All right, I'll indulge you, but you still haven't told me when Benjamin is coming over."

"Not for a while. I told you he's in Connecticut while Congress is in recess, didn't I?"

Her mother peered at Olivia. Her sharp eyes—rich brown with flecks of copper that flashed in the lamplight—bored into her daughter's blue ones. "I see…" She managed to put a full measure of speculation into the words.

"Mother, I'm warning you. No more vodka till we're at least past the first meeting."

Sydney grabbed the glass and held it tight to her breast. "You wouldn't dare!"

Olivia laughed, a tinkling, infectious sound. "Come on, give."

****

Boeing 377 Stratocruiser, 1958

"Come along, Sydney. Sergei is already in his seat. It's nearly time for takeoff."

"Mama, what is this building? It's not a house. It has wings, just like Sergei's toy, but this one has wheels. Where are we going? And who are all these people, Mama? Mama?"

"I'll answer all your questions once we get you strapped in, Sydney…There."

The little girl closed her mouth to keep the questions from spewing out. The days leading up to this adventure had been so confused, so rushed, and her mother seemed especially out of sorts. She wished her father would appear—he always made things better. Sydney plucked at the seat belt that held her fast. At least she could move her arms, but when she stretched them out they smacked into her brother's face.

"Leave me alone, Syd! I'm trying to look out the window." He tilted his head and peered out. "Looks like the rain has stopped. That's good, right, Mother? For flying, I mean?"

Sydney pouted. "How come I have to sit here and Sergei gets the window? I can't see anything. I can't move." Panic suddenly squeezed her chest, clutching at her with icy claws. "I don't like it here, Sergei. I want to get out!" The ceiling of the plane began to fall toward her. She cowered in her seat. "Sergei! Mama!"

Just then strong hands undid the clasp and pulled her into strong arms. "S'okay, Polly. I'm here. You can sit on my lap for a bit."

Sydney looked up into a dear face. "Papa, you made it. You're here!"

A dark-skinned man with a luxuriant black moustache chucked her under the chin. "You weren't worried, were you, Pollyanna?"

"No, Papa." The little girl snuggled into his chest

and sighed. The noise of other passengers boarding filled the cabin.

One childish voice rose above the rest. "This is one of the new transatlantic airliners, isn't it, Mother? It's bigger than I expected. When will we take off? We're going to fly across the ocean all night, right, Mother? So how…"

"Shhh, Elian. Your father has to take care of our luggage. After that, he'll tell you anything you want to know."

A tall woman in a well-tailored suit and heels tipped the steward and gently pushed a little boy into the row behind Sydney. Sydney nestled deeper under her father's arm but kept an eye on the comings and goings of the other passengers.

The boy subsided, and she heard the woman snap his seat belt. A minute later, his tinny voice cut through the hubbub. "Hey look, Mother. I can see people on the ground. Isn't it dangerous for them to be wandering around among these big machines? Couldn't they be crushed?"

"No, no, dear. They know what they're doing."

A steward made his way slowly down the aisle, checking the passengers. "Mr. Bellek? You'll have to put your little girl in her own seat during takeoff." He peered at Sydney, and she stared back as rudely as she dared, hoping to scare him off and leave her in the safety of her father's arms.

"Certainly." Her father lifted Sydney, but before he set her down, he bounced her a couple of times, which cheered her immensely. As her head came up over the seat, she spied the boy. He was staring out the window, rapt. She examined his profile. People's faces fascinated her. Her mother insisted that meant she'd be an artist—her father laughingly opted for detective.

This little boy sported a sharp chin and a long neck. Unusual for the time, his reddish brown hair had been allowed to grow over his ears, and a curl touched his forehead. She couldn't see his eyes, but his sturdy, well-shaped fingers plastered the window. He turned as she rose on the second bounce and smiled at her.

Just then the sun came out. It picked up the droplets of moisture in the air and made a rainbow out of them, streaking through the cabin. It touched the crown of the boy's head and curved toward her. Sydney sensed it could connect them if only she knew how to cross it. The little boy held his hand out, almost as though he wanted her to.

"Hi, I'm Elian."

Sydney could only stare at him, open-mouthed.

The steward returned. "We don't often have children fly with us," he said with a smile. "It's very brave of you." He looked at Sydney's father. "We've been advised that there will be a short delay before we can begin our taxi. The captain would like to invite the children forward to see the cockpit." Without waiting for an official parental nod, too often slow in coming, Sydney, Sergei, and Elian leapt out of their seats and fought each other up the aisle.

The captain and his co-pilot greeted the children. "My, my, we have some young folks here. I'll bet this is your first flight, eh?"

The distinguished man in the navy uniform couldn't help but intimidate and excite. Three grave faces nodded, staring at a dashboard that didn't look anything like the ones in their parents' Oldsmobiles.

"Well, we expect you all to behave according to protocol. It will be a long flight across the ocean, but you're not to worry. Captain Maxwell and I have done the trip many times. See?"

He pointed to a set of golden wings on his lapel. The children politely peered at it. He paused. "Say, would you like your own wings? We usually present them to passengers in honor of their first flight."

Three silent nods. Six very wide eyes.

"Edward? Do you have some wings for these young pilots-in-training?"

The steward held out three boxes. Sydney opened hers to find a small pin. It had silver wings and a logo that read "Pan American Airlines." She whispered, "Thank you," as she'd been taught, before allowing Edward to lead her back to her parents.

The boy Elian walked behind her. He punched her arm. "Neato, huh?"

His eyes gleamed. They were large and bright blue. Many years later, she would describe them as the color of the Caribbean Sea at high noon. Now they just seemed pretty. She punched him back.

"Sydney, come on." Her brother impatiently dragged her onto her seat. The engines rumbled, and the plane pulled slowly away.

"Are we floating, Papa? It feels like we're on water."

Her brother snickered. "You're such a lamebrain, Syd. We're on wheels. Like a car."

"Oh." Sydney refrained from pointing out that this airplane was a lot bigger than a car. They rolled over the tarmac, paused, then started to move fast, then faster and faster. She couldn't breathe. Thinking someone was pressing a hand on her chest, she looked down, but nothing held her.

Her father handed her a lollipop. "Here, take this and suck on it. Now, lean back and breathe in and out slowly."

Sydney didn't argue—she wasn't allowed candy very often, and she wasn't about to turn it down, even though a pile of heavy books crushed her chest. A moment later, they entered a bubble of stillness, like the eye of a storm. She couldn't have explained how, but she knew they were airborne.

Her brother leaned over. "Hear that grinding sound? That's the wheels. They tuck them right into the tummy of the plane."

Sydney stared at the back of the seat before her and reveled in the feeling of freedom. *I'm in the air. I'm in the air!* A sunbeam shot through the porthole, reigniting the rainbow.

The steward came down the aisle, hanging on to the backs of the seats to steady himself as the plane banked. It reminded Sydney of sailing the Atlantic in her grandfather's boat. The steward stopped at their row. "We will begin serving dinner in half an hour." He handed Sydney's father a card. "Here is the menu. I can take your orders now."

Sydney's father looked it over. "The children's menu offers roast chicken or a hamburger. Sergei?"

"Hamburger. Wow. Cool."

"Sydney?"

She refused to copy her brother. "Chippen please."

Her father laughed. "Chippen it is." He gave their orders to the steward and turned away to talk to their mother.

Soon after, a stewardess in a white blouse and perky little blue cap stopped a cart by their seats. She set their trays with silver cutlery embossed with the Pan Am logo and served their dinner from the cart onto bone china plates.

Sergei cuffed his sister. "It's as fancy as Grandmother's house, isn't it?"

Sydney said nothing, since she'd just taken a bite of chicken and she knew her mother would be angry if she spoke with her mouth full.

After dinner, many of the adults headed down a circular stairway. "Papa, where are they going?"

"There's a lounge downstairs. For grownups."

"Oh." Sydney couldn't imagine how a narrow little house like this could have so many rooms.

Her father patted her head. "Why don't you children stretch your legs while your mother and I go downstairs?"

Elian followed Sydney and Sergei down the aisle. They marched up and down without speaking for a bit, then Sydney pointed at Elian's loafers. "You're allowed to wear those?"

He looked down absently. "Sure. Why not?"

Sergei said, "We have to wear tie shoes all the time. Gee, you have big feet, kid. How old are you?"

"I'll be seven next month. You?"

"I'm nine." Sergei drew himself up proudly. "My sister Sydney here is five. We're going to Paris."

Sydney condescended to elaborate. "Pawes. It's in Fwance."

"I know." The boy let his gaze travel over her, as though he were memorizing her features. Sydney was too young to know she could have won the Gerber baby contest, or indeed any beauty contest, even at five. Her golden tresses framed a heart-shaped face, her nut-brown eyes were large and liquid, stippled with golden flecks like pyrite-veined jasper pebbles. Her sharp little chin mirrored Elian's. "I'm going to Berlin. That's in Germany. It's a war zone."

Since Sydney had no clue what a war zone was, she shrugged and asked, "Do you want to color with me?"

"Okay."

A few minutes later, Sydney's mother found them. "Time for bed, Polly." To Sydney's amazement, the stewardess pulled a trapdoor down, revealing a snug little berth. Her mother helped her up the ladder and tucked her in.

"Aren't you sleeping here, Mama?"

"No dear." She gestured at the seat below. "We'll sleep in these recliners—they're called Sleeperettes. They're very comfortable."

Sydney regarded them dubiously. Her little bed seemed much homier. She heard Sergei climb up into the next berth. "Wait'll I tell my friends," he whispered. "We're actually sleeping on a plane!"

He waited in vain for an answer. Sydney had fallen asleep.

The next morning the little girl awoke to a whole new world. Below her lay sparkling marble monuments and a ribbon of river that meandered through what looked to her like ancient ruins. Her father pulled her on his lap and pointed. "Paris. Your new home."

When the plane landed, Sydney looked for the little boy Elian. The terminal was crowded and busy, and she felt very small. Through the forest of bags and red caps and people, she spied a tuft of russet hair bobbing along between two adults. As she watched, he paused and turned to look back. He saw her and waved. She waved back.

Chapter Two

Alexandria, Present Day

"And you never saw him again."

"My dear, Olivia, you wouldn't be here if that were true."

"But he went off to Berlin and you to Paris. How did you ever reconnect?"

The older woman held her glass out. "Another tot, please, dear." She sipped thoughtfully. "My theory is that the rainbow created an unbreakable bond between us. Diaphanous, yes. Tentative and translucent. Wobbly, hard to walk on." She grinned. "But there. Whenever we hit the same part of the spectrum we'd meet up. And it wasn't always pretty."

"Okay, the second time? That was on your way to…" Olivia checked her notes. "Morocco, right?"

"Yes." Sydney lay back and closed her eyes. "So romantic, Morocco. So exotic." A slight snore came from the direction of the bed.

"Mother?"

"*Mmm.*"

Olivia rose and pulled the quilt up under her mother's chin. The quilt, her grandmother's, had been a fixture since her earliest childhood. Squares and triangles of faded calico were sewn in a comforting geometric pattern around the pieced picture of an airplane. She gazed with love at her mother.

"I'll see you tomorrow, then, shall I?" she whispered. Sydney waved languidly. As her daughter turned to leave, her mother opened one eye and reached toward her bedside table. Olivia knew she'd stay up half the night drafting missives and composing jeremiads. Sydney Bellek had started writing at the age of six and never stopped. She had no time for memoirs—that was Olivia's job. These days she scribbled myriad letters to editors, using trenchant metaphors that almost always stopped short of scatological to describe what she thought of their newspapers.

Olivia nodded to a woman in her sixties with close-cropped iron-gray hair, dressed in a severe black jersey dress and Peter Pan collar. "Good night, Alice."

Alice pursed her lips. "Writing again?"

"Yup."

"She'll be the death of me."

Olivia refrained from expressing her thought—*just to spite you, Alice*—and said instead, "The thought of Father keeps her young."

****

"I'm ready."

"I'm not." Sydney came out of the bathroom. "I'm having a bad hair day."

Her daughter held a thumb up and took Sydney's measure. "You are not. As usual, your hair is perfect."

"Yes, perfectly tousled. I'm too old to look like Meg Ryan."

"Meg Ryan's older than you are, you ninny." Olivia's brilliant cerulean eyes creased with laughter. She indicated the light woolen sheath her mother wore.

"I love that coppery color on you. It makes your eyes glow."

Sydney surveyed her frock. "Oh, this old thing? I had to wear something for our lunch outing."

"And the fact that it shows off legs that by rights should belong to a twenty-year-old is just serendipity."

By way of answer, Sydney retrieved her purse and gestured at the door. Olivia helped her mother down the stairs. "Did you call for the car?"

"Pickens had an errand to do this morning. He'll be here soon."

As the two women waited, Sydney remarked, "I'm looking forward to getting the Morgan back from the shop."

Olivia laughed. "Why? You can't drive the thing until your ankle heals."

"I know, but that should be any day now. I'm tired of Pickens shuttling me everywhere. I feel like that old woman in the movie…Miss Daisy, that's it."

"She was a curmudgeon too."

"Oh I see. I'm younger than Meg Ryan, but more cantankerous than Jessica Tandy."

A sleek Mercedes sedan pulled up to the curb, and a man of stiffly erect bearing in a forest green uniform stepped out. He handed Sydney and Olivia into the back seat and took the wheel.

Sydney eyed her daughter. "Have you heard from Benjamin?"

"Just an email this morning."

"Not even a phone call?"

"Mother, it's quicker and easier to send an email. He's on the road, and Senator McNichol has town halls and meet-and-greets every day for the next two weeks."

"How come Benjamin has to do all the district stuff? Doesn't the senator have a home office?"

Olivia darted a cross look at her mother. "Why are *you* whining? Ben's not your boyfriend." When Sydney didn't respond, she sighed. "The chief of staff in McNichol's home office is out on maternity leave, so Ben's in charge of the advance and prep work. Plus, Beth's not there. I told you the senator's wife stayed in Washington this time, didn't I?"

"From what I've heard she's not much use to him anyway. These trophy wives rarely live up to their name." Her mother spoke absently as they watched a tourist in Bermuda shorts and a T-shirt that barely covered his lamentable belly snap a picture of his large, milk-fed family. "I don't understand why McNichol's campaigning now. The election isn't for six months," she muttered with a vexed frown.

"I've already explained this to you." Olivia took a deep, noisy breath and blew it out. "He's not campaigning. The Senate's in recess for the Easter holiday, giving members a chance to communicate directly with their constituents. It's the most important part of the job. What with this controversial transportation bill in the works, it's vital that he hear from the voters."

"You sound like a campaign ad."

Olivia sighed. "You journalists. You think all politicians are slick liars whose only interest is in reelection."

"Well, aren't they?"

"No. Senator McNichol is a decent, hard-working man. Ben wouldn't work for him if he weren't."

Sydney grudgingly concurred. "I suppose he can't

be all bad since he's a veterinarian. I just wish he weren't from Connecticut." She lapsed into meditation as the brick townhouses of Old Town Alexandria zipped by them. The earliest Piedmont azaleas were in bloom, their delicate lavender spikes blending with the cheery yellow forsythia. Limning the bushes, gold-kissed daffodils peeked through their stockade of leaves. The cobblestone streets swarmed with delivery vans and construction trucks off-loading materials.

With a shriek of tires, the car suddenly skidded. The chauffeur spoke over his shoulder. "Sorry, ladies. There's still a bit of ice on the roads. Don't know if we're out of the woods yet weather-wise."

"In April? I do hope you're wrong, Pickens." Sydney touched her daughter's elbow. "Where are we going, Olivia?"

"I thought Vermilion. It's quiet for lunch and you can get on with your story."

"Ah, the next chapter."

****

Boeing 707, 1966

"So, Mama, what is this country…this…Mrucko… like? When does the plane leave? Do we get dinner? Why does Sergei get the window seat *again*?"

"You lost the toss, dear. The plane is on schedule. We get dinner. And dessert. And you'll see Morocco soon enough and will be able to make up your own mind."

Sydney slumped on the seat, but after a quick sulk, she sat up and scrambled onto her brother's lap. He wiggled out from under her and stood bent over in the small space between the passenger seats. "Hey!"

"I just want to watch the takeoff. Then you can

have your old seat."

As they rose into the air, Sydney's father handed her a lollipop with a wink. "For old times' sake, pretty Pollyanna."

She sucked on it thoughtfully. When she'd said goodbye to her friends at school, she had made a pretense of being world-weary and bored. "Tangier, yeah. I hear it has a great beach. Should be cool. Better than Kensington Junior High, anyway." She'd waited for Charlie to take the bait, but he just kept bouncing that stupid basketball.

Her best friend Sandy watched her watching him, then took her arm and dragged her down the hall. "Come on, Syd, you're wasting your time. Even if he cared, he wouldn't show it."

There's nothing more toxic to a thirteen-year-old girl's heart than indifference. She stuck her pointy little chin out and followed her friend, pledging to pour her feelings out to her diary before setting it on fire.

She wouldn't admit it even to Sandy, but she felt a little apprehensive now that they were really leaving. UNESCO had given her father a choice of Morocco or Berlin. Sergei wanted Morocco. Her mother wanted Berlin. As for Sydney, she claimed she'd be happy going anywhere—the lust for adventure that burned so strong in her father's heart found an echo in hers—but Berlin struck a chord. "Don't we know someone who lives in Berlin?" She had a quick memory flash of a cowlick and blue water.

Her father shook his head. "I don't think so. I must say, I'm leaning toward Morocco. Of course, I'll have to spend a lot of time in Rabat while you people loll around on the beaches of Tangier—but to set up a royal school for the king—what an opportunity!"

And so they went to Morocco. As the stewardess handed them pillows and blankets from the ceiling compartments, Sydney tried to remember her last international flight. "I was four, right?"

"No, five, dummy. Our flight to Paris."

She giggled and looked up. "I guess we don't get to sleep up there this time, huh?"

Her brother snorted. "They don't even have those reclining Sleeperettes anymore. And I bet there's no bar on the lower deck." He grimaced. "I bet there's no lower deck at all!"

His mother raised her eyebrows. "My heavens, what snobs you are. This Boeing 707 jet will get us to Paris a lot faster than that old Stratocruiser we took in 1958 did. We'll be there in about eight hours."

Sergei squirmed in his seat. "Yeah, but the old plane was a lot more comfortable. I feel like a sardine in here." He looked over the tops of the seats. "There must be over a hundred passengers on board. That's at least twenty more people than the 377 carried. Look at that big, fat fellow over there…Say, how much weight can this plane handle?"

"Sergei!" Sydney's father patted her head and glared at her brother. "That's not useful talk."

Sydney loved the attention from her often-absent father, so she didn't tell him Sergei's attempts at scaring her didn't work. Even at thirteen, she looked at every unanticipated event, every deviation from the path, as a chance to learn something new.

The three passengers in the row in front of Sydney—a couple about her parents' age, and a boy a little older than she—had been switching seats and arguing since the plane took off. As he moved from window to aisle, the boy scanned the back of the plane and caught sight of Sydney. Their eyes locked but quickly slid past each other.

"Hey, Syd, did you see that kid?" Sergei nodded at the boy. "He looks familiar. Friend of yours?"

"Are you kidding?" *Sheesh.*

Sergei lapsed into silence, and Sydney into thought. Sergei was right. Something about their neighbor's face…When he stood up again, she furtively checked him out. Tapered chin, russet hair a little too long. *And sticking up all over the place.* His blue eyes were pleasant, but the hook nose kind of overpowered the nice parts. *Also, his ears are too big for his head.* She supposed he might grow into them, but what if he didn't? Despite his unusual appearance, she couldn't place him. *The box boy at the A&P?*

She looked up in time to see the boy head up the aisle toward the bathroom. His mop of chestnut hair curled over his collar, one stalk waving in the air. *He has a cowlick! Poor slob.* Sydney's hand went automatically to the back of her head, smoothing the hair down. She hated her cowlick. It always made the hair lie awkwardly across the crown of her head. If only her mother would let her cut her hair short. Her friend Sandy claimed that would calm the cowlick. Sydney's tight braids only seemed to make it worse and yet her mother refused to let her cut them off.

"You'll thank me someday, dear. Your grandmother has hair down to her knees, you know. It's beautiful."

Yeah, yeah.

The boy returned. As he neared her row, he

stumbled and put a hand on his seat back to steady himself. She didn't turn away fast enough and caught the full brunt of his smile, his lips opening to reveal perfect white teeth. His blue eyes sparkled, and joy suffused his face. "Hi."

Sydney scrunched down in her seat, waiting for the blush to subside. "Hi."

The boy leaned over. "What did you say?"

Sydney looked up into a turquoise sea. Something caught in her throat. She finally dislodged it and shouted, "Hi!" so loud other passengers twisted to see where the noise came from.

The boy jerked back and stared at her. Then he abruptly sat down and began to whisper to his father. Sydney, for her part, considered her options and settled on melting into a little puddle of humiliation. With any luck, she could stay liquid for the rest of the trip.

She slumped down and shut her eyes tight. After a suitable interval, she opened them, only to find her vision filled with a sheaf of brown cowlick sticking up over the seat. She watched it bob and weave along with the boy's head. *Does he ever stop moving?*

Sergei took a walk up the aisle. On his way back, he stopped at the boy's seat. "Hey, have we met somewhere before?"

Sydney couldn't hear the boy's response. Sergei said, "I'm Sergei Bellek." He nodded toward Sydney. "That's my sister Sydney. We're on our way to Morocco. You?"

She leaned forward to catch the boy's answer. "Eddie. Eddie Davies. I'm going with the 'rents to Gibraltar."

"Really? I think we're supposed to take the ferry

from Gibraltar. You stopping in Paris?"

"Yeah, but just to make the connection. Then we fly to Spain."

"We're driving through Spain. Small world, isn't it?"

The rest of the conversation was too low for her to hear.

****

"We only have a short time in Paris, Sergei. I'm afraid we won't be able to leave the airport."

"Awwww, not fair. It's been so long. I hoped we could go to that little bistro—remember, Mama? The one we went to every Sunday when Papa was away?"

"You mean Le Café des Gourmands? The restaurant where we ordered the same meal every visit?" His mother sighed happily.

The remark reminded Sydney that her mother put up only grudgingly with the constant moves and travel that life with Father entailed. She'd once confided to her daughter that if she had her druthers, she'd live in one house for the rest of her life and never travel again. "I wouldn't even watch travelogues!" Sydney considered her mother slightly eccentric after that.

"Yeah, that place." Sergei recited with relish, "We always had escargots Bourguignonne, and steak *au poivre*, and—"

Sydney interrupted. "*Mousse au chocolat!*"

"So, can we go?" Both children directed imploring eyes at their mother.

She shook her head with real regret. "Maybe on the return trip, my dears. We don't have enough time now—your father has to start his job in three weeks, and we have to get settled in Tangier. As soon as Papa brings the car around, we'll be heading to Chartres."

Sergei leaned forward, eyes bright. "Chartres, and then the Loire Valley, and then Provence, right? I can hardly wait to see the Roman ruins down there. When do we get to Spain?"

"In about a week. Unless we run into bad weather crossing the mountains."

The boy frowned. "What's this Andorra place anyway? It sounds too small to have regular-sized people."

Sydney swatted him. "You big dope, it's a real live country." She closed her eyes in happy contemplation. "It's supposed to lie hidden way up in a mountain pass in the…in the…Pibblees—"

"The Pyrenees, dear."

"Whatever. And everyone smuggles. It's a…er…den of thieves." She sighed, transported to a thrilling land of pirates and brigands and devil-may-care adventurers.

"Well," grumbled Sergei, "I just want to get to Morocco. And the beach and the girls."

His sister stuck her tongue out at him.

"Sydney, manners!"

The young girl settled back on the hard plastic seat. She hated the endless waits in cold, unfriendly terminals that detracted from the excitement of travel. She kicked her legs out and in, counting the seconds.

"Ouch! Watch where you swing those!"

She curled the offending limbs under the chair. "Oh, er…Eddie? Sorry."

He rubbed his knee and eyed her thoughtfully. "I remember you. You were much littler—and you didn't have those dumb braids. Now where…" He surveyed the terminal. "That's right. We were on the same flight to Paris eight years ago. I was almost seven. That's when my family moved to Berlin."

"We didn't land in this terminal though," Sydney said smugly. "That was Le Bourget. This is Orly. You don't remember as much as you think you do." Satisfied she had put him in his place, she began swinging her legs again.

Eddie jumped out of the way. "I remember important stuff. Like you." He stuck his chin out and intoned, "People are a priority with me."

That did it. "Hogwash. Go find your parents. I'm busy."

He spun on his heel, making a painful squeak on the tile floor with his sneakers, and marched away.

****

Sydney's first sight of the great rock that guarded the entrance to the Mediterranean Sea, one of the Pillars of Hercules, came as something of an anticlimax. They'd arrived at the port of Algeciras in Spain, gone through customs, and sat on the dock waiting for the ferry. Sydney's stomach growled and acid kept bubbling around in it looking for something to chew on. "Papa, we haven't eaten in six hours. When can we get some food?"

"Whining will not get you dinner, my little Pollyanna. It's a short hop to Gibraltar. We'll get something to eat there before we sail to Tangier. Don't worry."

At last, they boarded a small ferry with one open and one closed deck above the cars. Men packed the enclosed part, standing in unruly rows like cattle sensing the approach of feeding time. "Day laborers," whispered her father. He led his family up to the open deck. They seemed to be the only tourists.

Her father gave Sydney a few pesetas and let her go down the gangway to the snack bar. When Sergei saw her purchases—two Cadbury chocolate bars and a Fanta—he complained. "Mother, look what she bought! That's that French orange soda. It's always flat. Yuck." While he and her mother argued, Sydney took her food to the empty bow. She sat, happily sucking on the soda for a few minutes, before looking up to see a tiny harbor luring them into a bustling port town. A huge black triangle of solid rock loomed over it. Here and there she could make out monkeys jumping up and over the pilings.

"Sergei, look! Monkeys!"

Her brother shrugged with indifference. "They're called apes. The famous Gibraltar apes. Didn't you read about them?"

Sydney didn't want to admit she'd been too busy mooning over the inattentive Charlie and reading *To Sweep the Spanish Main* to research the places on their trip. Except for Andorra, but then *there be pirates*.

Mr. Bellek gathered his clan. "Children, the ferry to Tangier has been delayed until this evening. Let's leave our car in the lot, then head up the rock to the peak."

They piled into a taxi and climbed the narrow road that ascended the hill in sharp hairpin turns. "It's like riding up Pecos Bill's mountain," Sergei groaned. "I don't feel so good." Their driver slowed down, but the switchbacks coming one after another kept Sydney's knuckles white as her hands clutched the armrest. They pulled off the road close to the summit and tumbled out.

Her father strode to a low wall and waved a hand at the view. "Sergei, come here. See that? That's Morocco. There behind us is Spain."

Sydney gazed out at the vast, empty sea surrounding them. Sky and water blended together in an opaque, muddy brown mist. The Mediterranean sure wasn't as blue as the guidebook described it. Her mother gave Sydney a coin for the telescope. As she fiddled with the viewfinder, a furry face suddenly filled the lens. A monkey about three feet high scrabbled over the machine and chattered at her like an angry hermit.

"Don't worry, he won't attack. He'll bite your hand if you feed him though."

Sydney turned to see the boy from the plane. His blue eyes glinted in the sun, and his cowlick waved a salute. Without thinking, her hand went to her hair. For some reason her lips stuck together, and she could only nod idiotically. Eddie didn't seem to notice.

"People call them apes, but they're not. They're monkeys—macaques. Used to live all over North Africa." When she didn't answer he said, "How was Andorra? Were you kidnapped by cigarette smugglers?"

She checked his face for smirks. "No."

He stared at her, apparently expecting further elucidation. Instead, Sydney concentrated on the sore spot on her tongue where she'd bitten it. Finally he remarked, "I guess you're waiting for the ferry to Tangier?"

She nodded, thanking God for the cool breeze that fanned her hot cheeks.

"Your parents Foreign Service?"

"United Nations."

He looked her up and down. "U.N., huh? My father's here as American trade liaison. We don't have a consulate, let alone an embassy, and no other Americans that I've met. I'll be stuck on this island for a whole year."

"Um."

"I hear Tangier has some good beaches." He waited patiently for a reply.

"I guess so."

Sergei came up behind them. "My sister's a bit…er…shy, Eddie." Sydney shot him a look that mixed gratitude and hostility in asymmetric proportion. "My father works for UNESCO—the United Nations Educational Scientific and Cultural Organization. He's been assigned to help King Hassan II build a school in Rabat, but we get to hang out in Tangier. It's supposed to be really nice. You should hop the ferry some time and visit."

Eddie glanced at Sydney and grinned. "Thanks. Say, Sergei, did you know this is a free port?"

"No…what's that?" The two boys wandered away, chatting amiably. Sydney headed toward a rock wall and gently banged her head on it.

Chapter Three

Alexandria, Present Day

"Who was this Eddie, and why are you talking about him?"

Sydney put down her glass. "Why do you think I'm talking about him? He's Elian, your future father."

"What's with the Eddie then?"

"Oh, he was at that age when he considered his real name geeky. Eddie sounded nice and normal and American."

"Everything he wasn't."

"Oh, he was *nice* all right, but the pseudonym sure didn't make the prospects for recognition any brighter."

Olivia buttered a tiny pumpernickel roll. "He went back to Elian when he became a famous journalist, I suppose."

"Yes. By then, he thought it had dash and vigor and would attract women."

"As it did. I never mentioned this, but when I was twelve, a friend told me my father had a weird name, so I looked it up. Do you know what it means?"

Sydney nodded, her cheeks dimpling with pleasure. "I do. It's Welsh for a moment in time. I always thought that very appropriate, don't you?"

Olivia opened her mouth to reply, but the waiter's arm obscured her view. "Your mixed beet salad, ma'am."

"Thank you. You did leave the dill out, didn't you?"

"As ordered. Beets and feta in a lovely yogurt vinaigrette." He set a plate before Sydney. "And for you, ma'am, the shaved Brussels sprouts with apples, dates, and blue cheese."

Sydney surveyed Olivia's plate. "That looks good."

"She heaves a long-suffering sigh. You want a taste, Mom?"

Her companion snickered. "You know it always looks better from over here."

Olivia took a large bite and ate it slowly, making *mmmm* sounds calculated to annoy. "What are you having for an entrée?"

"The shad is running. Albert says they have roe today. Who could resist? And you?"

"I think the Amish chicken sandwich. You don't often find broccoli rabe."

"Okay, then, let's get a bottle of Montrachet, shall we?"

The waiter materialized. "I highly recommend the 2009 Domaine Thomas Morey Les Truffières, madame. Spicy aromas of peach and gardenia, yet still dry, the way you like it."

"Sounds perfect. Olivia?"

Olivia ordered, and they settled back with their appetizers. "All right, Mom. Next stop, Morocco."

Her mother took a slug of wine—ignoring Olivia's sniff of disapproval—and set her chin. "Give me a minute to relax, won't you?"

Her daughter kept her eyes on her plate, knowing what was coming.

"Before I go on with my story, I want to hear when Benjamin is coming back."

Olivia muttered, "He didn't say."

"McNichol has a field staff. Why does his Capitol Hill staff director have to be back in the state?"

"I already told you, Mother. The senator's home office manager is having a baby. McNichol needs Ben to take care of constituents while he takes care of Beth."

"The trophy wife? I thought she'd stayed in Washington?"

"She did. Apparently, she requires a lot of long-distance hand-holding." Olivia scowled. "Women like that are so exasperating." She paused, evidently deciding a more diplomatic response was in order. "Ben says she's a bit of a handful."

"And those are just her boobs."

"Mother!"

They were interrupted by the waiter, who set down their entrees with a nice Italian flourish and stood back proudly. They dutifully took bites and nodded archly at him before he reluctantly moved off.

"That chicken sandwich smells delicious."

Olivia curled her hands protectively over her plate. "No, you don't. I intend to eat every last morsel."

Sydney affected indifference. "I'm just saying. My shad roe is more than satisfactory. Really."

Hoping to deflect more comments on her beau's boss's wife's bosom, Olivia remarked, "Besides, Connecticut is Ben's home. He doesn't often get a chance to visit with his folks."

"It's not his home anymore! He lives here. Why can't he accept that?"

"You're not making this any easier."

"I don't intend to. No reason you have to wait years like your father and I did. Benjamin Knox is handsome, kind, and a fiscal conservative. What more do you want?"

"How about romantic?"

"He gives you flowers and champagne every holiday, doesn't he?"

"Yes, the same flowers and the same brand of champagne. Every time. I want something...I don't know...*explosive*. A rock-my-world event. I don't think it's in him."

"*Hmm*. Well, I'll merely say this—having your world rocked on a regular basis is not all it's cracked up to be."

"Speaking of…"

"One more glass of that lovely Montrachet and I'll continue."

****

Morocco, 1966

"This is the life, isn't it?" Sergei rolled over to bake his backside. "What an incredible beach."

"Not bad. I wish Mother would let me wear a bikini though. I'm old enough."

"Trouble is, you're too good-looking." He caught the shell Sydney threw at him and lobbed it into the water. "Seriously, you know it's not acceptable in a Muslim country."

His sister looked around at the variegated beach crowd. "Come on, this is the most cosmopolitan place we've ever been. You know what I saw yesterday? A man with lipstick on. And nail polish."

"Yeah, but he wore a *jellabah*, didn't he?"

"Sure, a man's dress, but nothing under it. Why…"

"Hello there…Sergei and Sydney, if I'm not mistaken?"

A boy of about fifteen stood between them and the sun. Sergei jumped up. "Eddie! Glad you could make it over here. How long are you staying?"

"A week. The 'rents want to see all of Morocco. We head to Marrakesh after this. So, can you show me the sights?" He gave Sydney a hopeful glance. She didn't respond, distracted by the discovery that—while his nose remained hooked—Eddie seemed to have grown six inches and his ears had dwindled to a point where they actually fit his head.

Sergei broke the silence. "Sure. Where are you staying?"

Their voices faded as the two walked off down the beach, leaving Sydney to blush and watch the reddish-brown cowlick bob along next to her brother. She seemed to be always watching him walk away.

****

By luck or accident, Eddie's parents had chosen the hotel next to Sydney's apartment building, so they saw him every day. She and Eddie spent hours scouting the beach for what Eddie dubbed *valuables*—shells and sharks' teeth and interesting flotsam. They kept their treasures in a shoebox under Sydney's bed. Life seemed as good as it would ever be, or so Sydney told her diary.

The day before he had to leave for Marrakesh, Eddie met her at the front door of the hotel. "Let's go down to the port. Ali says he has a surprise."

They made their way to the bustling docks. Dwarfing the usual jumble of fishing boats and ferries at the wharves, a huge gray destroyer lay at anchor, its

American flags flying proudly. "Wow, what's that?"

A sailor passing by them said, "It's the USS *John Paul Jones* of the Sixth Fleet. She's come in for a weekend's leave. See that little kiosk over there? You can get tickets for a tour if you like."

Sydney started toward the kiosk, but Eddie held her back. He pointed at a gaggle of local kids standing near the ship pointing and yelling. "There's Ali. Let's see what's going on."

They ran along the pier, gawking at the sailors in their brilliant white uniforms who stood at attention on the decks. A couple of the other kids waved their arms, calling the sailors. Eddie grinned at Sydney. "You wanna jump in and see if they'll throw us something?"

"What? Eew!"

"No, it'll be fun. Ali says he and Yusuf do it all the time." He took a flying leap and landed butt first in the oil-ringed water. He came up spluttering and waved at her. "Come on in, the water's disgusting!"

When you're thirteen years old and in love, you sometimes do the darndest things. Holding her nose, Sydney dove off the pier. She made the mistake of opening her eyes before she surfaced and was nearly blinded by a silt soup thicker than the Nile at flood stage. Something nipped her toe. She shot up out of the depths, kicking frantically at whatever slimy sea creature lurked in the muck. Together they swam over to a couple of brown-skinned boys and waved and shouted along with them. "Hey, sailor! Throw us sumpin'!"

"Hey, mistah!"

Pretty soon, they had a crowd of uniforms hanging over the railing, tossing cigarettes to them. Sydney wondered what her mother would do if she saw her little Pollyanna screeching and spitting out scummy water while she fought over soggy Winstons. To be on the safe side, she yelled in French. That way the headlines wouldn't read "Underage American girl caught fraternizing with the Sixth Fleet." One sailor leaned far out, pointed at her, and sent his Dixie cup hat floating out. She lunged for it, but instead her head slammed into Eddie's. Dazed, she threw her arms out hoping to find something to grab on to and hit a bare chest. Two arms went round her, and before she could struggle out of them, two lips came in contact with hers. A moment later, they were gone. A hand took hers and guided her to the dock. "You okay?"

"Eddie!" Then she couldn't think of anything else to say.

He grinned at her. "We'd best get back." He pulled her out of the water.

They picked up their towels and walked home. Sydney kept her mouth closed, the better to savor the tingling feeling the kiss left on her lips. At the door to her building, he stopped. "We're leaving tomorrow morning early. I'd…I'd like to see you tonight. Can you get out?"

She shook her head. "I've used up my three late nights. I have to stay in." She hoped the tear that welled up wouldn't fall.

Eddie's face fell instead. "I don't want to say goodbye, Sydney. What happens if…"

"If we never see each other again?" A sudden weight crushed her sternum, reminding her of that first climbing ascent in a plane when she was five. *Never?*

"Look, I'll figure something out." He checked the

sun. "I've got to go. I promise, I'll see you tonight." Before she could move, he bent forward and kissed her again, then threw his towel over his shoulder and strolled jauntily away.

****

Sydney's throat hurt. *Crying nonstop for an hour will do that to you, silly ass.* She'd gone to her room after supper to mope in peace over her impending heartbreak. Her room looked out over the back of Eddie's hotel. She giggled, thinking back to the night she, Sergei, and Eddie had hurled eggs out the window, aiming for the belly dancer performing poolside. They'd missed eleven times, ducking down after each one, but the last one hit its mark—they could tell by the squawk and the attendant laughter. She squeezed her eyes shut, thinking miserably that life couldn't get any worse. Finally, she turned back to the bed and lay down.

The bright Moroccan sun warming her face woke her. She sat up and attempted to pull her nightgown off but encountered denim instead. She wrinkled her nose. *I fell asleep in my clothes!* Peeling her jeans and T-shirt off, she went to the bathroom to splash water on her stinging eyes. As she came out, she glanced toward the window, a heavy sigh escaping her lips. A scrap of paper fluttered under the latch. She slid the window open and peeled it off. Just then Sergei knocked and yelled through the door. "Come on, Sydney, we're all supposed to go down to the hotel to wave Eddie and his family off."

"I'm coming." She read the note.

Dear Sydney, I hoped for one last kiss. Goodbye, my dear.

Holding it, she contemplated the ground eight stories below. *How did he get it up here? He couldn't have...No.* She scrambled into a light summer sheath, combed her golden tresses out, braided them quickly, and ran out of the room.

Sergei met her at the elevator. "You look tired. You didn't stay up after curfew, did you?"

"No." She banged the elevator button. "I didn't sleep well."

"Oh." They rode down in silence. Standing at the doors to the hotel, Mr. Davies signaled for a taxi while bellhops brought out several large pieces of luggage. Eddie appeared, shielding his eyes from the sun.

Sydney stood rooted, trying to memorize every feature of his face. She prayed she'd never forget those cobalt eyes, or the slightly pointed ears that reminded her of an elf, or those curly locks the color of burnt sienna. Especially the one that stood straight up. Eddie saw her and came over. Taking her hand, he led her away from the group. "Did you get my note?"

She nodded. "What did it mean?"

He looked perplexed. "What do you mean, what did it mean?"

"I mean…" She laughed at her own confusion. "How did it get there?"

His face displayed embarrassment, pride, and disappointment in successive waves. "I put it there. I climbed up the balconies."

"Eight stories? On the outside of the building?"

He hung his head. "It was the only way I could think of to get to you. To…kiss you goodbye. I banged on the window, but you were dead to the world."

"Oh my God, Eddie. You could have been killed!"

He took her hand again and swung it shyly. "It would have been worth it."

"Come on, Son! Time to go!"

Sydney watched the old woody station wagon pull out to the street, leather bags tied haphazardly to the rack on top, and turned away, smiling peacefully. Sergei caught up with her by the entrance to their building. He glanced at her contented face.

"What's with you, Syd? Aren't you crushed that your boyfriend's gone?"

"That's all right. I'll see him again."

"Yeah, right. You, sis, have a rich fantasy life. How on earth could your paths cross again?"

"I don't know how, but they will."

Sergei shook his head. "Girls…Hey! What just hit me on the head?" He looked up at the sky. "Look at that—it's raining." Sure enough, a small gray cloud hovered directly over them, leaking droplets of water. They drew back under the awning. "It won't last—it never does here."

Sydney said nothing. She watched the little cloud, waiting for the sun to cast it off and shine again. Sure enough, a minute later a round, yellow face peeped out, shooting light rays in all directions. One beam struck the last droplets hanging suspended in the air, creating a shimmering spectrum highway. She pointed. "Look, a rainbow!"

Sergei glanced up. "Yeah, yeah. At least the rain's stopped. Hey, race you to the beach."

****

Alexandria, Present Day

"Aw, an adolescent crush, how cute."

"You sound bitter, dear."

Olivia handed the waiter the receipt and rose. "Not bitter, restive. You have to admit, you're taking your sweet time getting to the juicy bits."

Sydney gave a haughty shake of her head. "Just because you're required to throw in a sex scene by page thirty in your novels doesn't mean I have to." She picked up her purse and followed her daughter out. "I'm building a theme here—a romantic one. You know, the rainbow connection?"

Olivia eyed her and settled onto the back seat. "You are aware that's a shameless rip-off from the Muppets, aren't you?"

Her mother folded her hands complacently. "You don't have to use that exact expression, love. That's why you're writing the memoir and I'm not."

When they reached Sydney's house, Olivia kissed her mother and went to her car. "Be ready about eleven tomorrow, all right?"

"Yes, yes. I'll spend the interim finding some way to spice up my sorry life's narrative."

****

"Hurry, Mother. If we miss the curtain call, they won't let us in until the second set."

"I'm coming." Sydney retrieved her cane and stepped carefully down the steps to her daughter's ancient Volvo. "I don't see why I can't drive the Morgan. It's finally working again, and the weather's so fine."

"The doctor said one more week off the ankle. Anyway, it's supposed to rain."

Sydney grumbled all the way to the Kennedy Center. "I don't know why you like these rehearsal thingies so much. Why not go to the actual performance?"

"Because it's fun to listen to the musicians argue. And I don't have to stay up late and miss my dinner."

"Okay, fine, but promise you'll go with me to the *Turandot* opening. Domingo's singing Calaf."

"Wouldn't miss it."

Sydney lay back against the torn leather seat. "Why can't you buy a new car? You're making enough money now. The last book sold a thousand copies only last week."

"That doesn't translate into much as far as royalties go, Mother. I'm doing fine financially, but I don't want a new set of monthly payments hanging over my head. Besides, Betsy only has ninety-five thousand miles on her. If the consumer reports are to be trusted, she's good for another hundred thousand."

"I can't tell if you're sensibly conservative or the cheapest creature on earth." Sydney glanced at her daughter. Large diamonds sparkled in her ears. Her ivory silk dress practically screamed designer. Not a rich chestnut hair out of place, not a split nail. "Well, at least you clean up good."

Olivia smiled but kept her eyes on the road. "I simply prioritize how I spend my money."

Sydney patted her daughter's arm and pointed to the right. "Turn here for the garage." As her daughter pulled the parking ticket, she mused, "I'm glad your writing has been so lucrative. I'd hate to have to subsidize you in my old age."

"I told you, the only growing segment of the literary market is romance. Everybody likes a happy ending."

"That may be true, but a good story doesn't

telegraph the ending. To be really satisfying, there has to be conflict—some smidgen of doubt that it will all work out."

"Like your romance?"

"Or yours."

"I don't need actual romance—I have my books for that."

"You've changed your tune then. Yesterday, you told me that Benjamin was in a rut, that you longed for some zing in the relationship. Which is it?"

Olivia pulled into a parking space, and they walked toward the escalator that would take them to the mezzanine. "I don't know, Mother. I guess I'm just bored."

"*Bored?* I can't imagine being bored. Ever. And I can't imagine that my daughter, the best-selling author of romantic suspense novels, could be either." She touched Olivia's hand lightly. "What is it? What's wrong?"

Olivia took her mother's arm and half-dragged her to the concert hall doors. "*Shh.* I'll tell you later. Do you have your ticket?"

****

"You were right, Olivia, I enjoyed that, especially when the two sisters played dueling banjos on their grand pianos. For one heady moment there, I thought they'd go for each other's jugular."

"I suppose that would have considerably enhanced the entertainment value for you?" Olivia pulled up to the curb. "Go in and find us a table, there's a dear. I'll park."

"I'll wait for you." When Olivia joined her, she limped into Landini Brothers.

The maitre d' rushed to her side. "A quiet table by the window, madame, mademoiselle?"

"Certainly. Olivia will have iced tea. Bring me a vodka martini, will you? Two olives and a twist. Quickly. I need fortification."

He laughed and trundled off. A few minutes later, her mother thoughtfully sucked on a toothpick emptied of olives.

"Are you ready for Round Three?"

"Not yet. I've been thinking about this ennui of yours."

"Mother, we've less than two weeks before your trip. I'd like to get at least the first draft done."

"I know, but I want to resolve this matter of your state of mind first. I don't want it hanging over my head in Paris. Now, something has happened. What is it?"

Olivia signaled the waiter. "A basket of bread, please." She fussed with her napkin and straightened her cutlery. When she reached for the butter plate, her mother put a hand out.

"Olivia."

The younger woman sighed. "Okay, here's the thing. Do you remember Rémy de Beaumec?"

Sydney's eyes softened. "Me, remember the elegant Frenchman you almost married your junior year? Do I remember those long, slim, aristocratic hands, the glossy ebony hair tied back in a ponytail that somehow didn't detract from his fervid virility, his eyes the color of hot fudge and just as delicious? That Rémy? I think so."

"I'm going to save that image for my next hero. Anyway…I…er…heard from him. A week ago."

"I see."

"Is that all you can say?"

"You haven't told me enough to pass judgment."

Olivia examined her glass carefully. "Fair enough. Ben left Tuesday for Connecticut. On Thursday, Rémy called. He's in town for a conference on French wines. We met for a drink."

"It's been how long—five years since you've seen him? Is he still as passionate? And as gorgeous?"

Olivia smiled. "Yes, Mother. He sent his respects."

Sydney sat back, satisfied. "Go on. You slept with him?"

"No, of course not!"

"But?"

Her daughter signaled the waiter. "We've...uh...spent the last week together. Every waking minute. Mother, it's been...well...grand. We've reminisced, laughed, talked nonstop about everything under the sun. I've been...happy."

Sydney waved the waiter away. "Give us another minute, Frank."

Olivia's face crumpled. "Mother, I'm so confused. Am I merely nostalgic for the salad days of college? Or am I still in love with Rémy? What does any of it say about my relationship with Ben?"

Sydney patted her daughter's hand. "Let's get something to eat. Muddles can't clear up on an empty stomach."

"You and your food." But Olivia picked up the menu. Her forehead unfurled a bit, and the twitch below her eye began to smooth out.

When the waiter had taken their orders, Olivia glanced at her watch. "Oh, look at the time. If we're going to meet the deadline, we have to get back to you."

Her mother put on a long face. "I suppose. Let me finish my wine first." She took tiny, slow sips until Olivia took her glass away and pulled out her notebook.

"*Rendezvous in Paris*. Or, *We Meet Again*. How's that for a title?"

"Your father would hate it."

"He's not around to complain, is he? So, you're twenty-one. You're flying to Cairo to study Arabic, but the plane has stops in Paris and Athens…"

****

Douglas DC-7C Seven Seas, 1974

The old Douglas DC-7 had obviously seen better days, but those must have been glorious. The seats were huge, as were the windows. Sydney twisted around to look at the semicircular lounge taking up the rear of the plane—like a harem, only with blue vinyl banquettes. A belly dancer would certainly not come as a surprise, nor be unappreciated. On her way to a year in Cairo, Sydney wanted to bone up on Egyptian culture, including the national pastime. Her Arabic teacher at Harvard told her that little Egyptian girls could roll their tiny hips by the age of five. She wondered if she would rise above her puritan squeamishness and learn to love it.

The stewardess flipped on the intercom. "Welcome to the last flight of the Seven Seas, our luxury piston-engine airplane. Launched in 1956, she was the first airplane capable of making transcontinental, transatlantic, and even transpacific flights nonstop. Alas"—here the young woman allowed herself a poignant sigh—"with the introduction of jet engines, she must now make way for a new age." The stewardess's voice faltered on the last words, but she rallied. "You'll notice that your view from many of our windows is expansive—one advantage of piston over jet engines. Once the captain has turned off the seatbelt sign, feel free to make your way to our comfortable lounge in the rear." Sydney could almost hear the unspoken words—*another luxury you won't find on jet planes.*

She pulled the curtains closed and settled back. It would be nice to have a layover in Paris. She hadn't been back since she was fifteen. After the summer in Tangier, UNESCO recalled her father to its headquarters in Paris for another two-year tour of duty. She had fond memories of the city even though her parents dumped her in a convent school. Her brother Sergei had gone to the international school and loved to rub it in.

"I don't have to wear a uniform. I don't have to speak French all day. I don't have nuns hounding me. Nyah, nyah."

"Yeah, well. I can walk to school, and you have to take the train." Not much, but then she didn't have much to work with.

The stewardess came by. "A young man asked me to give you this." She handed her a folded note and went on. Sydney opened it. The letterhead gave an address on Park Avenue and sported a crest.

She read, "You look awfully familiar. Do I?" The scent of anise filled her nostrils, and she looked up into very blue eyes framed by thick, chestnut brown curls. He'd tied the curls back in a ponytail, revealing slightly pointed ears. A tiny diamond stud sparkled in one lobe.

Her lip curled. *Another prep-school pseudo-hippie.*

"I don't think so."

He drew back, his eyes closed to slits. "Oh, I see." His head disappeared.

She'd almost fallen asleep when the seat before her shook as someone struggled out of it. The note writer stood in the aisle, revealing torn jeans, a Lacoste polo shirt, and several strands of homemade beads swinging around his neck. She shuddered. *My God, he's worse than I thought.* He reminded her of too many of the boyfriends she'd shucked in her four years of college. By her senior year she'd decided two things—first, she'd never date a man who couldn't explain clearly and succinctly why he voted a certain way, and second, that she'd be a journalist. Not a journalist like the current crop who wanted to *change the world* and *make a difference*, but one who went after the truth, no matter how ugly, and reported it. She wanted to be an authentic journalist, a conduit for facts, not a filter.

Her dream would have to wait, though. She'd committed too much time to her Middle East studies not to take advantage of this fellowship. Full tuition, airfare, and a monthly stipend larger than the average Egyptian bureaucrat's salary couldn't be refused. Besides, once she'd learned Arabic and traveled the Arab world she'd have more to offer a news service. That was her plan, anyway.

When the young man returned, she gave him her best supercilious air and noisily opened her magazine. She heard him chuckle. "*Vanity Fair*? That doesn't seem *you* somehow."

"I'll have you know you can find some very good reporting in here." *Why am I defending it to this slug?*

"I see. What the world needs to know about leggy

blondes and lipstick shades. You know what impressed me most? The in-depth study of front-closure versus back-closure bras. Wow." When she didn't respond, he smirked and pointed to a headline on the front cover. "Perhaps you prefer 'Bikini Wax—Friend or Foe'?"

Sydney flipped the pages and pretended to ignore him. After a minute, she raised her eyes to find his still trained on her, mischievous humor glinting in them.

Her obvious hostility didn't seem to rattle him. "So where are you headed?"

Good manners forced her to reply. "Cairo." He continued to stare, obviously expecting her to reciprocate. She finally muttered, "And you?"

"Athens. I guess we have a stop in Paris, though. That'll be nice. I haven't been there in, oh, eight years."

"I've lived there on and off. It will be nice to be back, if only for a few hours. I have a layover."

"You do? So do I. Perhaps...but no."

He made as if to turn around. For reasons she didn't accept, she touched his arm. As he swung back, she noticed his ears again. Perfectly shaped except for the slightly pointed tips, they lay flat against his head. The diamond earring enhanced the impression of an Ariel-like sprite. "Are you staying near the airport?"

He smiled, and his blue eyes flashed like a sunbeam-riddled tropical wave. "Orly Hilton."

"Oh, me too. Perhaps...perhaps we could have a drink there."

"Perhaps."

He sat back down, leaving her vaguely dissatisfied. She'd expected him to be enthusiastic. *Isn't that what he was going to ask me? To have a drink?* She drew the blanket up to her chin and tried to sleep.

She woke to the stewardess announcing their imminent landing in Paris. Below her, the city of lights lay brilliantly white in the midday sun. As they flew southeast toward Orly Airport, she made out the white lines of the Palais de Chaillot across the river from the Eiffel Tower. Even from that height, she could hear the cacophony of Paris traffic.

"Welcome to klaxon city." The young man cocked his head as the Étoile's radiating avenues jam-packed with cars came into view on the other side of the airplane. "I thought they passed an ordinance banning horns."

Sydney laughed. "And your point?"

"Oh. Yeah."

She lost sight of him as they went through customs. A long line at the ladies' room held her up, and she caught the last shuttle to the hotel. Still no sign of her purported date as she checked in. What began as mild disappointment grew into full-blown vexation when she realized he hadn't bothered to give her his name. *Why did I stick my neck out? The fellow was probably just bored and flirted with me to pass the time. What a fool I am!* As she pulled out her toiletry bag and kicked off her shoes, the hotel phone rang. "Sydney? Sydney Bellek?"

"Yes?"

"This is Elian Davies. I believe we have a date?"

Elian Davies. That sounds familiar. "I wasn't sure, since we hadn't exchanged names. How did you find me?"

"Oh, I engaged the concierge in conversation about beautiful young women recently arrived in Paris, and your name came up. He kindly put me through to your room."

"Oh, he did." *So much for security.* "You're very clever, aren't you?"

"Yes, yes I am. That's why I'm a journalist. Now, can I meet you in the bar? Is six o'clock okay?"

She almost said, "You'll be the rich American in plastic beads and designer jeans, right?" but thought better of it. *A journalist.* "Sure."

As she showered and pulled out a travel dress the color of warm caramel that matched her eyes, she thought about Elian Davies. Setting aside the less than professional apparel, he wasn't bad looking. Tall, thin to the point of lanky, he reminded her of her favorite actor Jimmy Stewart. The slight left hook to his nose, together with the rather elvish ears, lent him a fey aspect, not unattractive to her love of the exotic. She rather liked his wry sense of humor, too, even if most of his jokes were at her expense. Her reflection in the full-length mirror made her wish once again she had bigger breasts and maybe just the teeniest wave in that straight, blonde hair. *Oh well.* At least she'd been spared baby blue eyes, though that hadn't stopped her family from nicknaming her Pollyanna. *Better than Miss Goody Two Shoes, I suppose.* She swished the long skirt. *Too bad he can't see my legs.* Phil—or was it Peter?—one of those short-term boyfriends anyway—had once pronounced them tens. Miniskirts couldn't come back in style any too soon for her.

She got her purse and headed to the elevator. *A journalist.* She'd been worried that the year in Cairo might interfere with her plans in that arena—this meeting could be a godsend. *I'll ask him about the profession and how he broke into it. He doesn't look much older than me—maybe a couple of years.*

The bright red neon letters flashing "Le Bar" led her to the hotel lounge. Elian swiveled on his stool and pointed at the sign. "I guess you didn't have any trouble finding the place."

"No. They're literal-minded folk here in France." Sydney had been stewing over what drink to order. At twenty-one, beer was her drink of choice, and she hadn't branched out into anything more complicated yet. Heaven forbid Elian thought her unsophisticated. *That Park Avenue crest probably means he's terribly cosmopolitan.* She tried desperately to recall what her mother had told her about cocktails. Old Fashioned. Pink Lady. Manhattan. Martini. Her parents, world travelers, turned up their noses at bourbon drinkers, she knew. Scotch, Scotch is the only whiskey for the enlightened. *Alrighty then.*

"What'll you have?"

Sydney bit her lip. "A Manhattan?"

The bartender pulled out a tumbler. "What kind of whiskey, mademoiselle?"

"Scotch, of course." The stutter was too faint to wake the dead, so she surveyed the other patrons with flushed pride. No one paid her the slightest attention.

"Let's take our drinks over there." Elian ushered her to a low table surrounded by overstuffed chairs. She sat and took a sip, only barely hiding the grimace. *Execrable.* She noted with a dash of envy that Elian held a frothing mug of pilsener.

"So, you said you're going to Cairo? What for?"

"I'm studying Arabic at the American University in Cairo."

"Junior year abroad?"

She bristled. "I graduated from Vassar in June, thank you very much."

He looked her over critically. "You don't look old enough."

"I'm twenty-one!" She held up the glass, sorely tempted to knock it over so she could order a beer.

"Oh, I see…" His sharp chin trembled.

He had better not laugh at me. "You're stopping in Athens?"

"Yup." He took the change of conversation in stride. "I'm working for the *Baltimore News-Register*, doing a piece on the Greek revolutionary movement." He indicated his ponytail and earrings. "Hence the hippie look."

She warmed to him.

Several beers later, they wobbled out to the lobby holding hands. Sydney had learned enough to know this Elian was a complex person and really, really cute. When they reached her room, he backed her against the door. She could feel his penis throbbing through his jeans and took a minute to revel in the desire the friction kindled before pushing him away. He set his arms on either side of her and regarded her with serious eyes. "You still don't remember me, do you?"

She shook her head. She didn't really want to recognize him. Placing him in some other context could only be deflating. She liked him now, a tall, thin, russet-haired man with a pulsing member and inviting mouth, currently blowing a tidal wave of pheromones in her direction.

He continued to stand there, making none of the moves she wished he'd make. Finally, she took a step toward him and held out her lips. Leaning in, he took them with his. The link pulled the rest of their bodies together. Arms went around waist and neck, bellies ground against each other, thighs intertwined. Sydney fell into a long, dark, winding tunnel that squeezed her, taking her breath away. She no longer felt corporeal, but more like a soft piece of quivering tissue, the bones dissolving, reduced finally to a pool of liquid heat.

He broke away, panting. "Now do you remember me?"

Her arms empty, she tried blinking to drag herself back to the present. Elian swam into view. His cerulean eyes shot signals, signals that she couldn't decipher. *What does he want of me? Why can't we live for the moment? Just be in the here and now?* For an instant she thought of lying, but somehow she knew he would see through it, that it would only push him farther away. "I'm sorry."

He lifted his hands, then dropped them in frustration. He gazed at her, pleading. She couldn't help him. Bits of him seemed familiar—as though those features belonged to someone else she'd known a long time ago. Other bits, like his deep, gruff voice and his air of insolence, were strange and new. A fleeting sense of abandonment passed through her. Whoever he reminded her of had left her once before. She didn't want that loneliness again. She turned from him and put the key in the door. He caught her arm. "We'll meet again, Sydney."

She tried to match the hope in his voice. "Perhaps we will." She ran inside and threw herself on the bed. After a good cry and a call for room service, she paced the room, trying to get a grip on her emotions. Something deep in Elian's eyes drew her. She didn't recognize his face, but she felt a nexus, a bond with him. An affinity shared, but long ago. She understood him, *knew* him. A face rose before her, but all jumbled as though she looked at it through a kaleidoscope. Eyes, chin, nose, cheeks, all split up into triangles and rhomboids, making the face as inscrutable as a Picasso painting. She gave up.

Halfway through the chicken cordon bleu, she stopped, fork stalled two inches from her mouth. *Why does he care whether I recognize him? What is this rapport I sense? Is there some deep, dark secret I should know? Oh my God, is he my long-lost brother?*

Chapter Four

Alexandria, Present Day

"I can't believe you still didn't recognize him."

"Why should I? He'd changed dramatically in eight years, as had I. Thirteen to twenty-one, with all that comes in between, makes for a huge gap in consciousness, not to mention physical development. I cherished the memory of a romance with a boy in Morocco. I couldn't have picked his face out of a lineup by 1974. Don't forget too, that I knew him only as Eddie in Tangier."

"That's right. He thought it would make him fit in. I guess he got over that soon enough."

Sydney said musingly, "Plus, his voice had changed. It's amazing how a scent or a voice brings back memories more efficiently than a face." She sipped her drink. "At any rate, it didn't occur to me that they were one and the same boy. It's not like I didn't have lots of boyfriends in between. Lots."

"Yes, Mother." Olivia watched the pedestrians as they stopped to read the restaurant's menu. "How come he remembered *you* then?"

"He was fifteen in Tangier. There's a big difference between thirteen and fifteen. Plus, I think braving certain death for a farewell smooch kind of sticks with a fellow."

Olivia took a piece of French bread from the basket, tore the crust off in one piece, and began chewing on it. "You mean, climbing eight stories up the outside of a building? Yeah, you might be right."

The waiter slipped a crispy filet of trout before Sydney. She squeezed lemon over it and tasted one of the boiled potatoes. "They do fish so well here. How's the Meursault?"

"Excellent. Now continue."

"You're such a slave driver. You want to know if we slept together that night in Paris?"

Olivia held a hand to her mouth in mock dismay. "You *did*?"

Her mother smiled impishly. "Of course not. He left me at the door, like I said. Thankfully I'd never quite acquired the habit of one-night stands...what do they call them now? Friends with benefits?"

"It's not exactly the same thing. I thought the seventies was the era of free love?"

"Another urban myth. Anyway, I wanted him, but I liked the romance more than the sex. It's hard to moon over someone once you've seen him with his pants down."

"Now there's a sentence."

"Besides, what if he *were* a long-lost brother, given up for adoption at birth? I may be liberated, but I draw the line at incest."

"Did Grandma ever mention a sordid affair? A birth in the night? A babe in swaddling clothes left on the church steps?"

Sydney took a bite of fish before replying. "Well, she wouldn't, would she? At least not to her legitimate daughter."

Olivia poured more wine. "This is an unproductive line of conversation if ever there was one. We know Pop wasn't your brother. So go on. You saw him again?"

"Oh no, I want to go back to the current crisis for a bit. My romance can wait. Have you talked to Rémy about…well…about your mixed feelings?"

Her daughter pursed her lips. "You know, it's funny. He was always such a smooth operator in college. The life of the party, the center of attention. I liked him, but as to substance…"

"Too rich?" Her mother's eyebrows rose.

"No, that didn't bother me. I liked being the only girl in my dorm with a boyfriend who could pick me up in his Ferrari and afford imported beer. No…I just sensed that the more I let my affection for him grow, the more he would fade away…that the distance between us was fixed. If I approached, he would back off."

"So you never took stock of your feelings?"

"I knew I cared very much, but I had a feeling he'd be gone if I bared it to the light of day."

Sydney let the waiter remove her plate and ordered coffee. She watched her daughter, a tiny smile on her face. "And now?"

"Now?" Olivia reached a hand out and squeezed Sydney's. "He's changed, Mother. He's…I guess you'd call it ebullient. Joy practically spurts out of his pores when he's with me. He…he *dances* all the time."

"Dances? You mean like a jig?"

"More like a waltz."

"Oh good. I don't think I'd like him jiggling."

"If you continue to tease, I won't tell you any

more."

Sydney zipped a finger across her lips. "Has he said anything to you?"

"No, not in so many words."

"Does he know about Benjamin?"

"Yes. I told him when we first reconnected." Olivia avoided her mother's gaze.

"I gather you haven't brought it up since."

"Er, no."

"And you say you haven't slept with him?"

"Mother!"

"Well?"

Olivia slumped. "Point taken. Tit for tat on the personal questions. But this is different!"

Sydney picked up her purse and stood. "Sweetheart, why don't you relax and let whatever happens, happen? I know that's hard for you. You like things clear and precise and settled. Just like Benjamin does." She ducked in time for the wadded napkin to miss her head. "I'm going to the ladies' room. Let's get some dessert. It will perk you up. Then I'll tell you all about the sex dream."

"What?"

****

Paris, 1974

Sydney had it all planned. If she checked out of the hotel early and got to the ticket counter, she could miss Elian entirely. That way she wouldn't have to face either his disappointment or her admittedly bizarre suspicions.

No such luck. As she gave her instructions to the taxi driver, the door opened and a familiar head stuck in. "Going my way?"

Caught, she could only nod.

He hopped in. "What airline are you taking? Middle East?"

Sydney gave up. "Yes."

"I'm on Sabena."

They lapsed into an uncomfortable silence for the remainder of the short ride. Sydney jumped out of the cab and paid the driver through the window. Elian caught up with her near the Middle East Airlines counter. "Look, I'm sorry if we got off on the wrong foot. Here's my card. If you get over to Athens, I'd…I'd love to see you again."

As she took the card, she felt something crack in her chest, and a feeling that wasn't acid indigestion invaded the cavity. Foreboding? Grief? *How totally stupid is that?* She made a feeble effort at a smile and waved him off.

The clerk at the counter took her ticket and paused, clicking keys on her computer. "Mademoiselle Bellek? I'm sorry, but your flight to Cairo has been cancelled. I can put you on a Sabena flight to Athens with a connection to Cairo."

"I beg your pardon? Did you say Athens?" *Now the damn thing's gone from cracking to fluttering.* "That's fine. When does the flight begin boarding?"

"Fifteen minutes. Let me check you in."

Sydney waited, tapping her foot gently and humming. When the attendant held out the ticket, she grabbed it and sprinted down the terminal. She spied a familiar tie-dyed shirt disappearing down the jet bridge to the plane. As she followed it, she noticed a twig of brown hair sticking up and out of the ponytail. *A cowlick. Too funny. Now where…?*

Panting only slightly, she dropped into the seat next to Elian. He turned in surprise. "Sydney?"

"They cancelled my flight, so here I am."

"Well…that's…nice."

A warning gong went off. *Danger Will Robinson.* "I…um…I'm just playing through. We stop in Athens, then go on to Cairo. I don't think I'll be able to get off the plane."

"Oh, you'll have to—security's super tight now. I hear they're frisking everyone."

"Oh."

Sydney sensed Elian's discomfort. Not sure of the cause, she whispered, "What's wrong?"

He held a finger to his lips and pointed at the row ahead. "My contact," he mouthed.

Too late Sydney remembered his assignment, to infiltrate a revolutionary group in Greece. Her only experience with intrigue came from shows like *Man from U.N.C.L.E.* and *The Avengers*. *How should I act?* Would it help to pretend to be his lover? Or better, to feign non-recognition? She decided to take her cue from Elian. She took a box of mints out and offered it to him. "For your ears."

He took three and popped them in his mouth. Then he pulled a notebook and pen out of his backpack, scribbled something, and handed it to her. She read, "Dangerous to know me." No response came to mind, so she gave him a thumbs-up and sat back.

The plane rose heavily in the air as though it felt the weight of world politics riding in it. Sydney wished she could sleep. She tried to relax, concentrating on one body part at a time as her mother had taught her, starting with her toes. She'd reached her thighs when she felt something. Fingers. She cracked open one eye. Elian's hand had casually dropped on her thigh. It must have sent an electrical impulse through her skin, because not only her thigh but her whole nether region rose a few degrees in temperature. She snuck her hand down and touched his. He didn't look at her but squeezed her fingers. They sat rigidly, holding tight to each other's hand, staring straight ahead.

At last Sydney fell into a fitful sleep, in which twining bodies and skin slick with sweat featured prominently. She'd never had a sex dream before, and she wiggled in her seat, wanting it to last as long as possible. In the dream, Elian stood naked before her, his cock perpendicular, thick, and pulsing. He closed the gap between them and fastened his lips on her erect nipple while his fingers climbed under her skirt and twisted and pulled at her sensitive skin. She tore off her clothes, grasped his penis, and pulled it toward her. Hitching herself up, she circled his waist with her thighs, and helped him enter her inch by slow inch. She rolled her hips, drawing him in. He stared into her eyes—his red-rimmed with lust—and began to pump. Her body felt stuffed and whole. They rocked, his ball in her socket, back and forth, faster and harder, until his cock froze. Something wet ran out of her and down her legs, and she fell to the ground.

"Are you okay?"

Sydney opened her eyes. Elian was watching her anxiously. She realized she held his hand in a crushing grip and let go. "Oh…er…" Still lost in the dream, she perceived only hazily that she hadn't in fact made love to her seatmate. For a minute she considered going back to sleep—*do it to me one more time*—but shook it off.

"I'm fine. Just had a…vivid dream."

"You were moaning. In ecstasy. Or so it sounded." He gave her a quizzical smile. "What were you dreaming about?"

She sat up hastily. "Nothing. Really. Um…when do we land?"

"About an hour. Relax. Go back to your dream."

She looked at him quickly. *My God, he knows. I'm going to kill myself.*

He wrote something on his pad and handed it to her. "May I join you?"

The heat rising from her face could have boiled an egg. She turned away from him and pulled a magazine from the seat pocket.

****

They had no time to talk at the airport as two tall Greek policemen led Elian away. Before she could call or run after him, a hefty woman in a uniform clearly borrowed from a much smaller person took her elbow and directed her behind a curtain to strip. The guard—*please God let her be happily married*—checked her body cavities quickly and efficiently and left her to dress.

Sydney had to stay in the security area until her plane left for Cairo and could only wonder what had happened to Elian. The atmosphere in the airport was strained. Passengers and security guards eyed each other with distrust. At one point, a swarthy man with a large duffel bag entered the waiting area and trudged through the silent crowd, which split like the Red Sea at his passing. She knew political tensions ran high, not just between Egypt and Israel, but within Greece itself. She wished she'd asked what revolutionary group Elian planned to investigate. Depressed, she headed to her gate, fearing she would never see him again.

****

Alexandria, Present Day

"Except in your dreams. What a dirty mind you had, Mother!"

Sydney smiled a Mona Lisa smile. "It was our first encounter. I believe Elian knew full well what I'd been dreaming about. He seemed genuinely…er…gratified."

Olivia wiped the disapproving frown off her face with a napkin. "I'm not sure I need to hear this level of detail."

"I did warn you, dear. How about this? I promise when the hot and heavy sex starts up, I'll send you out of the room."

"Yes, I think that would be a good idea." Olivia stuck two fingers in her glass of water and rubbed her temples.

"Dessert, mesdames? We have a fresh *tarte tatin*. Or a tiramisu perhaps?"

"Coffee for me. I'm watching my figure. I want to look my best for Paris."

"Tiramisu please."

Sydney turned to her daughter. "Now, about Rémy."

Olivia sighed. "I don't know. Next to him Ben seems so…so tepid, so bland. Rémy and I have so much more to talk about."

Sydney considered. "One woman's tepid and bland is another's strong, silent type. By the way, did Rémy take over the family vineyard?"

"Yes, as well as several other estates. He leaves the day-to-day operations to his managers, so he can concentrate on the marketing end of the business. That allows him to jet around to conferences like the one here."

Sydney sipped her coffee. "How long will he be in town?"

"Another week or so."

"I see. Well, keep me informed. Perhaps he should come to dinner."

Olivia put her cup down. "But…"

"Tell him I'd love to see him again. His natural courtesy will force his hand."

"Just don't try to force mine."

Her mother sedately folded her hands. "*Moi?* Now, do you want to hear what happened in Cairo?"

****

Cairo, 1974

It wasn't until she reached the airport in Heliopolis that she realized she had left her carry-on in Athens. As she stood in the middle of the terminal, her mouth open in shock, a man appeared and touched her elbow.

"Miss Bellek?"

"Yes?"

"I'm from the university. Sayyed Ibrahim at your service. I can take you to the campus if you're ready."

The stress of travel suddenly rolled over her like a giant tractor, and she began to cry. "I left my suitcase in Athens," she blubbered.

"Oh, dear. Not your passport, I hope?"

She pulled out a tissue and blew her nose. "No, all my important papers are with me, but the carry-on bag held my diary and…and…other things." Better not mention the lingerie, and definitely not the lemons tucked in among her niceties for safekeeping. While it may have been unwise to mention ladies' underthings to an Egyptian man, it was positively dangerous to mention lemons, since President Sadat had prohibited all food imports in an unpopular plan to showcase Egypt's self-reliance. Fruit in her luggage could mean a fine or, for a citizen, jail.

Sayyed Ibrahim took her arm. "If you go to the embassy, I'm sure they can do something. Did you have any other luggage?"

She shook her head. "Only my trunk. That's coming by sea."

He halted, hand to mouth. "We'd better hook you up with the matron right away then. She'll help you buy a wardrobe and other necessities."

"Why?"

He hesitated. "You don't really expect to see the trunk any time soon, do you?"

Sydney let him lead her to a taxi while contemplating this new world of delightful inefficiency.

A few days later, she found her way to the U.S. Embassy. The vice-consul, a Mr. Plum, failed to be helpful. "I'll have my assistant contact the Athens port authority. We'll be in touch when we hear from them." She left with the distinct impression that, aside from the Independence Day celebration to which the eminent Plum had invited her, he would not, in fact, ever be in touch.

An hour later, sitting in the euphemistically labeled "family" section of a café—meaning where the women who didn't want to be treated like prostitutes sat—she pondered her next move. The tiny cup of coffee sat untouched. Its bitter taste did not sit well with a stomach only recently introduced to Middle Eastern food.

"I bet you ordered it *sade*, didn't you?"

She started at the familiar voice. "Elian! How did you get here?"

He pushed a small valise between her legs and sat down. "One of maybe four words I know in Arabic. *Sade* means plain. American coffee may taste good black, but Arab coffee is much too harsh to drink that way. Next time, order it *masbout*."

"Medium sugar?"

"Yes. Now if you ask for *sukkar*, it'll come super sweet—disgustingly so. You don't want that. So you'll—"

Sydney pushed her cup aside. "Elian." She hoped the menace in her voice would move the conversation along.

He grinned. "I couldn't let you languish without your diary, could I? When I saw your little case sitting there like a lost teddy bear, I claimed it and hopped the first plane to Cairo to deliver it personally."

"You didn't! How did you know where to find me?"

He hung his head, but she could see no blush. "I rifled through your bag, fondling and sniffing, to find an address." He shivered a little at her look and went on. "Perhaps I should clarify. I fondled and sniffed the *lemons*, not your unmentionables. By the way, I left them back in Greece, to be on the safe side. The lemons, not the lingerie. We don't want to be thrown in an Egyptian dungeon for smuggling citrus, now, do we?"

Sydney examined the lock on the case. "At least you didn't break it."

Elian rolled his eyes. "That's the thanks I get. Aren't you going to show me around? Take me home with you?" He cocked his head at her.

The effect of his blue eyes on her libido descended to unexpected quarters. She squirmed in her seat, wishing the damp warmth in her loins would dissipate. Elian continued to gaze at her, conveying the uncomfortable impression that he knew the effect he had on her. Finally, he stood and held out his hand. "Come. Show me your apartment."

Mohammed the *bawwab* jumped to attention at the entrance. They greeted him and climbed the stairs to the third floor. The building, owned by an Armenian, housed mainly American students but offered few modern conveniences. Sydney unlocked her door. A tiny kitchen lay to the right. Straight ahead, a very long hall led to the rest of the flat. Elian mimed throwing a bowling ball.

Sydney laughed. "I knew I'd find some useful purpose for this alley." The end of the hall opened on the high ceilings and rococo decoration of a typical Victorian room. The paneled walls were painted soft yellow and baby blue. French windows opened onto other people's gardens. Sydney twirled in the middle. "Like it?"

Elian walked to the tiny balcony and leaned out. "Wonder if I could reach that mango." He indicated a tree in the next backyard. "Here, hold my legs…"

"No! Elian, behave." Sydney felt suddenly shy. "Would you…would you like something to eat?"

He came back in. "Sure."

"I'll see what I have in the icebox." The word made her giggle—no refrigerator for Mr. Anabelian's tenants, no sir. None of those newfangled contraptions here. She ran back down the hall to the kitchen and opened a wooden cube that sat on a table. Next to a half-melted block of ice she found a dish of yogurt, some cherry jam, and two beers. She grabbed them and loped back, dropping them on the table, then sat down, panting only slightly.

Elian popped the caps off the beers and gave her one. "Cheers. This is my first Stella."

"The big bottles are only sold locally. I've discovered that the quality can be...er...uneven."

He took a long swallow. "Not bad." He touched her hand lightly. "I wish I didn't have to go back so soon. I'd like to see more of Cairo."

"I've only been here a few days—I'm not sure I'd be a very good guide."

"Well, then, we'll do it the next time I come visit." He casually dropped his arm over her shoulders.

She felt her stomach tighten. *What am I—some sort of feline in heat?*

"Which is your bedroom?" He asked it oh so casually.

She pointed to her left.

He finished his beer—no small feat since the local Egyptian beer came in liter bottles—and rose. "Come."

Somehow it seemed the sensible thing to do, so she went.

Chapter Five

Alexandria, Present Day

"Wait a minute—why are you stopping? Mother!"

"You said you didn't want to hear the actual sex parts." She indicated the waiter. "Especially not here."

Olivia gaped at her. "At least give me a hint. You did make love that day, didn't you?"

"Oh yes. He was magnificent. A stallion." Sydney's lips curled upwards.

Olivia tut-tutted. "Yeah, right. I bet it was awkward as hell—just like most first times."

Sydney made a face. "I did my best not to laugh. First, he couldn't figure out how to unhook my bra. Then he tripped over his pants and fell face first on the bed. Well, to be more specific, on the cat."

"Oh, dear."

"Little Archimedes did not take kindly to the intrusion and scratched Elian's nose. After I cleaned him up and shooed the cat away, things veered toward…uncomfortable."

"You mean, even more so?"

Sydney smiled reminiscently. "Nevertheless, we soldiered on." She closed her eyes. "Once we sorted ourselves out and found the correct apertures, it went swimmingly. Your father was indeed magnificent. If only Elizabeth hadn't turned up."

"Your roommate?"

"Yes. She did not, shall we say, act the good sport, and took finding us in *flagrante delicto* with about as much grace as Archimedes had. Poor Elian had to throw his clothes on and hightail it back to the airport."

"No goodbye kiss?"

Sydney's face crumpled. "No goodbye kiss. In fact, I didn't hear from him again for four years."

"Four years!"

Sydney put her napkin down. "I need a nap, dear. Let's pick this up later, shall we?"

Olivia paid the check, and they walked back to the car. The blue sky and bright sun augured well for an early summer. Restaurants had even set a few tables outside, immediately snatched up by basking customers. The two women wove gingerly through leashes and excited dogs and tables and long legs stretched out. "Look at that. I swear, half of Alexandria's population is dogs."

"I know." Sydney laughed. "I read one letter to the editor that described this as a 'family-friendly' town."

"Right. That only works if you understand that most Old Towners think of their dogs as children."

Once in the car, they wound their way through the byzantine streets of Alexandria and crossed the bridge onto the parkway. Sydney hummed the tune to an Edith Piaf song. To stop her, Olivia chirped, "So how come you didn't see Pop again?"

"What? Oh, too busy learning Arabic and fending off Egyptian boys who wanted to touch my hair to see if it was real. I had my life and he had his."

"Didn't you miss him?"

"At first, but I soon met a nice fellow, and Elian

faded into the background."

Olivia slowed and turned to stare at her mother. "The love of your life *faded*? That makes no sense."

Sydney put a warning hand on the steering wheel. "Sweetheart, watch your driving. I want to get to Paris intact. As to your dear father, he didn't call or write either. At that point in my life, I had way too many fish to fry. It's not that I didn't care. I had the typical attention span of a twenty-something-year-old and moved quickly on to new adventures."

Olivia zipped around a slow-moving SUV. "So you forgot him."

"No, no. I followed his career from afar. That was hardly difficult."

"You knew he'd been captured by the revolutionary group he'd hoped to infiltrate?"

"Oh yes, his exploits were plastered across every newspaper. At least the part about his abduction. No one knew he'd planned it that way until he began publishing his series."

"It certainly blew the lid off their Communist ties. They'd been pretending to be nationalists until Pop uncovered their money conduit to Moscow. After that, it all fizzled."

Sydney beamed. "I was so proud when he won the Pulitzer."

"What do you mean? You didn't have anything to do with him. You hadn't seen him in years. In fact, you told me that his endless string of scoops irritated the bejesus out of you."

"They did. What can I say? He'd made an impression on me. I didn't admit it even to myself, but no man ever really equaled the standards he'd set."

"What standards? You hardly knew him."

"Physical things. Those pixie ears, that cute little cowlick, his eyes...and his sense of humor—wry, a little strange—stuff like that. And his courage."

"Some would call a man who deliberately got himself abducted by a bloodthirsty gang—"

"And climbed an eight-story building to be with his lady love—"

"—an idiot. Or a fool."

Sydney ignored her daughter. Dreamily she went on, "Anyway, I'd find myself looking for those things whenever I dated a man. Silly really. And after Cairo..."

Olivia pulled into the circular driveway before a graceful white-painted brick house. She helped her mother out, and together they went inside. Once she'd gotten Sydney settled, Olivia went to the kitchen to put the tea kettle on. Back in the living room, she picked up her notebook and sat down. "You were saying? After Cairo...?"

"Oh, I don't have to tell you all the gory details of my meteoric rise in journalism, do I?"

"I only know what I've read in the newspapers." Her daughter grinned. "I'd like to hear it first-hand. Your rivalry and your adventures. Go on."

"Get the tea, would you? And call Rémy. I'd like him to come tomorrow if he's available and Mrs. Doughty amenable. If you do that, I'll indulge you for a little while."

****

Washington DC, 1979

"Hey Sydney, did you see the latest installment in the exploits of Spiderman, aka Elian Davies?"

"No. Leave me alone, Sanford. I have real work to do."

"He's treading on your turf now."

Sydney pushed away from her desk. "What are you talking about?"

The copy boy beamed with malicious pleasure. "Iran. He's wangled a room at the American consul's home in Tehran, the better to broadcast events as they unfold."

"At Peter's? How on earth?"

"Apparently, he knows the consul's wife. Met her in Russia. When he broke the news of the big split between Brezhnev and Kosygin."

Sydney slammed her fist down, missing the one clear part of her desk. Her knuckles glanced painfully off a stapler. "And I suppose Craddock is going to let him go."

Her colleague shrugged. "This is what happens when newspapers collide…I mean…merge. The big name gets the big story."

"We haven't merged. We've been bought by the same conglomerate. Ronald Duncan insists we'll maintain separate staffs and separate focuses."

"Foci."

"What?"

"Never mind. You can't honestly believe that the *News-Register* and the *Observer* are going to remain separate but equal, do you? We've been rivals for three decades. Look at you, Sydney. You want to report on the fomenting Iranian revolution. What do you suppose Craddock over at the *News-Register* expects Davies to do?"

She put her head in her hands. All the years

slogging through the style section, the city desk, the national desk, to finally break out into international affairs, only to have her best chance at a major story ripped from her clinging hands. *And by Elian Davies.* "Sanford, get Nancy to cut me a ticket to Tehran. I'll be in Malcolm's office."

She wended her way through the cubicles to the editor's office. "Malcolm? You busy?"

A dramatically bellied and bewhiskered man who could pass as a younger Andy Rooney did not look up. "Yes, you can go." Sydney saluted and turned to leave, but the editor-in-chief called her back. "That's unless and until Duncan decides to merge the papers. And since his fifth wife turned out to be a lesbian, I hear he hates all women, so you know who'll get all your assignments."

Sydney bristled. "Not if I can show him who gets the real scoops. Without tricks and disguises. And crap like that."

"Gotcha. Write when you have something solid to offer me."

****

Alexandria, Present Day

Olivia couldn't ignore her mother's second yawn, particularly since it lasted so long. "That's it? Can't we at least get to Iran?" She tried to keep the frustration out of her voice.

Sydney checked her watch. "Not now. I need my beauty sleep if you want me at my best for your young gentleman." She surveyed her daughter. "You could use some shut-eye too. Your cheeks are sunken."

"You're always so supportive."

"Yes, I am." Sydney folded her hands in her lap

and gave her daughter a smug smile. "That's why you turned out so well."

Olivia rose and kissed her mother's forehead. "Funny, Pop always claimed his timely interventions at critical moments are what saved me."

Sydney pouted. "Well, he would say that, wouldn't he?"

"I'll see you tomorrow. Good night, love."

"Good night."

****

"Welcome, stranger." Sydney offered her cheek. The chiseled features of the man at the door inclined toward her with polished grace. One perfect ringlet of ebony hair sidled down his temple. He kissed her and drew back, his black eyes sparkling.

"You grow more beautiful every year, Madame Davies."

"I see you still have that silver tongue." His hostess gave a gentle laugh to soften the criticism. "Olivia, why don't we go into the drawing room? Would you like a cocktail, Rémy? Or champagne?"

Sydney kept the conversation light, dwelling on politics and religion rather than the weather. The tense muscles in Rémy's shoulders gradually relaxed as the evening wore on and the wine flowed. He even began glancing at Olivia now and then, something he had studiously avoided at first. *He hasn't forgotten about Benjamin. That's good.* Sydney watched her daughter. She sensed Olivia had been opposed to this dinner—whether out of shame or apprehension Sydney wasn't sure. Even now her face remained inscrutable, annoying her mother. *Just like Elian.*

"Dessert?"

"No, thank you."

"Coffee then?"

"Yes, please."

When they were served, Sydney rose. "Why don't you two take your cups to the living room? I have some things to do to prepare for my trip. I shall return in a few minutes." She let them go, waiting for a sign. Sure enough, as they passed out the door, their hands found one another and squeezed. She sighed and headed upstairs.

****

"Must you go so soon? The evening is still young."

"Yes, madame." Rémy's hooded eyes kept her from deciphering his state of mind.

"We'll see you again before you return to France?"

He twisted to look at Olivia. The pause lengthened. Olivia stared into his eyes, silent. "I hope so."

When he'd gone, Sydney indicated a chair to her daughter. "Tell me what happened."

As if she knew there was no escape, Olivia sat and squared her shoulders. "He asked me to go back to France with him."

"Ah."

"I…I said I'd think about it."

"Ah."

Olivia stood and started to pace. "I wish…"

"You wish Benjamin would show up out of the blue, sweep you off your feet, and carry you off to…er…"

Her daughter halted. "I do?"

Sydney shrugged. "If you up and took off with Rémy, would you ever know what you'd do if he did?"

Jaw slack, Olivia stared at her mother. "Say that

again?"

Alice stuck her head around the door.

"Ladies, Mrs. Doughty would like to know if she can talk you into some of the lovely apricot crisp she made for dinner."

"Thanks, Alice, none for me. I'm saving up for a napoleon in Paris. Olivia will have some."

Olivia stuck out her tongue at her mother. "A *large* piece would be most welcome. With whipped cream if there is any."

Alice cracked a cold smile. "I'll check."

Olivia sat down. "All right. You win."

Her mother pretended not to understand. "I have?"

"I'll call Ben." Alice came in with a tray. "Now, let's get back to the story. I'm in the mood for a happy ending. When last we talked, you were headed to Tehran."

"Yes, into the inferno, although we didn't know it then."

****

Boeing 747-100 Queen of the Skies, 1979

Sydney settled into her seat. How cavernous this 747 felt compared to the 707 and the DC-7 she'd flown before. *The term jumbo jet is sure apt.* She surveyed the packed rows, three seats to a section, and multiplied. *It must carry more than four hundred and fifty people.* The stewardess tapped the intercom. "Good evening, and welcome to the Queen of the Skies, the first wide-body airliner developed for inexpensive and efficient transatlantic service. You'll be flying the largest and heaviest airplane in the world, and the first to use fuel efficient, high-bypass turbofans. If you have any questions, be sure to ask. And thanks for flying Pan

Am."

Sydney supposed that should impress her, but somehow it all seemed too much. She accepted a plastic cup of tomato juice from the stewardess and looked out the window as the jet took off. Lights were beginning to come on all over Manhattan. She could make out the spire of the Empire State Building and farther away, the square façade of the new World Trade Center building that always reminded her of a giant steel Gumby.

Sydney had never flown into Tehran before. The last time she'd been in Iran she'd traveled by local bus through Kurdish country, subsisting on KitKats and apples. To this day she couldn't abide either one. She had met Peter Buckley and his wife while there and, now, when revolution threatened, had acted on their longstanding invitation to return. *So what if Davies is there? They're* my *friends.* It didn't hurt that their house would provide a perfect location from which to watch the festivities.

"Lady, you do know about the troubles in Iran, right?" Her seatmate, a balding, sweaty man in his fifties, nudged her. "Not a great place for a little gal like you."

She nudged him back, a teensy bit too hard. "Luckily I have a black belt in karate. And an AK-47." At his look of dismay, she said brightly, "It's okay. It's in my checked bag."

That took care of any further conversation, and Sydney could enjoy the landscape unfolding beneath her. They'd flown from Istanbul over the rugged mountains of eastern Turkey. One peak speared through the clouds. The steward pointed it out. "Mount Ararat is always cloud-covered. That's where the Ark landed."

Sydney recollected seeing it from the ground. She had survived the harrowing trip in an ancient bus that careened down the narrow switchback road from Erzurum, only to land with a jolt on a pancake-flat expanse of ground spreading across the flood plains of the Tigris and the Euphrates. In the midst of the plain—like Prometheus breaking his chains and reaching toward the sky—rose a huge mountain. It made sense that the Ark ended up there. *Any port in a storm I guess.*

"Ladies and gentlemen, if you'll return to your seats and fasten your seatbelts, we will be landing at Mehrabad International Airport in a few minutes."

The Queen of the Skies floated down into a morass of trucks and humanity. Three jeeps teeming with soldiers met the disembarking passengers and escorted them to customs. Sydney left her seatmate, his four suitcases roped and tied by his side, arguing with a taxi driver. A man in a chauffeur's uniform approached her. "Sydney Bellek?"

"Yes. You're Gregory?"

"At your service." He took her bag and led her to a car parked at the curb.

The Cadillac battled through the streets of Tehran, finally reaching a leafy, quiet suburb. It pulled up in front of a green stucco house with a wide veranda. "Ivana!" Sydney ran up the steps and into the arms of a slender woman dressed impeccably in Chanel, her graying hair folded into a luxurious chignon.

"My darling Sydney, I'm thrilled to see you again. It's been so lonely since the girls went back to school in America. It's wonderful to have the house full once again!"

With a sinking heart, Sydney realized she meant

Elian. "I hear you have another guest."

"Yes, yes. I don't know if you two know each other. Elian Davies is almost as famous a journalist as you are."

Sydney laughed and hugged her. "I hear you met him in Russia?"

"Just once. To be precise, his mother knows my mother, and when he asked so sweetly if he could stay here, I saw no harm in it." She glanced at Sydney with mild trepidation. "You will get along, won't you, dear?"

"Of course, Ivana. Now where's Peter?"

"He's at the office. Things are turning very ugly here. I'm glad you saw the beauties of Tehran the last time you were here—I'm afraid the mobs are wreaking havoc downtown. They're even threatening to overrun the palace. What if they destroy the Peacock Throne? Or all those beautiful malachite urns?"

"There, there." Sydney made as if to head into the house, but someone blocked the door. Taller than she remembered. Thinner. Shorter hair. *That's good.* Something glinted in the sun. *He's still got that diamond stud in his ear.* A fleeting sensation of heat in her loins startled her.

"Sydney? Sydney Bellek? At last we meet."

Sydney paused. For a moment, she almost believed him and discovered to her chagrin that her mood worsened a bit at the thought. "What do you mean—at last? We've met."

He didn't miss a beat. "Ah, you're right of course. I'd nearly forgotten." He peered at her from under the crop of thick chestnut hair, a slight smile playing over his lips. "With a name like Bellek, you would have to remember me."

Sydney stared at him. Ivana put a soft hand on her arm. "You've been studying, Elian. How clever of you to know that Bellek means memory in Turkish."

Elian gazed down at the mortified Sydney. "You don't always live up to your name, though, do you?" he whispered. Aloud, he declaimed cheerfully, "Athens, wasn't it? Where we last met? I'm afraid subsequent events kind of pushed the memory aside. Being kidnapped takes its toll." He winked at her.

Firmly suppressing the ridiculous hurt feelings, Sydney reminded herself that this blue-eyed creep stood between her and a Pulitzer. His careless—and inaccurate—remark could only be the product of an enlarged ego and not a deliberate attempt to sting. "Are you going to let us in?"

He bowed with a flourish and stepped aside. The two women swept in arm in arm and took the stairs. "We'll see you at dinner, Elian," called Ivana.

****

Elian kept up a light banter throughout dinner. Sydney had forgotten how delicious conversation could be with three very cosmopolitan travelers at the table. Ivana proved a gracious hostess and lavish with the wine—"It's Georgian. I have a secret conduit." She blew a kiss to her husband. "Peter, these young journalists are here to report on events. You must tell them what you can of the current state of affairs."

Peter Buckley, a cheerful man with florid cheeks and a bulbous nose that bespoke much happier times, laid his napkin down. "I can tell you what the ambassador announced today. Our latest directive is to begin preparations to close the consulate. I spent the day sorting and burning papers. We are continuing to monitor the riots. No one has seen the shah in days."

Elian leaned forward. "My sources in the Guard say it's only a matter of time before he is captured."

"Really?" Sydney couldn't resist. "*My* sources tell me that the shah has already left Tehran." She stared Elian down.

"Well, the embassy would appreciate any and all information from any source. The atmosphere is quite…er…disquieting." Peter stood and waved toward the door. "Shall we have port in the study?"

Sydney followed him, chuckling inwardly at the way diplomats could minimize the most virulent conditions.

Later, as she trudged up the graceful circular staircase to her room, Sydney felt rather than heard someone behind her. A scent of something spicy and sweet filled the air. She whirled.

Elian stood one step below her, his narrow chin sticking straight out and his cowlick straight up. He jumped back and stumbled down the stairs, landing hard on one knee. Nursing his foot, he glowered up at her. "What did you do that for? I could've wrenched an ankle!" She could hear the muffled word *bitch* even from the top of the stairs. She turned and marched up to the landing without a word.

He caught up with her at her door. She raised a hand to slap him, but the look of pain on his face made her pause. "I'm sorry, Elian. Are you hurt?"

In a voice that dripped self-pity, he said, "No. I guess not."

"You gave me the willies, sneaking up on me like that."

"I wasn't sneaking. I was coming to bed."

"Excuse me?"

He indicated a door down the hall. "Unless…" He smirked at her.

For an instant, she suspected he hadn't forgotten Cairo and their less than spectacular lovemaking. She straightened and glared at him. "I don't have to tell you what the answer to that is." She bent to the doorknob.

"Ah."

The silence made her turn. He stood smiling, then, in a lightning quick movement, leaned forward, took her face in his hands, and kissed her. Before she could say anything, he whispered, "That's what I would have done our last night in Tangier." He left her with her mouth open and limped down the hall.

Sydney went in and fell on the bed. *Tangier? Could it be? Could he be…?* No. *Elian isn't anything like that boy.* That boy was fun-loving and daring and exciting. This one called her names and beat out every scoop she ever had. In fact, this one didn't even have the same name. She concentrated on her memories of that summer at the beach. She saw a fifteen-year-old boy, gangly, all limbs. Sure, he had a shock of rich russet hair, a resolute chin, and blue eyes too. Different name though. What was it? Eddie. His name was Eddie. Not Elian. And he smelled like…licorice. This man, this Elian, smells like…She wracked her brain. Fennel. That's it. Maybe anise. Entirely different.

Satisfied, she undressed and fell asleep within minutes.

****

She found a note slipped under her door in the morning. Holding her breath, she opened it.

"Miss Sydney, I will meet you at Arq Square at eleven o'clock. Cover your head, and wear something shapeless. Cyrus."

So, her contact had news. She tapped the note on her forehead. Elian had a reputation for pilfering his rivals' tips. How to get out of the house without raising his suspicions? She found Ivana. "Do you have a *chadur* I can wear?"

The Russian nodded in agreement. "Good idea. With things the way they are out there, it's best not to draw attention to yourself. Especially when you're American. I'll find one." She went down the hall calling to her maid.

An hour later Sydney, covered in the traditional women's black cloak, slipped out of the house and headed to the center of the city. She didn't see a shadow hail another cab and follow her.

Cyrus, a young man of about eighteen, loitered casually on the steps to the Golestan palace. Although the square was crowded with people, they seemed fairly calm. Without directly acknowledging Sydney, he ushered her into an alley.

After checking for eavesdroppers, she slipped the hood off her head. "What can you tell me?"

Her informant brought his hand down in a gesture that clearly meant *keep your voice down*. "Not much. The Ayatollah Khomeini is readying himself to return to Iran from Paris. The shah has disappeared."

"I knew that already, Cyrus. Can't you tell me anything else? Have you heard where the shah is? Or his family?"

The young man craned his neck, searching the area. His voice dropped to a mumble. "They are hiding near the airport. The crown prince was rumored to be on his way back to Iran, but I heard from my cousin in New York that he will not come, that the shah has ordered him to stay in America. The younger son, Prince Ali Reza, has been seen in the company of—"

A yowl like a furious band of hyenas sounded from the other end of the alley. Five men with scarves across their faces erupted from behind some garbage cans. They waved heavy sticks and ran toward Sydney. Cyrus took off.

She pivoted and ran smack dab into a hard chest. One that smelled of anise. "Elian!"

"Hurry!" He grabbed her arm and dragged her down the street. The men stopped at the entrance to the alley and melted back into the darkness.

They ran a few more blocks until they reached a vegetable market. Elian stopped at a juice seller and pointed at one of the pictures displayed on the cart. The boy threw chunks of fresh green honeydew melon, sugar and water into a blender and let it whirl. Sydney had to wait till her breath slowed before she could take a welcome sip. "What were you doing in my alley?"

"Me? My usual. Nosing around. Appropriating other fellows' sources. That kind of thing."

"You followed me!"

"I did."

"You…you…filthy ass."

"Ooh, I'll bet that's not as colorful a curse as you're capable of. Anyway, you'd be in a whole heap of trouble if I hadn't. As a matter of fact"—he pushed a curl behind her ear—"I had a feeling you might need my help."

The touch of his fingers would have soothed her if

she'd let it, but her annoyance took precedence. "Look…"

He interrupted her. "Look yourself. Let's get out of here. I'm beginning to think the revolution is much farther along than we thought. There's rioting everywhere. Millions of people have filled Shahyad Square. I want to get back to Peter's and file a report. You coming?"

Sydney checked the market. It bustled the way markets do, but in an eerie silence. She caught furtive glances from the women and open stares from the men. The atmosphere reeked of hostility. She nodded.

Together, they hopped in a taxi and roared north to Majidiyeh. They found the door open and the house empty. A note lay on the hall table. "Elian and Sydney. We've just gotten word to close down the consulate and go for sanctuary in the embassy. Hurry there as soon as you can. Love, Ivana."

They looked at each other. "Is this it?"

"What do we do?"

Elian started up the stairs. "I'm getting my things. You get on a plane."

"I don't think so."

"Sydney, I've heard rumors that a small clique of radicals are planning to storm the U.S. Embassy. If true, it won't be any safer there. We're dealing with all kinds of different factions—religious, Marxist, nationalist, Kurdish independence, you name it. The only thing they have in common is they all want a piece of Americans and the shah." At her rueful face, he smiled at her and ruffled her hair. "Look, I'll see what I can find out, and then meet you at the airport. Don't worry, I'm no hero, Sydney."

Even though they were miles from the center of Tehran, her journalist's antennae told Sydney danger was closing in. She longed to go with Elian but knew it made more sense to get out now. "I know you're not. Okay, I'll head to the airport, but I'm not promising to get on a plane right away. Cyrus—*my* informant—told me the shah and his family are hiding in Ekbatan and on their way to the terminal."

At Elian's shocked face, she grinned and pushed past him to her room.

Chapter Six

Alexandria, Present Day

"Wait a minute. You went to the airport and he stayed in town? You didn't escape together?"

"No—why would you think that?"

"You once told me—or at least you implied—that you had se…er…made love in Tehran." Olivia glared accusingly at her mother. "Since that has yet to be described, I think you're trying to skip over the juicy parts."

"Olivia! You don't really want to have that image stuck in your brain, do you? I've tried to shield you from our more…lascivious activities."

Olivia poured her mother a second cup of herbal tea. "I'm trying not to think of it as you. It's just a story—a very romantic story—about a couple of journalists who fall in love while cities and governments topple around them. So far you've only had a wet dream about Elian."

"You've forgotten that encounter in Cairo. And anyway, women don't have wet dreams."

"Oh, really? What would you call it?"

Sydney accepted the cup with a pensive air. She closed her eyes, a reminiscent smile playing across her lips. "What would I call it? A portent. Of what was to come."

"Mummy! You've spilled your tea." Olivia mopped it up.

Sydney didn't move, lost in the past. "That was January 1979. I wouldn't see Elian again until four years later, in 1983."

"But you corresponded."

"Oh, yes, in a way. We wrote dueling columns in our newspapers and sent mean-spirited anonymous letters to one another's editor."

"Now you're confusing me. Didn't you just admit you were lovers by the time you escaped Iran?"

"Lovers? No. I wouldn't call us lovers. A few amorous moments in the throes of youthful exuberance. Mostly we were haters. You know what Elian did to me? He let me get on the plane thinking he would follow. Sure, I got a scoop on the departure of the shah and his family, but he stayed in Tehran and sent dispatches from the front for months after that. The ones that won him his second Pulitzer. The bastard kept reporting until the revolutionaries took over our embassy in November 1979. Then he hitched a ride on a lemon truck and snuck out overland to Iraq."

Olivia's eyes went soft. "And you feared for his life every day, didn't you?"

Sydney shook herself. "Me? Not on your life. I was so pissed at him"—she made a snipping motion in the air—"I would have performed a battlefield vasectomy given the chance."

"Right. That would not have made a good ending to the story. Especially for me. So, then you didn't have…um…relations in Iran?" Olivia couldn't suppress the blush. This was, after all, her parents' sex life they were discussing.

Her mother grinned mischievously. "Oh, yes."

"Huh? Wait a minute…"

Sydney checked her watch ostentatiously. "More than a minute, I fear, my dear. Let's take the story up tomorrow, shall we?"

"Mother! You drop a bevy of teasers in my lap and you want me to *sleep on it*?"

"You can stay up if you like."

Olivia pursed her lips. "*Hmmph*."

Sydney smiled fondly at her daughter. "I'll take that as a good night."

****

"Have you heard from Benjamin?"

Olivia dropped into a chair. "How about if I let you know when I do? Are you ready to go?"

Sydney picked up a voluminous purse, slipped into some flats, and grumbled, "Why can't I just shop online? It's so much easier."

"Because you can't buy shoes without trying them on. Especially shoes for travel. Oh, and the dress has to be fitted."

"This whole trip to Paris is getting more and more complicated."

"Would that everyone were so lucky."

Sydney frowned and stared at her reflection in the mirror. "Is it really worth it?" The woman who stared back at her had too many wrinkles to be ignored, although her light blonde hair, caught up in an elegant French twist, stopped just short enough of white to keep her youthful. The rich, brown eyes Elian had remarked on so often still glinted with flecks of gold, and the throat—*thank you, patron saint of jowls*—remained slender and taut.

"I'm not the one to ask. Now, can we get moving? We also have to finish the Iran chapter today, and I have a date tonight."

Her mother pounced. "Rémy?"

Olivia declined to take the bait. "Yes. Now come on."

****

"All right, my trousseau is complete. Now, before we get back to my story, tell me where Rémy is taking you."

"Trousseau?" Olivia's eyebrows rose.

"It's just an expression. Spill."

"On a picnic."

"A picnic? Tonight? Isn't it still a little chilly for that?"

"We'll figure out a way to stay warm."

Sydney let out a snigger, followed quickly by a glare. "I do not approve. You must resolve the issue with Benjamin before you go bed-hopping."

"Mother, I haven't slept with Rémy. He's being very sweet about it. He's giving me plenty of space."

"How about time though? Isn't this the man who wants to take you back to France with him? Is he here indefinitely?"

"He can stay awhile longer."

"Must be nice to be a man of leisure. Doesn't he have a plane ticket?"

"He…er…has his own plane."

"I see."

To stave off further questions, Olivia blurted out, "He says he has a surprise for me."

Sydney sat forward, her eyes bright. "A surprise? Ooh, I wonder what it is…"

"You'll be the first to know. Now, can we get back to Iran?"

****

Tehran, 1979

Sydney kept her *chadur* on and had the taxi driver take the long way to the airport, so they wouldn't have to go through the center of the city. He grumbled about women and gasoline and accepted with ill grace the handsome tip. The flights to Paris and Rome were sold out, so she bought a ticket to Frankfurt. With four hours to wait, a walk seemed in order. She left the building and wandered over to the freight terminal. An unlocked gate let her into a compound where a small airplane sat on the tarmac. Somber men in black surrounded it, suspicious bulges at their hips. They appeared to be waiting for something. Sydney drew her cloak closed and retreated to a strategic spot to observe.

Sure enough, a few minutes later a small group emerged from a Quonset hut on the other side of the compound. Sydney counted three people—one tall, straight-shouldered man marching ahead of a woman and a man in uniform. Mohammad Reza Shah Pahlavi and the Empress Farah. But where were his children? Were they prisoners? Fear for the innocents seared her throat. She swallowed. *Nothing I can do about it. This is news. Time to do my job.*

Slowly, she drew out her camera and took a bead.

She managed to get quite a few shots as they climbed into the private jet. No one gave the woman hidden under a headscarf and shapeless cloak a second glance. When she ran out of film, she found a Dumpster and slipped behind it. Kneeling, she emptied the camera and carefully dropped the film into a canister.

"So where are you going to hide it? In your chastity belt?"

"Elian! You did make it. Oh, thank God."

"Aha. The lady does care." He said it lightly, but she heard an undercurrent of apprehension in his voice.

He doesn't want me to. Care that is. He had a reputation in the press community of wooing and ditching women like so much waste paper. One tag line had caught on and now followed him everywhere—"blue-penciled by Elian." *No-strings Davies.* She hoped her shrug conveyed sufficient indifference. "I'd be glad anyone—even you—survived. We're looking at a widespread rebellion here I think."

"I think you're right." He nodded at her camera. "What were you taking pictures of?"

"The shah and the empress flew out a few minutes ago." She ignored his look of outrage—*has he ever been scooped before?*—and whispered, "Elian, I didn't see any children. Have you heard anything? Are they all right?"

"The youngest two left yesterday for the States. Prince Reza and Leila are already there."

"That's good news."

He stuck his head around the Dumpster and looked out. "Did you get a ticket?"

She waved it at him. "One of the last seats on the flight to Frankfurt. It's leaving in two hours. Where's yours?"

Instead of answering, he said, "Okay, you'd better stay here. It's not safe out in the open."

She eyed the Dumpster. It was cleaner than the alley, but not by much. "You want me to climb in there?"

"Don't be absurd. Come." He led her around the corner to an unmarked door and rattled the handle.

"It's locked. What are you going to do now, Mr. Cleverkins?"

He grinned, which only irritated her further. "You'll see." He took out a credit card and slid it up and down between the jamb and the door. They heard a click. "After you."

She walked into a small storeroom. A wheeled gurney sat in the middle, and the walls were lined with shelves of medical supplies. "This must be the first aid closet."

Elian picked up a box marked *Tongue Depressors* and hefted it. "Let's hope no one needs these for a while."

She tossed her cloak on the floor and sat on the gurney. She bounced twice. "Seems comfortable enough."

He said nothing.

"Elian?"

"Yes?"

"I might remember a boy in Tangier. He had a cowlick, and pointed ears, and…and…he smelled like licorice."

He moved toward her. "Anise."

"All right, anise."

Their eyes locked. "Sydney?"

"Yes?"

"Kiss me."

She floated toward him, fetching up against his chest, where she rested, bumping gently. Her head rose like a helium-filled balloon, her lips drawn inexorably toward his. She hesitated, suddenly afraid. *What if this is real?*

"It is real, Sydney. It's always been real. You just refuse to recognize it. Or me." His hands went to either side of her face.

The wall crumbled. Tears falling, she wrapped her arms around him and kissed him deeply. They stood swaying, holding on by mouth, only breaking apart to allow a frenzy of kisses to rain on each other. Hand between her breasts, Elian bent Sydney back and gently pushed her onto the gurney. He kissed her throat and planted kisses down her sternum as he unbuttoned her safari blouse. Motionless, she concentrated on the burning spots where his lips had touched her skin. When he reached her belly button, he undid the zipper and continued on.

She writhed on the bed, hoping, hoping he wouldn't stop. He tugged at her pants, letting them drop on the floor and buried his face between her legs. She felt the orgasm approaching, a fast train on a slow track, and pushed him away. "Come to me."

He lifted his head to look at her face, his own muddied with desire. In one swift movement, he tore his jeans off and threw them aside. He climbed up on the gurney. As in her long ago dream, his cock pulsed, beating against her belly. With one hand, he spread her thighs and let his penis run up along the inner flesh and deep into her. The gurney began to roll, but neither of them paid any attention. He pressed into her, a steadily accelerating motion, reaching ever closer to her heart. They rolled back and forth, a symbiotic wave crashing against the shore, until she whispered, "Elian, we're there…oh….Elian." Her clitoris trembled and gave in, just as the gurney hit the wall with a crash. They heard a shout.

"Quick, quick." He tossed her clothes at her and pulled on his jeans. Except for a single exhaled breath, he showed no evidence of what they had just done. Sydney stifled the stab of pain his cold dispassion gave her—*blue-lined by Elian*—and followed his orders.

The shouts had died down, and the two quietly left the room, sidling along the wall until they reached the main terminal.

"You have your ticket?" he murmured.

She nodded.

"The Middle East Airlines counter is down to the left—now run!" and he gave her a mighty shove. She didn't have time to argue. Behind her, a uniformed brigade marched into the terminal, singling out foreigners and checking their passports. She handed the stewardess her boarding pass and hurried out to the plane.

As she reached the bottom step of the airstairs leading up into the plane, she felt a hand on her shoulder. "Elian!" She turned in relief, but before her stood a stranger, a young Iranian boy. He held out a folded note.

She took it and read. "Sydney, I forgot something in the room. Go quickly, don't look back. I'll find you again. I've always remembered you. Someday you'll do the same."

With shaking hands, she put the note in her pocket and gave the boy a rial. Before she settled in her seat, she searched the other passengers for a familiar face. It occurred to her that despite the thousands of plane trips she'd taken, the only ones that counted were the ones she'd shared with him. *It's funny, I feel as though I've known him all my life—but that's ridiculous.*

She closed her eyes. Two azure eyes, a crooked nose, a diamond-studded ear, together with some very manly parts, swam onto the lens of her mind. *Maybe it isn't so ridiculous.* Somehow the thought cheered her up, and before she dropped off to sleep, she chuckled. *Well, at least I now have more than a wet dream to dwell on.*

****

Alexandria, Present Day

"Okay, so you *did* make love in Tehran. Whew. It didn't sound any more *magnificent* than the first time, though."

"I can't argue with that." Sydney grinned. "Sex can be a challenge when you're blundering around on a hospital gurney smashing into things."

Olivia cocked her head. "It sounds very romantic, though."

"Everything sounds romantic to you, dear. That's why you write such tripe."

Olivia didn't take offense. She knew her mother had read every single one of her romantic suspense novels, and for the last few years she'd pressed copies on every relative and friend they had, including the men. "More tea?"

"I think not. I'd like to put my ankle up for a bit. It's still a little sore. Don't you have some tripe to write?"

Her daughter laughed and picked up the tray. "I have to get ready for my date. I'll be back tomorrow. I'm on pins and needles to hear what happened next."

"I'll do my best to idealize your father's and my sordid affair."

"Promise?"

"If you promise to come clean about that phone call to Benjamin."

Olivia raised her eyes heavenward. "Phone call?"

"I know you made it. What did he say? What did you say?"

"He said he was very busy and didn't think the senator could spare him just now." When her mother continued silent, Olivia snapped petulantly, "What was I to do, tell him I'm considering running off with another man and want his opinion?"

The silence continued. Olivia finally barked, "*What*, Mother? I can't sit around and wait for him to show up. I'm tired of pushing him, of being the engine of this relationship. If he won't make an effort, I can only conclude he doesn't care."

"You know better than that. You've known Benjamin for what? Three years? He loves you dearly. I can see it in the way he looks at you, the way he takes care of you."

Olivia threw herself on the couch and wailed, "Why can't he show it then? At the very least, he takes me—us—for granted. He doesn't think he has to keep up his end of the bargain. Mother, I'm just…tired of it."

Sydney softened. "What will be, will be, I suppose. But don't give up yet, if only for me."

"Why don't I get back to you on that tomorrow?"

"You want to see how it goes with Rémy tonight."

"Yes. Things should fall into place tonight."

****

"Your breakfast tray, Your Majesty."

"Thank you, minion."

"I believe you meant to say *mignonette*."

"Perhaps, perhaps." Sydney took the silver cover off. "Eggs and sausage. This should keep me going."

Olivia watched her mother eat. "I can't believe you've stayed so thin over the years with an appetite like that."

"I'm making up for all those field assignments when I considered myself lucky to find a dung beetle or two to munch on."

"You never ate dung beetles."

"Well, grubs, then."

"At any rate, you're as beautiful as you were when I first laid eyes on you."

"That doesn't say much. Every muscle in my body trembled with fatigue, you were covered in slime, and we were both red and squawling."

Olivia remarked sadly, "I wish Pop had been there."

"Don't start that again. You know he had no idea you existed and no way to get there if he'd known."

"Why didn't you try to send word to him?"

"Because I thought…I thought he was dead."

Olivia carefully set her coffee cup down. "Tell me."

"I will. But it will take a while. First, let's hear your news."

"News?"

"Yes. What happened at the picnic? What was Rémy's surprise?"

As Sydney watched, a tear welled up in her daughter's eye and dribbled down to her chin. She wiped it away absently. "I don't want to talk about it."

Her mother continued to wait patiently, sipping her coffee. She knew Olivia would eventually break down.

Their closeness ran wide and very deep, a devotion born of trust validated many times over. She knew Olivia needed to confide in her.

"I…we…went to that park near National Airport—what's it called? They play soccer there. Across from the Lady Bird Johnson Park?"

"Gravelly Point. Such an unimaginative name, don't you think?"

"What? Oh. Yes. Anyway, we found a picnic table right down near the water and watched the planes take off and land. Did you know the moon is full now? It was huge."

"Yes, it's supposed to be the brightest in a decade. So what did you eat?"

Olivia's somber face broke into a smile. "I knew I could count on you to zero in on the important stuff."

"Well?"

"He brought a lovely champagne—before you ask, Bollinger—and truffle paté and cornichons and a voluptuous cheese he called Délice d'Argental that he smuggled in on his jet, and—"

"Let me guess, the first raspberries of spring. Oh, and a baguette still warm from the traditional French oven he's installed on board the jet."

"Very funny. Yes, as a matter of fact."

At the look on her mother's face, she burst out laughing. "If I didn't know better, I'd say you were jealous."

"Am not. So…moving on. The surprise?"

Olivia began slowly. "I know the same thing had occurred to you—that it would be a ring. Not so."

Sydney set the tray to one side and put her hand under her chin to listen.

"We talked about travel and how much we both love it. You know Ben hates to fly. That's been the biggest challenge to our relationship."

"I know—he could have coined the phrase 'There's no place like home.' It's not Benjamin's fault—he comes from a long line of stay-at-home men. Once the first Knox scrambled ashore at Plymouth, the family figured they'd done enough traveling for a century or two."

"Oh, Mother." Olivia put a hand over her mother's thin one. "I don't think I could stand to spend the rest of my life in that musty old house in Connecticut! Did you know his mother refuses to change anything—even the wallpaper? It's been the same horrible floral pattern for almost fifty years. I'd go insane!"

Sydney studied her daughter. "You were saying? Rémy's surprise?"

Olivia's face transformed into fondness. "A TripTik."

"A what? You mean like one of those triple-A maps?"

Olivia nodded. "Except he made this one up himself. A round-the-world trip. Just the two of us." Her pleading eyes sought out her mother's. "What do I do?"

Sydney rose and went to the door. "Alice! Would you mind fetching the tray?" Then she picked up her hairbrush and began to brush her hair, counting the strokes under her breath.

As she took a step toward the bathroom, Olivia gave a warning growl. "You can't ignore me forever. I need help."

Sydney paused. "Call him."

"Ben?"

"Whichever one you want."

Olivia threw up her hands. Alice slipped in and picked up the tray. "How are you ladies coming with the biography?"

The two women stared at her. "Um."

The old nurse pursed her lips. "You don't have much time left, you know. Best get on with it. Miss Olivia, will you be here for supper?"

"I...I don't know yet."

"I see." Alice's simple phrase, as always, struck fear in the hearts of her subjects. She left.

Sydney indicated a chair. "Orders received."

Olivia nodded. "I believe we were at the part where Pop was dead."

"No, we weren't. You were wondering how Elian came to be a no-show at his daughter's birth. At that point, I believed him dead, but back in 1979, he was very much alive and made sure the whole world knew it."

"So, you're saying I'm not going to hear how I came to be conceived any time soon?"

"Yes. I mean no. Look, do you want the story of my life or just the bits that involve you?"

Olivia made a show of puzzling over the question.

Sydney swatted at her. "Be patient. We won't get to your part in the story for another four years. We're getting way ahead of ourselves."

Olivia waited just long enough to annoy her mother. "Fine, tell it your way."

Sydney sipped her coffee. "Like I said, it would be four years before I saw your father again. The bastard escaped Iran by his fingernails..."

"Bastard?"

"He managed to get all kinds of glamour shots of himself scaling border fences and leaping onto moving buses. By the time he returned to civilization, he was hailed as a superstar. My own secretary tacked a poster of him to her cubicle wall. She came in late one day and found it like this." Sydney ripped a piece of paper into small pieces and tossed them like so many broken bones on the table. Olivia gave a little shiver. "He even had a fan magazine. And a chat room before they were really hot."

"Chat room? I've heard of those. Weren't they a sort of primitive Facebook?"

Sydney glared at her daughter. "Hey, before you twitter…I mean titter…think how quickly we went from the first so-called *bulletin board* in 1978 to a social medium that handles three-hundred and fifty trillion tweets a day. Your father was way ahead of his time."

"I love it when you defend him right after trashing him."

"Well, back then, in the early eighties, I had nothing good to say about him. And I had to give a direct order to my secretary forbidding her to moon over him."

"All right, all right, when will you get to the part where you thought he was dead?"

"Soon, soon." Sydney rose and spoke to her mirror. "We have lots of adventures to relate before that and…some of that stuff you have to leave the room for."

"Mother!"

"Well, you wouldn't have been conceived without

it. Just let me finish dressing and I'll tell you."
****
Boeing 747-300 Big Top, 1983

Sydney pulled out her crossword puzzle, mints, pen, glasses, embroidery, and tissues and set them on the other seat before stealthily slipping the miniature bottle of Jack Daniels into the magazine pocket. She checked her ticket once again. They'd be in Rome tomorrow morning and from there the flight to Beirut should be less than five hours. As she searched for her seat belt, a husky voice behind her ear said, "Excuse me. I believe I have the window seat?"

The scent of licorice filled her nostrils. She looked up into a pair of deep indigo eyes, half-obscured by a tangle of hair the color of cordovan. He used his angular chin, cloaked in reddish brown stubble, to indicate his seat. She looked him up and down without moving and pronounced, "Elian Davies."

He drew back, an expression of mock surprise on his face. "Sydney Bellek? Could it be you after all these years? My, how you've aged…I mean matured."

Whatever joy she'd felt at seeing him faded. "You."

He scooted around her knees, grabbed her stuff, dropped it in her lap, and sat down. "Me."

She opened her crossword puzzle and pretended to work on it. He pointed a tanned finger at a spot on the page. "Eleven down is Oslo."

"Duh."

The stewardess came by. "Please buckle your seat belt, sir. We'll be taking off in five minutes."

"Oh, Miss…" He peered at her name plate. "Petula? What a lovely old-fashioned name!" He beamed at her. "Would you mind bringing me a glass of ice before we begin to taxi?"

The stewardess opened her mouth, then opened her eyes wide. "Why, you're Elian Davies, the famous photojournalist, aren't you?"

"At your service, Petula." He bent in a graceful half bow.

"Right away, sir. I'll be back in a jiffy." She tore down the aisle, knocking into passengers' elbows and knees along the way. Holding a glass high, she ran back like a bartender in a Bastille Day race, and proudly plunked it and a packet of peanuts on Elian's knee.

When she'd gone, he took a furtive look around and pulled a miniature bottle from his pocket. Sydney's annoyance dissolved in giggles. "You too?" She pulled her own small whiskey out.

"Oh good, we'll share this first one, shall we?"

She couldn't say no, and besides, sipping kept her busy. *Elian.* She'd spent the last four years trying to hate him. It should have been easy. His reputation as an ace reporter and first-class scoop jockey had only grown since Tehran. Too many of her colleagues told stories of him racing across the tarmac just ahead of them to catch the final words of an escaping dictator, or jumping into a helicopter for a one-on-one interview with said dictator upon his triumphant return. Along with his derring-do came the even more infamous reputation as an inveterate ladies' man, which the recent episode with Petula only confirmed.

She studied his left hand as it popped a peanut in his mouth—steady, strong, tanned. It looked familiar. *Oh yes, I watched it unbutton my blouse in a supply room in Tehran.* She turned away to hide the blush.

When her cheeks had sufficiently cooled, she turned back only to have him glance away quickly.

Staring out the window, he inquired in a casual voice, "So how's your boyfriend holding up while you're off on these wasted efforts to follow in my footsteps?"

Her momentary affection melted away. Old Blue-Pencil Davies at it again. *Prick.* "They're all moping of course, poor babies. And yours?"

"Me? I don't hold with leading women on."

"That's not what your adoring public thinks."

He swung around on her, the customary smirk on his lips gone. "They're wrong, Sydney."

The remark—and his deadly serious face—threw her. To cover her confusion, she sipped her drink. After a minute, he turned back to the window. As she watched his shoulders gradually relax, she reviewed the stories about him. From what she'd heard, women who crossed paths with him considered a one-night stand the standard reward. *Could he be telling the truth?* Just then Petula passed, slowing as she neared their row and heaving a soulful sigh. Sydney remembered the lovelorn look on her secretary's face. *He may not lead women on, but he sure draws them in.*

Passengers began to fill the remaining seats. The airplane reminded her of the Pan Am Stratocruiser she'd flown in when she was five. Far more spacious than the Queen of the Skies—the 747-100 she'd taken to Iran in 1979—this one had only two comfortable seats on each side, rather than the three-five-three configuration she'd stuffed herself into on the last flight. She'd almost sprung for first class when she heard they'd reinstated the old Sleeperettes, but

Malcolm had put his foot down.

"No reporter of mine is going to hobnob with the elite. You'll lose your edge."

Elian followed her eyes. "They call this plane the Big Top. A definite improvement on the old 747s, don't you think? This stretched upper deck is considered economy class, but I feel positively pampered." He'd lifted the glass to his lips to catch the last drop of whisky and jiggled the melting ice. A thick white line about two inches long ran across the back of his right hand.

She touched it tentatively. "How did you get that scar?"

He glanced at it. "I'd almost forgotten about it." He grinned at her. "I've had it for, oh, about four years. Happened in Tehran."

"Really? During which of your fabulous exploits were you wounded?"

He hung his head. "Well, I wouldn't exactly call it an exploit. It involved a girl…"

"I don't need to hear about it then."

"You might have known her. She stood about five feet two, with long blonde hair you could wrap yourself in, and eyes this kind of warm, cinnamon toast color. Her—"

"Hey!"

He drew back, the shock rendered perfectly. "Why, it was you! Now I remember."

At that moment, the plane, which had taxied for over an hour, finally took it into its head to take off. They were thrown back in their seats, and Elian's drink sloshed in his lap. The big jumbo jet rose wheezing into the air, complaining its way to cruising altitude.

When things had settled down and Elian had talked Petula into two more glasses of ice, he produced more miniatures from a secret cache and poured Sydney another. She took it and, curiosity conquering her better judgment, reluctantly asked, "You were saying?"

"Saying? Oh, about this beautiful girl and how I got this scar. It's not a very romantic tale."

Sydney thought of a gurney, slippery with sweat, and the sight of very manly bits disappearing into her vagina. *No, not very romantic. But...*

He put a hand on her arm and spoke softly. "We'd made love in a small room with a tempest simmering outside the door. I'll never forget how her eyes gazed into mine with so much desire. I'll never forget how warm her skin felt, how her curves fit mine, how satisfying our ultimate convergence. I often wonder if she remembers." She felt rather than heard the question that hung in the air.

He didn't look at her, but she felt his body tense beside her. She longed to tell him she did remember, that that moment was still precious to her, that she'd never experienced any union so fulfilling. She opened her mouth and closed it again. *I can't. He left me at the plane four years ago. He abandoned me.* She hadn't understood until now just how much his desertion had hurt. A great rush of agony and near-hate surged from her head to her heart. She clutched at her chest, willing the pressure to subside. Something—she had to say something to distract him.

"You haven't told me how you got the scar."

He gave her one look from under his brows, and his face closed down. He downed his drink and in a bantering tone replied, "In a fight over a lady's trinket."

"A trinket?"

"After I'd seen you off on the plane, I went back to the supply room. I thought I'd heard the clink of something metallic hit the ground while we…we…were—"

"Go on."

"When I opened the door, I found a beggar inside. He'd obviously been stealing medical supplies, but when he turned to face me he was holding something shiny."

Sydney gasped and circled her pinkie with her hand. "My ring, my mother's ring. So that's where I lost it."

"Yes. At any rate, the beggar inexplicably refused to let his windfall go without a fight. So I gave him one. Unfortunately, I was unarmed and he was. Armed. With a large dagger. Which he used to slice a piece of my hand off."

"What happened to the ring?"

"Thanks for the sympathy. The beggar considered a diamond earring an even trade for it, and we went our separate ways."

Sydney missed most of his last sentence, lost in unexpected joy. "You…you still have it? My ring?"

He held out his other hand and opened the palm. On it lay a plain, rose-gold band. Her mother had given it to her the day she died, and Sydney had worn it ever since. That is, until Tehran. Its loss had nearly broken her heart. She slipped it on.

He touched it lightly. "It's been in my pocket a long time. I'll miss it."

"Why didn't you send it to me?"

He drew back. "You know, I never thought of that.

I guess I assumed we wouldn't go four years without seeing each other."

His words left Sydney wondering if the time apart had bothered him. And why he'd kept the ring on his person all these years. He couldn't have known she'd be on this plane. Could he?

The stewardess brought their dinners. Elian pulled the plastic off the sectioned plate. "Ooh, yummy, my favorite—brown meat in mystery sauce." He grinned at Sydney. "I always ask for the *special* meal."

Sydney took a bite of her roll and a swig from the wine. "I take it you're also covering the Lebanese civil war? So how did you land this plum assignment?"

"Same way you did. Hostilities are on the upswing. A dinky little struggle for control between the Maronite Christian minority and the Muslim majority in 1975 has now evolved into a full-scale regional war."

"I know. At last count there were four Christian militias, seven Communist groups, the PLO and four splinter groups, Sunni Muslims, Shi'ite Muslims, Druzes, and now Israel and Syria with their fingers in the pot."

"Why can't these people take up a hobby? Oh, yeah. They've got one."

"Mayhem."

Elian nodded. "My vaunted facility with disguises and my ability to infiltrate any group from Australian aborigines to Aleuts makes me the obvious choice to report on such a complex array of enemies. Plus, Craddock always sends me where there's more than an eighty-percent chance of being shot."

"You want to take a breath after that speech?"

"Nah, I'm good. I had to get it all in before you

interrupted me. So how come you're en route to yet another 'conflict that doesn't determine who is right but who is left'?"

"That's a quote, right?"

Her seatmate saluted. "Good for you, but it's by the late great Anonymous, so I take full credit. You haven't answered my question."

"I'm the only one at the *Observer* who knows Arabic."

"So, we're both headed into the maelstrom because no one else wanted the job."

"I guess so." Sydney took a tentative taste of the square object labeled *Brownie* and quickly swallowed the rest of her wine. "Has Israel withdrawn yet?"

"Nope. According to them, it's a security issue—they don't like Palestinians and militants on their northern border."

"Beirut isn't exactly on their border."

"Which brings me to the alternate possibility, that they're hoping in all the confusion they can annex southern Lebanon."

"You don't think someone would notice?"

"Hey." Elian counted on his fingers. "You've got your Lebanese Front, your Lebanese Forces, your Fatah, your South Lebanon Army…I know I'm forgetting a bunch. And now with the U.S. and Saudi Arabia sticking their noses into it, the time is ripe for a sideswipe at even more Arab territory. Wouldn't put it past them. That's how they got the Golan and the Sinai. They pick some minor attack, claim they have to retaliate, and voila—Greater Israel."

"They tried it in 1978, didn't they? It didn't work then."

"Well, the situation in Lebanon hasn't exactly improved, has it? Look, I think I'll get a little shut-eye before we land in Rome." He snuggled under his blanket. Less than a minute later, she heard his rhythmic breathing.

She watched him sleep, his face serene, even cherubic, his insolent nature well-disguised in repose. *Something's different about him.* The same chestnut tendril spiraled down his forehead, the same firm, almost pugnacious chin shook when he snored, the same slightly pointed ears...*That's it. The diamond stud is gone.* She remembered him saying, "The beggar considered a diamond earring an even trade." *For me. He did it for me.*

A rush of emotion dropped a veil over all but the tiny world of the two people in seats 11A and 11B, in a jet plane floating somewhere over the Atlantic, in a still moment in time.

****

The plane set down amid jeeps bristling with automatic weapons and the soldiers that carried them. It reminded Sydney unpleasantly of Tehran.

Passengers started to move down the aisle. Elian retrieved Sydney's carry-on. "Where are you staying?"

"The St. George. How about you?"

"Oh, I found a little place near the Corniche."

Sydney made her voice deliberately off-hand. "So...what angle are you working in all this?"

Elian winked at her. "Right, like I'm going to tell you. By the way, I read in the news clips that you're planning a series of heart-tugging interviews with street kids. You writing for *Good Housekeeping* now? Say, how about you pick up some nice recipes for your readers while you're at it?" He zipped down the aisle just ahead of her claws.

Customs took forever, since the agents refused to give up on the possibility of a bribe until they'd exhausted every approach. By the time Sydney reached the city, people crammed the narrow streets, trying to get home before the sirens began.

Once settled at the hotel, she called the chief of the Beirut news desk to check in. "Malcolm says hi, Ted."

"Hey, Sydney, glad you made it. Are you at the St. George?"

"Yes. What's that background noise at your end?"

"That? Oh just a little air war going on. No big deal. I suggest you get over here early in the morning—safest time—and I'll issue you a flak jacket and helmet. Do you want to meet with General Kirkonnen? I can arrange it."

"Who? Oh, the commander of the Multinational Force? Maybe later. My primary assignment is to get in touch with Fawzi al-Hurriyeh. He's the leader of a faction called"—she checked her notes—"the Shepherds of the Cedars. Now that Ariel Sharon's been demoted from defense minister I want to see where their loyalties lie."

"Good thing you're here then—I haven't been able to spare a man to check that group out. It's not clear what their position is. After the uproar over the massacres at the Sabra and Shatila refugee camps, they've been downplaying their association with the Israeli occupying forces. On the other hand, Fawzi's brother was assassinated last year, it's said because of his close ties to Israel. So somebody out there thinks they're still linked."

"Who killed him? Do they know?"

"A Christian."

"Oops."

The bureau chief chuckled. "Since then the Christian militias are in a bit of disarray."

"Sounds like this could be an interesting assignment."

"Yeah, yeah. Sydney, be careful in your dealings with al-Hurriyeh—his brother's death definitely spooked him. Make any false moves and I can't vouch for your safety. I presume you've done your homework, but facts on the ground change almost every second here. I can't keep all the acronyms clear in my head—and I've been here almost five years!"

"Message received. I'll see you tomorrow, Ted."

****

A productive day, yes. Sydney had managed to set up a meeting with al-Hurriyeh for the following morning, and she'd taken a jeep tour of the central city. Her guide, Amin, told her they called the most recent period of this seemingly endless civil war "the battle of the hotels." She gawked at the shell of the Holiday Inn and at the gaping holes in the once beautiful promenade along the Mediterranean known as the Corniche.

"I used to swim off those rocks near the university," she said, a tear in her eye. "At least the campus has escaped much of the destruction."

"The buildings, yes, but not the psyches of the students, I'm afraid. My friend Nageeb still hides under his bed when he hears sirens."

"It's so different from the American University of Beirut I knew when I was a student back in seventy-four. The toughest building to get in and out of then was the girl's hostel!"

Amin shook his head sadly. "AUB no longer draws the cream of European and American students." He waved a hand at the rubble of a bombed-out building. "Someday…someday we'll rebuild, and Beirut will once again be the Paris of the East!"

The driver dropped her off, and she managed to get a shower and her face on before the mandatory afternoon power cut. As the sun set, she stood at the concierge's desk waiting for a list of recommended restaurants, thanking God her days of staying at hostels were long over.

"Mind you, mademoiselle, there are no truly safe places to eat in the city anymore, but these four tend to be less frequented by tourists and foreigners so they're not often targeted."

She chose one and hailed a taxi. As the maitre d' led her to a table, a now familiar hand touched her shoulder. "May I join you?"

She noticed the long white scar on the back of his hand and felt a stab of guilt. "Sure."

They sat quietly for a minute. Sydney felt an unfamiliar shyness descend on her as the silence continued. She searched for something intelligent to say. "So…you like Indian food too?"

"Me?"

Sydney fought the urge to say something sarcastic. From the look on Elian's face, he was doing the same thing. *Quick, Syd, jump in before he does.* "Ted Hampton—he's my bureau chief here—said Hamdi's has the best Indian food outside of the subcontinent. Have you eaten here before?"

"No, but I heard the same thing." He ordered an

India Pale Ale and shot her a questioning glance. "Sydney?"

"I'll have one too. It goes better with spicy food than wine I think."

Elian ordered lamb biryani, and Sydney asked the waiter about the pork vindaloo.

"It is a southern dish, mademoiselle. Very spicy. Are you sure you want to order it?"

"Why not? I pride myself on my iron stomach." She puffed out her chest and gave said stomach a fond pat.

The waiter's face grew even more dour. "We shall see, mademoiselle." He set down a dish of the thick yogurt sauce called *raita* and a basket of flat bread. A few minutes later, he returned with their orders.

Elian tucked into his lamb. "Perfect—just the right blend of spicy and sweet." He nodded at the waiter and gave him a thumbs-up. "Ted's right—the food is excellent."

Sydney stared at her plate. Threads of steam rose from the vindaloo. She took one sniff and snapped her head back to give it time to stop whirling.

"What's wrong? Aren't you going to take a bite?" Elian asked, his eyes twinkling.

That did it. No way would she back down now. She scooped up a teaspoonful and dropped it on the tip of her tongue. "Oh. My. God." Her hand went to her throat as her esophagus tightened to the diameter of a pin in an attempt to expel the stuff. She gasped.

"Hot?"

Sydney was in too much pain to respond, though his curled lip cried out for a good slap. She sat quietly, praying for release. Finally, she pushed the plate away, drank off her beer, and dragged the bread basket toward her.

"Hey, you're not going to eat *all* the bread, are you?"

She nodded, dipping the warm *naan* in the yogurt sauce, and signaled for another beer.

By the time Elian had finished his dinner and smacked his lips often enough to elicit a growl from his companion, the effects of Sydney's unfortunate choice of dish had worn off and she could breathe without coughing. He paid the bill with a handsome flourish and held out his hand. "Shall we?"

The night was young, the guns were asleep, and they decided to take a stroll along the bits of sidewalk still left in the famous district known as the Hamra. Elian took her arm. "Let's walk down to the shore."

Peals of laughter and wreaths of smoke followed them, a bit eerie considering they were in the midst of a conflagration that had already left two hundred thousand dead or homeless and an enmity between sects hitherto unheard of. They found a flat spot of ground between two boulders and sat, listening to the crash of the waves. Elian's words came softly out of the dark. "This sea has seen so much blood, so much death."

Sydney couldn't see his face, but she could hear the sorrow in it. "I didn't think you cared that much about anything."

She felt him twitch. "You know me so little, Sydney? After all these years?"

"Years? What do you mean, years? I've met you"—she counted on her fingers—"twice in some ten years. How am I supposed to know you?"

"Twice? No. Way more than that."

"What do you mean?"

He didn't answer.

Sydney had begun to focus on her assignment and the approaching meeting with al-Hurriyeh when he spoke again. She could barely hear him above the pounding of surf on rock. "Every time we meet it's like I've known you all my life, Sydney. I know your voice, your eyes, your scent—Fidji, isn't it? By Guy Laroche?" At her gasp, he chuckled. "Easy for an investigative journalist like me, snookums. Anyway, I bet I can guess what you're thinking right now."

Sydney felt suddenly defensive—or was it vulnerable? "I bet not." She tried to empty her mind of thought.

"Well, a minute ago you'd lapsed into work-related musings. When I caught your attention with my little…er…recitation, you began to worry that I'm right—that you're an open book to me. Have I got it?"

"I…I…." She was spared the necessity of coming up with a suitable retort by the touch of his lips on hers. "Elian…I…"

"Sydney? Shut up and kiss me."

"Okay."

A long kiss later, she settled back in the crook of his arm. "So what am I thinking about now?"

"Probably cookies." He cut her giggle off with another kiss.

The return walk was restful. Elian left her at her hotel and went off whistling "Sweet Betsy from Pike." Sydney called in a loud whisper, "*Shh*—snipers shoot whistlers."

The music cut off with a snap. She almost ran after him to make sure he was all right when his face appeared out of the darkness. He blew her a kiss. "Night, love. See you *mañana*."

Chapter Seven

Alexandria, Present Day

The doorbell rang. A minute later, Alice trudged up the stairs. "Rémy de Beaumec to see you. He says you are expecting him."

Sydney gave her daughter a thoughtful look.

Olivia avoided her eyes and turned to greet the tall, broad-chested Frenchman. He bowed to Sydney and took both Olivia's hands in his. "You told her?"

Sydney had never seen her daughter quite so red-faced. Olivia hiccupped and sat down. "I told her, but we haven't had a chance to discuss it yet. We're trying to finish the book before Mother leaves for Paris."

"Discuss it?" His thick, black eyebrows rose. "What is there to discuss? You need only announce, *non*?"

"Um, Rémy, now is not a good time. Mother and I are at a critical juncture in her story."

He threw up his hands. "But you told me to come this afternoon, Olivia. So that we may tell your mother of our intentions."

Olivia peered helplessly at Sydney. "I...I haven't had a chance to explain to her."

Rémy stood, hands rolled into tight fists, his normally exquisite manners clearly taking a back seat to his resentment at this new hitch in his plans. "Darling, you're a grown woman! I don't see that we need your mother's permission to go." He swiveled quickly and caught Sydney's belligerent expression just before her face went blank. The hesitation lasted a mere instant before he continued smoothly, "Forgive me, Madame Davies." He cast a calculating eye toward Olivia. "Naturally, your blessing would be most appreciated."

The soft spot Sydney used to have for the Frenchman went *pouf*. "Rémy, Olivia is correct. We have much work to do before I leave for Paris. I understand from her that you have your own jet here. I assume you have a flexible schedule then?"

He shook his head, baffled. "Yes, but—"

"Then I suggest you go home and come back tomorrow."

The tone of her voice brooked no discussion. "I will do as you instruct." He kissed Sydney's hand and held out his arms for Olivia. She moved toward him and pecked his cheek.

"Ah, you wound me, *ma chère*," he whispered.

Sydney shooed him out and swung around to her daughter. "Olivia…"

"What?"

"Why do I get the feeling you accepted his invitation?"

Olivia's attempt at an indifferent shrug fell flat. "I didn't exactly say yes."

"But you didn't exactly say no." Sydney fiddled with the desk clock. "Rémy is clearly under the impression that this is a done deal."

"I know," groaned Olivia. She flung herself on the chaise. "What do I do, Mother?"

"Olivia, as Rémy said with admirable accuracy,

you're a grown woman. I leave in ten days. You have to resolve this before I go."

"I will, Mother. You're right as usual. I'm being a coward." She put her coffee cup on the tray and sat at her mother's desk. "Now, where were we?"

Sydney lay back on her bed and shielded her eyes. "Where indeed? That lamentable interruption has made me lose the thread."

Olivia consulted her notes. "You had an appointment with the Christian militia leader, Fawzi al-Hurriyeh."

"Oh, yes."

****

Beirut, 1983

The jeep picked her up at six a.m. the next morning and drove her through quiet, meandering streets. At one point, the driver pulled over and tied a blindfold on Sydney. That had been part of the agreement, so she didn't quibble. The Phalangist leader she was going to meet had every reason to be cautious after his brother's assassination.

They drove for another hour. The sounds of the city faded, and a fresh-scented breeze fanned her face. "Have we left Beirut?"

The driver didn't answer. She felt the jeep tilt up. The blindfold muddled her sense of direction, but the fact that they were climbing, and that the road seemed to wind in dramatic hairpin turns, could only mean they had reached the mountains east of Beirut. She felt for her bag. Her Nikon and notebook lay inside, but the other camera, a tiny one the size of a matchbook, hung from a chain around her neck. The bureau chief had given it to her, along with her helmet and flak jacket.

"It's a prototype. Elie got it from his girlfriend in the physics department at AUB. Looks like a Byzantine cross, doesn't it? There's a knob on the bottom edge you press to take a picture. Don't touch the stone in the middle. That's the lens."

The car slowed, and the driver exchanged a few words with someone. She heard a gate open and women's voices rising above the bleating of goats. *We must be in a compound.* She waited for her blindfold to be removed, but no one touched her. Before she could take matters into her own hands, two strong arms helped her out of the jeep and shoved her into a room. She pulled the scarf off, but her eyes met only darkness. "Fawzi? Is anyone there?"

For answer, she heard a whistle, only this one didn't have a melody. A deafening crash sounded, and stars twinkled in the pitch black sky. *They're out awfully early*, she thought stupidly. As she lost consciousness, her brain wandered off on its own, pondering how she could have missed the forecast of an eclipse.

When she awoke, the darkness had lifted only slightly. Her arms were tied behind her, and she seemed to be sitting on the ground. A sharp rock dug into her thigh. She opened her mouth to call and discovered the hard way that someone had stuffed a rag between her lips.

"Spit it out."

She followed the voice's instructions and was pleased to feel the gag fall out. "Elian?"

"At your service."

"Where…where are you? Are you…are you…"

"Isn't this cozy?"

"What do they want? How long have you been here? Have you seen al-Hurriyeh? When—"

"Easy." Elian's laugh ended with a cough. "Your questions will likely be answered soon. Once the word gets out that Fawzi's kidnapped two American journalists, he won't have much time to do whatever he plans to do."

"Huh?"

"Never mind. Someone's coming."

They heard shouts and the clucks of angry hens. A door blew open, letting in broad sunshine. Their captor stood on the threshold, legs spread and arms akimbo. Sydney could have sworn he wanted to beat his breast like an enraged demigod. "Ah ha!"

"Ah ha yourself, Fawzi," grumbled Elian, which earned him a swat. "What do you want? The helicopter's due any minute."

Sydney tried to glimpse Elian's face to gauge whether he was bluffing. If she could tell, so could Fawzi.

Bluff or not, it must have worked, for Fawzi turned and yelled to someone outside. Sydney thanked her eight years of Arabic that she could almost understand him. "You, Jamil, check the skies at the lower end of the compound. Youssef, watch the gates." He turned to his prisoners and said in English, "We'll make this quick then, shall we?"

He pulled a chair up to Sydney and sat down backwards on it. "*Ahlan wa sahlan*, Sydney Bellek. Welcome to my humble abode."

"*Ahlan bīk*, Fawzi. I guess."

He continued to eye her, smiling mysteriously.

Finally, she broke down. "What are you doing?"

"Waiting."

"What for?"

"The helicopter."

Urp. "What if it doesn't show?"

"Oh, it'll show." He pointed a thumb at Elian. "Davies never lies. Do you, Elian?"

Sydney's confusion grew. "Look, Fawzi, I thought you'd agreed to this interview. Why kidnap me? What is El…Mr. Davies doing here? What do you want with us?"

"You don't know?" Fawzi spat on the ground, just missing her foot. "Good, then your acting will be more genuine." They heard a whirring sound that quickly grew to ear-splitting proportions. Wind swirled in and out, blowing dust and mercifully unidentifiable items around the small hut. Fawzi excused himself and went outside.

"Elian," Sydney whispered urgently. "What the hell's going on?"

He raised his eyebrows toward the sky. "Mossad."

"Israeli intelligence? What are they doing here?"

"I imagine to negotiate with the Shepherds."

"About what?" A thought occurred to her. "Wait! It's about those massacres in the refugee camps, isn't it? The Israelis claimed they had nothing to do with the actual killings, and the court only declared that Sharon was lax in his supervision of the Christians. There's more to it, isn't there?"

"*Shh*. What do you think?"

Sydney recalled the facts as she knew them. Israel, taking advantage of the Lebanese civil war, had invaded twice to obtain concessions. Yet their biggest diplomatic issue remained the thousands of Palestinians displaced from their ancestral homes during Israel's expansion, now living in squalid refugee camps in Jordan and Lebanon. The Arab governments had so far refused to absorb them, increasing the pressure to establish a viable Palestinian state, which Israel wanted to avoid. That left only elimination as a solution. However, if Israel took matters into its own hands, the world would turn on it. Even the U.S. might reconsider its support for the Jewish state. Hence the reliance on the Phalangist forces to take care of the problem.

She whispered to Elian. "The massacres occurred last year. Sharon's been demoted. What are they doing here now?"

Before he could speak, the door opened, and Fawzi and his bodyguards stepped inside, followed by two men in crew cuts and rumpled suits. They stopped short when they saw the two captives. "Who are your prisoners, Fawzi?" One of the men eyed Elian and continued in Arabic, "His face is familiar."

The other one stepped over and raised Elian's chin with a none-too-gentle hand. "He's that American journalist, isn't he? The one we heard was missing." He turned accusing eyes on the Arab.

Al-Hurriyeh shrugged. "We caught them trying to infiltrate the camp." He turned to one of his guards and barked, "Coffee."

"Are they spies?"

"No. At least…" A gleam shone in Fawzi's eye. "I don't think so."

"Why don't you kill them?"

"Ah, then they'd be of no use to us, would they?"

The Israeli waved an indifferent hand. "The U.S. would do nothing to rescue them. They don't deal with hostage takers."

"That's not what I've heard. I've heard Israelis are the hard liners." Al-Hurriyeh leered at the second Israeli, who remained silent. Sydney wondered if Fawzi referred to something specific.

The first agent, who seemed to be in charge, indicated the table. "We're here to talk. Take your prisoners elsewhere."

Al-Hurriyeh threw up his hands. "I've nowhere else to put them. We're expecting a rocket attack any moment from the Syrians. This is the only safe house in the compound. Besides, they don't speak Arabic. Americans never bother to learn any language other than English." He winked at the agents and turned a hard stare on Sydney.

He knows I speak Arabic. Why is he doing this?

Elian bent toward her and said in a low voice, "Pawn to King Three."

This might have been helpful if Sydney knew how to play chess. As it was, she could only give Elian a look she hoped conveyed *Checkmate?*

The two Mossad agents gave Elian and Sydney a wary berth and sat down at the table. They began to speak in whispers, but it didn't take long for the voices to rise.

"What do you mean, you won't give us the weapons? You promised!"

"We made no promises."

"You did. Sharon did anyway. He said if we cleaned out the camps at Sabra and Shatila we'd get the grenade launchers and assault rifles we asked for. We did what you asked."

"General Sharon never instructed you to attack

anyone. Israel doesn't condone massacres."

Fawzi's mouth fell open. One of his underlings muttered, "Only the ones they don't get away with."

Sydney watched expressions of anger, disgust, aggravation, and fear chase each other across the militia leader's face. He settled on anger. "You told us to go into the camps. You promised us support."

The Israeli spat. "Look, we have no interest in your petty tribal struggles. We gave you money and weapons on the understanding that you would create a buffer against a Palestinian takeover of Lebanon. You have proved unable to accomplish that. Why, you can't even agree with your fellow Christian groups long enough to drive the Syrians out. We've come to tell you you're on your own." He rose. Al-Hurriyeh lunged at him. His two guards went after the other Israeli, who pulled out a Glock pistol and began firing wildly.

Sydney felt Elian's hands behind her. *What the—? Is he free?* "How did you—"

"*Shh*, while they're fighting, let's git."

"Git?"

Instead of responding, he cut the ropes on her legs and pushed her through a window. The combatants paid no attention. Elian landed beside Sydney with a thud and lay very still. After a minute, she nudged him. "You okay?"

"*Shh*. I think I cut myself."

Sydney noticed blood pooling next to his thigh. "You weren't shot?"

"Er…maybe." He gave a wry chuckle. "Shot trying to escape. There's a headline. Look, why don't you scout around? See if there's a way out at the back of the compound. I'll stay here and hold the fort."

Obediently, Sydney crept to the corner of the hut. A camouflaged chopper purred in the center of a large open area. She could see the pilot through the windshield, but no other men, Israeli or Arab, around. *The two agents must have come alone.* Other than a small knot of children and women huddling under a lean-to on the far side, the place was empty. The din inside the hut seemed to be reaching a crescendo. She went back to Elian.

He lay panting, a rag pressed to his leg. Blood still leaked. She looked closer. "Elian, I don't think you're holding it against the actual wound."

Her companion did something she wrote about much later and with great relish. He blushed madly. "I know." He lifted his leg and she could see a small tear in his pants just on his left buttock.

"Oh for heaven's sake, Elian, he shot you in the *ass*?" She tried unsuccessfully to stifle the titter.

"It's not funny, Sydney. It hurts like hell. Can you…" He peered up through his thick auburn lashes like a crestfallen beagle.

Sydney rolled him over, scrunched up the rag and bore down with steady pressure on the wound, then tied the torn bits of trousers together. "It's not that bad. Looks like the bullet only grazed you. I read somewhere"—she sniggered—"that but*tocks* bleed a lot."

"Oh, Christ. You remind me of my fourth grade teacher. Sheesh."

For answer she pulled his arm. "Come on, we've got to get out of here."

She half-dragged Elian to a wooden gate and pulled him through into a small olive grove. She looked around. "There isn't much cover here. Maybe we should try to get behind that other house."

"I think I can walk now," panted Elian. "On the count of three..." But Sydney had already dashed across the path and into a tiny alley between two houses. She beckoned. They huddled behind a curtain of shirts hanging on a clothesline and listened. The gunshots and screams diminished and after a few minutes stopped. As they watched, the helicopter rose in the air and took off.

"Do you suppose Fawzi killed the two agents?"

"Either that, or the pilot decided to abandon them. Provides more deniability. Come on—Fawzi'll see we're gone now. If he's still alive, that is."

Sydney hooked an arm under Elian's shoulder and together they staggered through the alley. Beyond the houses lay a stretch of rocky scrub that rose up to a cedar forest at the top of the hill. They worked their way up, crouching behind boulders and checking the scene below. All was a-bustle, but no one seemed to be looking outside the compound for them. They reached the trees just as the sun set. Elian lay down on a soft bed of needles and closed his eyes.

Sydney snuggled beside him. "How's the butt...er...wound?"

"Better. I think the bullet glanced off the wall as I climbed over the sill."

"I wonder—Israeli or Phalange?"

"It doesn't matter...oh, you're making a joke. I see." After a minute, he rolled on his side to face her. "Thanks for helping me, Sydney." He pulled her hands between his large paws. "Are you cold?"

"A little. What do we do now?"

"Sleep."

"Okay." Sydney lay as still as she could, but Elian's nearness bothered her. His hands warmed hers, while something else worked on the rest of her body. A drop of perspiration dribbled down her forehead, and a tendon pulsed near her groin. Cool lips touched her face.

"Sydney? You asleep?"

Her whole body tensed. She waited for another touch, another kiss, terrified and longing at the same time. "No." Would he kiss her again? His hands released hers and went to her waist. He drew her to him and somehow found her lips with his. A dove cooed in a tree nearby. The darkness was complete, except for a blue gleam from the vicinity of Elian's eyes. She pressed against him, crushing her breasts on his chest, and circled his neck with her arms.

"Sydney…" His voice came in a hoarse groan of desire. "Sydney."

For answer, she snaked one hand down between them and undid the button of his jeans. She let her fingers worm their way in to find his cock, hard and hot. *So that's what was pulsing.* She rubbed it tentatively, and it responded by straining against the zipper. She unzipped the pants and pulled his penis out, caressing it with soft fingers.

He kissed her hungrily. "I want you. I want all of you, Sydney. I want your mouth, and your breasts, and your toes, and your fingers and…" The last word was a mere sigh.

"What? What did you say?"

"Nothing. Help me with this thing."

She dutifully opened her blouse and undid the bra.

He lifted out her breasts and brushed his lips across them, nibbling on the nipples. She rose to meet him. He licked around the breasts and traveled down her stomach to her belly. Fingers pulled her jeans and panties down and cupped her ass, forcing her toward his mouth. His tongue flicked the top of her clitoris. Without warning, her orgasm ripped through her and lifted her off the ground. She shuddered, bucking against him.

"Hold on, love, I haven't even started."

She heard his muffled command and tried to relax. But the orgasm had a mind of its own, and she felt it peak. "Oh dear. I'm sorry, Elian."

"S'okay. Somehow I think we'll see another one." He traveled up her body, cheek to skin, until he reached her face. His hands separated her thighs and pulled them up and around his back. As she worked to keep her breathing regular, the head of his cock touched her opening. *Oh my God he's right, I'm going to come again. Slow down, Sydney. Savor it.*

Elian inched his hard rod slowly into her vagina, scraping the walls with a delicious roughness that exquisitely scratched the itch. He backed out a bit, then entered a little more, each time bringing her to new heights of desire.

She grabbed his head. "Faster," she grunted.

"In a minute." He kept up his forward motion, gradually accelerating each entry and exit, until he was fully inside her. He took a deep breath and started pistoning, faster and faster, driving his penis into her, each time grazing the sweet spot and pulling away.

Her climax climbed with him until she moved faster than he, sucking him into her body, swallowing him whole like quicksand, like a whirlpool, until the two became indistinguishable, indivisible. She knew better than to scream and panted, "Oh God, Elian, we're…we're coming."

As they glided down into contentment, he lay across her, his penis still pulsing inside her. She reached down to release it, but he pushed her hand away. "It's all right," he breathed. "It's just reliving the moment."

Chapter Eight

Alexandria, Present Day

Olivia kept her eyes fastened on the notebook page. Sydney paid no attention, lost in the past and the feel of warm, wet flesh. At the sound of a step on the stairs, they both jumped. Alice peeked around the door. "It's getting late, ladies. Will you be wrapping up soon? Mrs. Doughty would like to serve supper."

Olivia opened her mouth and closed it with a snap. "Uh…"

Her mother rounded on her. "What's the matter? Oh!" She clapped a hand to her mouth. "I forgot to warn you, didn't I? The…affair evolved rather precipitously." Her lower lip jerked twice. "Sorry."

Olivia hastily gathered her things. "I…er…think I'll head home and…" *Gulp.* "…type up these notes. I'll see you tomorrow, shall I?" And she beat a hasty retreat, trailed by muffled snickers.

****

"Miss Olivia, Mr. de Beaumec is here."

Olivia turned unseeing eyes toward Alice. "I…what?"

Sydney nodded at the old retainer. "He's downstairs?"

"Yes."

Olivia pulled herself together, only to dissolve into

a new crisis mode. "Oh, dear, oh dear. He's early. I haven't decided. Mother, I need time!"

Sydney put the coffee cup down. "Tell him that then. Nothing has to be decided now. Did you email Benjamin? Have you heard from him yet?"

"No." Her voice quavered. "Mother, I told him everything. All about Rémy and these past few weeks. I said I needed to see him."

"No reply?"

"Not a word."

Someone knocked.

"Come in."

Rémy, immaculately dressed in a slim European-cut suit, his Princeton University tie perfectly knotted, stood on the threshold. "Miss Alice told me I could come up." He held out a long, white box. "Madame Davies."

Sydney opened it. Two dozen red roses lay inside. She lifted them out and held them to her face. "They're lovely. Thank you, Rémy." He pivoted gracefully to Olivia and presented her with a small velvet bag. She took it with a slightly trembling hand.

He smiled, his white teeth flashing in the dark face like a young Omar Sharif. "Aren't you going to open it, my dear?"

"Yes, yes, of course." Instead, she laid it on the desk. "Rémy, I…I…Would you mind waiting downstairs for me?"

His ebony eyes glinted, and his mouth set in a thin line. He opened his mouth to speak and shut it again.

"Rémy?"

"Yes. I will go now." He spun on one foot and stalked out. They heard heavy steps descending the stairs.

Sydney turned to Olivia. "Whew. He's no fun when he's angry, is he?"

Olivia sat heavily. "It's not a laughing matter."

Her mother watched her daughter with a speculative air. "He thinks you accepted his proposal. Doesn't he deserve an explanation?"

She shook her head. "No, this is his fault. I never explicitly said yes. Every time I tried to demur, he would change the subject to the weather or food or something. You know what I think? I think he knows I have doubts, and his strategy is to ignore any interruptions and hope I give in and go along with his scheme."

"If he knew you, he'd understand that ploy is not a recipe for success. Do you want me to talk to him?"

"No!" Olivia stood. "No, please. This is my responsibility. I just wish he'd give me more time." She headed toward the door. They heard the bell ring downstairs. Her hand on the knob, she hesitated. They heard Alice greet someone. Sydney strained to hear but the voices were too low. Finally Alice came up.

"A gentleman to see you, Olivia."

"What? What are you talking about? Rémy is already here—he's in the living room, isn't he?"

"Mr. de Beaumec is in the morning room." Alice's tone reeked of displeasure. Sydney, however, who knew her much too well, recognized an underlying hint of amused indulgence. "You have a second caller. I put him in the living room."

Olivia stamped her foot. "Are you going to tell me who it is or not, Alice?"

Sydney put a soothing hand on her daughter's

shoulder. "I can guess. Benjamin?"

Olivia could only stare at her mother, who smiled and said, "You didn't think you could control fate, did you?"

Silence reigned. Sydney listened to the mantel clock tick and waited. She hated to admit it but, like Alice, she found her daughter's dilemma agreeably diverting. Poor Olivia! Forced to choose between two handsome, accomplished, loving men. Men who represented polar opposites. Rémy, dashing, rich, world traveler—*French*. Benjamin, dependable, reasonable, domestic, American to his Pilgrim core. Apparently, he had finally woken up to the fact that he could lose Olivia, or he wouldn't have come.

"Will you excuse me a moment, Mother?"

"Certainly."

Olivia walked purposefully out of the room.

Ooh, ooh, what's she gonna do? Sydney wasted a precious minute trying to recall the title of the old country song about failure to commit—"Amy's Song." *That's it!* She hummed the tune, practicing patience.

Time passed slowly. At one point, the front door slammed. Which one of them left? Or had Olivia made a run for it? She toyed with the idea of calling Alice but rejected it. She needed the old retainer down there as the scene unfolded.

Just as she began to nod off, Olivia came in, her face a mask of woeful resignation.

"Well?"

"They're both gone for now. I told Rémy you weren't feeling well, and I had to take you to a doctor."

"And Benjamin?"

Olivia sat down and put her head in her hands. Her

words were barely audible. "Ben…said I could go with Rémy. That he wouldn't try to stop me."

Sydney took her daughter in her arms. When the sobs had subsided, she said, "How exactly did he say it?"

Olivia wiped her eyes. "What do you mean, how?"

"I mean, what was his tone? Was it stoic? Did he seem indifferent? Upbeat? You know Benjamin—he wants you to be happy above all, and if he thinks it's what you want, he won't make a fuss. It's not in his nature."

"I know." Olivia's glum smile broke her mother's heart. "He's so…so…solid, Mother. So respectful of my wishes. Oh God, how I wish he'd just take charge once in a while."

Sydney smiled. "And tell you what to do?"

"Yes," she wailed.

"*Hmm.*"

"*Hmm?*"

"Is he gone?"

"Yes. He had to drive back to Connecticut. He only came down to…to…see me off."

"If you go."

"If I go."

Sydney rose and went to her bureau. She ran a brush through her honey-blonde hair before twisting it into a knot at her neck and drawing a black lace snood over it. She checked her watch. "Well, we've successfully wasted the whole morning. I've got an appointment at the dentist at eleven."

"Oops, I forgot. Say"—Olivia managed a weak grin—"my little fib to Rémy wasn't a fib after all!"

"Come on. Since you've fought off your swains for

the nonce, we can spend the afternoon together. We need to get cracking on my story."

"Ready when you are."

****

"Has the Novocaine worn off yet?"

"I fink so. Do I found funny?"

Olivia laughed. "I guess that answers my question."

"Oh dear. We'd better wait for awhile, then."

"All right. You rest quietly for a bit and I'll check back."

****

"All recovered?"

"Yes. See? My s's are as sibilant as ever."

Olivia patted her mother's head. "Shall I order something for lunch?"

Sydney gazed beyond her daughter at the tulip magnolia in the front garden. In full bloom, its large cup-shaped pink and white blossoms opened in a lavish paean to spring. "It's another beautiful day. Let's take a picnic down to Belle Haven Park, shall we?"

"What a nice idea! I'll make some sandwiches for us and then run and pick up some of those chocolate cookies from Balducci's you like so much…Do you want champagne?"

"Of course. We're celebrating my first trip to Paris in ten years, aren't we?"

"I'll be back in a few minutes then. You'd better change into something more comfortable. Oh, and get Alice to set the picnic basket out."

Alice saw them off, and Olivia drove north to the riverside park. "Let's head over to the water."

Olivia lugged the basket to a picnic table under an

ancient sycamore. She spread out a tablecloth and set down a plate of sandwiches, a bowl of cucumber slices, and a white cardboard box marked Balducci's. Sydney popped open a bottle of Piper-Heidsick and twirled it in an ice bucket. On a branch just above them, a bluebird tweeted. "Looking for a mate, I suppose."

"Not a handout?"

Sydney nodded at the starling edging toward them. "No, but he is." She tossed the bird a crumb and filled her plate. They sat eating and watching the crews practicing on the water in contented silence for a while.

"This is the life, isn't it?" Olivia stretched lazily and poured champagne into her plastic wine glass.

Her mother eyed her. "You're awfully complacent considering your predicament."

Olivia dropped her arms with a sigh. "You have such a knack for pummeling a person with reality. Okay, why don't we get back to work then? Are you finished with that sandwich?"

Sydney handed the plate to her daughter. "I am. Now, where was I?"

Olivia paused. Her blush lent an attractive rosy hue to her cheeks. "You…er…you had just had…er…"

"Oh, yes, that's right." Sydney chuckled. "We'd fallen asleep in the woods." She gave her daughter a sly look. "There's more of that. Are you sure you want to hear it?"

Olivia tossed off her champagne. "It's part of the story, isn't it?"

"Integral."

Her daughter grimaced. "Hit me with it then."

****

Lebanon, 1983

She woke to the touch of cold steel on her forehead. "My, you Americans can have sex under any circumstances, can't you?" Fawzi's grinning face loomed above her. "Even when your lives are in danger."

She made as if to rise, but he kept the gun pressed at her head. She impatiently pushed it away and sat up. "If you were going to kill me, you would have done it already." She noted his well-wrapped form and shivered in the morning chill.

The militia leader stuck the pistol in his belt and sat back on his haunches. With his right arm he shook Elian, who rolled over and began to snore.

Sydney surveyed her captor. He sported a black eye and carried his left arm stiffly. "I see you survived your little altercation. What happened to the Israelis?"

"You mean the foreign businessmen? They preferred to…er…disappear, rather than face their…er…CEO with the news that Fawzi al-Hurriyeh and the Shepherds of the Cedars did not accept their terms and expect their company to live up to its bargain." He rapped his chest, then winced. "These Isr…I mean, foreign businessmen, they think they can get away with cheating us because we're Arabs."

"What are you going to do?" Sydney hoped she didn't come across as too eager, but her journalistic instincts had kicked in. In her excitement she stood up, forgetting Fawzi's first words. Following his leer, she stole a furtive glance down. Her blouse hung open, and her jeans had fallen to her knees. As she redeployed her wardrobe, she glanced at Elian. He seemed to be respectably attired. *Whew.* Her lover slept on, unaware of their scrutiny nor that his hands had been tied again.

"What will we do?" Fawzi raised his good arm and shook it. "We shall continue our fight against those who want to dominate Lebanon. Now at least we have a clearer idea of who our friends are." From the snarl on his face, Sydney didn't think any Israeli overture would meet with success at this point. "Now come on, we go back to the compound."

Sydney's stomach growled. "Can I have some food?"

"When we get there. You'll be staying awhile." Fawzi indicated a coil of rope with his chin and one of his guards tied her hands.

Sydney laughed. "You don't think you can handle a widdle girl like me?"

Fawzi indicated his stiff arm. "I am not at my best at the moment, Mademoiselle Sydney. I'm taking no chances."

The guard bent down to Elian, who woke, cursing and trying unsuccessfully to dodge the slaps.

A jeep stood a few yards away. Fawzi's men dumped Elian in the back and jumped in next to him. Fawzi escorted Sydney to the front seat and started the engine. They bumped down a rocky path toward the compound. Sydney decided to take advantage of his good mood. "Fawzi, why did you kidnap us? What do…did…you want from us?"

"You speak Arabic. The Israelis didn't know that."

"So?"

"So now I have American witnesses to their perfidy. The U.S. doesn't believe anything Arabs say, even us Christians. They condemned us for the refugee camp attack. Now you can explain to them that the Israelis arranged the whole affair. The Americans will not be able to defend their little Jewish sister against your charges."

Sydney doubted whether America's deeply ingrained support for Israel, bound as it was to decades-long Cold War loyalties, would come undone simply on the word of one journalist, who didn't after all hear any actual evidence. But then, she'd learned that Arabs were eternal optimists.

When they reached the camp, Fawzi deposited Sydney and Elian in the same hut as before, untying them but locking the door behind him. Sydney inspected the room for bullet holes but found no evidence of the shootout. Boards had been haphazardly nailed over the window, allowing just enough light to see by. A few minutes later a woman clad in a head scarf, short jacket, and baggy pants entered with a tray. She laid a carpet down on the dirt floor and spread several dishes out. Without a word she left, locking the door again.

Sydney fell on the food. A piece of bread and white cheese in one hand and a handful of olives in the other, she finally noticed that Elian hadn't joined her. He leaned against a large embroidered pillow, his eyes closed. "You're pale. And you're not eating. Are you all right?"

"Me?" He opened one eye. "Sure. I…think I may have sprained something last night." He gave her a wan smile. "And my butt is killing me."

Sydney sighed and put the bread down but not before taking a huge bite. She crawled over to Elian. "Turn over."

He did. She inspected his left buttock, not without a slight intake of breath at the memory of the maneuvers of the previous night, took a ewer of water from the makeshift table, and poured it over the wound. He flinched. She looked around for something to clean it with. Her backpack lay by the door. She rummaged in it until she found the small tube of Neosporin she always carried. She rubbed it gently over the wound in a steady clockwise motion.

"Stop that."

"Stop what?"

"You're deliberately arousing me. "

"Me? I'm applying ointment." She giggled. "I didn't want to be too rough."

"It's the rotation. It's having an effect. Stop it."

By way of answer, she rolled him on his side. Sure enough, a large bulge indicated the unintended result of her ministrations. She unzipped his pants.

"What are you doing, you witch?" But he didn't move away.

"Completing the therapy." She curled herself over his penis and gave it a long, wet lick. With one hand she hefted his balls, then squeezed them.

"Ah, ah, Sydney." Elian threw his head back. "Pray continue." His chest rose and fell. Her mouth wrapped around the base, and she worked her way up, squeezing with her lips and sucking the tip hard. He arched his back. "Don't stop."

"Which is it? Stop or don't stop?" She didn't wait for an answer but kept licking and sucking and rubbing until the penis went still.

He lay back, then jerked forward suddenly. "Ouch!"

"Oops, I forgot. So sorry." She grinned at him.

He kissed her nose. "Okay." He checked his watch.

"We should have time. Face away from me."

Wondering what he had in mind, she obeyed. He spooned her body, while his hand came between them and pushed her jeans and panties down to her knees. "For quick retrieval," he whispered.

She felt a hard nub pressing her from behind. "Are you…are you…"

"Yes. Have you ever?"

"Once."

"Do you want to?"

Suddenly she wanted to do anything and everything with him. He swept away all her old inhibitions, and there, in that squalid hut, on the floor, in the semidark, surrounded by platters and dishes, she opened her heart and body to him. "Yes."

His cock pushed at her lips, nudging them open. Grunting with each thrust, he slapped her ass cheek gently. That did it. She bucked backwards against him like a bronco, wiggling and turning, trying to get closer. He kept up the pressure until she mewled, "I'm coming, I'm coming." He collapsed on his side.

Both hands went round her middle and squeezed. "Wow."

She clasped his hands and rested.

When they awoke night had fallen. The dishes had been removed and a lamp lit. Sydney sat up and looked straight into the face of her captor. "Fawzi! How long have you been here?"

"Only a minute or so. After your…exercise I thought you'd need some rest." He snickered.

Her face hot, Sydney attempted to wrap the shred of dignity she had left around her. "When are you going to let us go?" she asked sharply.

He shook his head ruefully. "Of that I am not sure, Miss Sydney. I must confer with my generals. I wanted you here to act as witness to the treachery of the Israelis, but now I am not sure how best to utilize you." He dropped his chin into his hand. "If we let you go now, you could immediately report on this little encounter with our colleagues. That would be good. On the other hand, perhaps you will consider my hospitality less than exemplary and tell the story in another way, one that will do harm to my reputation."

He spun around to regard the sleeping Elian. "On yet *another* hand, holding hostages can be useful in itself. The Israelis reneged on their promise of supplies. Perhaps we can work a deal with the Americans. Or the Syrians." He slapped a knee. "So you see, we must think on this. There are many possibilities, many ramifications. I have my soldiers to think of." He smirked. "And my career."

He stood up. "Leila will bring food anon."

When he'd gone, Elian opened an eye. "What did he say?"

"You don't understand Arabic?"

"It's Greek to me." He grinned. "That's a joke. We met another time, years ago, you know. I was on my way to Athens."

"And I was heading to Cairo. I remember you vaguely. Now." She saw no need to tell him how the memories had rushed back along with the scent of anise mixed with lovemaking.

"So? Are we to remain prisoners?"

"He hasn't decided."

"You mean he hasn't figured out how we can be of use to him."

"He kidnapped me to act as witness at his meeting with the Israelis."

"As insurance, you mean. Because you know Arabic. I gather he lied about your language ability to them?"

"Yes. So at least I'm more useful alive than dead."

"And that leaves me where?"

She longed to say *up a tree* but somehow didn't think Elian would take it in the spirit in which it was intended. "I don't know. Look, what were you doing here in the first place?"

"Me? I was out for a walk. Just taking in the view."

"Oh really?"

He hung his head. "Fawzi caught me trying to sneak into the compound."

"And?"

"And what?"

"Come on, Elian, out with it. I can't help you if I don't know what you're involved in."

Elian got up, winced, sat down, winced, and stood again. He leaned casually against a wall, arms folded. "I've been investigating secret channels of communication between the Phalangists and Mossad. The cozy relationship with the Israeli military is well known, but my sources told me that Israeli intelligence agents had recently infiltrated the Christian militias and were making deals. The big one went down at Sabra and Shatila. I wanted evidence that Mossad had planned or supervised it, and that they were offering military equipment in exchange."

"You knew the helicopter was coming."

"Like Fawzi says, Davies never lies. I was waiting for it just like Fawzi."

"You were right—they did have a deal. And the Israelis backed out of it."

"I gathered that much. I may not know Arabic, but I can read body language. Plus I got shots of the two agents."

Sydney's hand went involuntarily to her breast. The necklace still hung there, its tiny camera intact. She'd counted on the Christians respecting the cross. "Do you have a camera?"

He shook his head. "They confiscated it. But"—he patted his ankle—"I have the film."

Sydney toyed with the idea of keeping her camera a secret, but since he no longer had one she had the advantage. "That's good—I couldn't get to mine."

"Yours?"

She touched the necklace. "Turns out it's not all that clever a gadget when you have your hands tied behind your back."

Elian nodded. "We'll be able to use it now though. With my photos of the Israelis and any subsequent ones you can take, we should have a fairly comprehensive report."

"That would be great, if we were working together."

Her companion grinned. "You don't forgive easily, do you? Look, we're in this together now. Divided, we don't have much. Together, we have a chance to break this story wide open. You game?"

Sydney stared at him, emotions warring in her head and heart. His glance lulled her, called to her. His lips formed a kiss, but she noticed his hands were balled into fists and a vein pulsed in his neck. *He thinks he can sweet-talk me into this. Can he?* "I'll think about it."

Only when his shoulders sagged and he let out a long breath did she realize how tensely he'd awaited her answer. She almost wished he would argue with her. "I—"

The door opened to reveal a woman's backside. Leila turned around with a large tray. The two prisoners pretended nonchalance until she'd gone, then went down on their knees before the food. Between bites of juicy tomato slices and lamb kebab, Elian kept up a steady stream of idle talk.

Finally, Sydney interrupted the flow. "We've got to get out of here. Do you have a plan? Or were you thinking you'd just talk Fawzi to death?"

Elian took a sip of tea. "Of course I have a plan."

"And?"

"I'm working out the details."

"I see. I suppose," Sydney returned sarcastically, "it involves a *deus ex machina*."

"That would be nice, but no. I think we should run away."

"We didn't get very far the last time."

"We didn't have a lot of time. If we wait until the camp's asleep, we can get over the mountain and down to Beirut before al-Hurriyeh rounds up a posse. Once we reach the Marine headquarters, he can't touch us."

"You want to go tonight?" She looked him over. He still winced whenever his rear touched a surface. "Why don't we wait a day? By then we may know what Fawzi plans to do with us."

"I'm betting he'll try to shake the Americans down."

Sydney put down the bread. "That could be our break. Once they know he's keeping Americans prisoner, they'll have to do something."

"Like rescue us? I doubt it. Colonel Riley, the Marine commandant in Beirut, told me in no uncertain terms that I would be on my own while pursuing my investigations. He hates journalists. Probably just as happy to let al-Hurriyeh string us up."

"Ah," Sydney simpered, "but when he learns it's a female that's being held hostage?"

Elian gave her a long, slow examination, lingering on her feminine parts. She fought the urge to squirm. "Maybe. Okay, we'll wait a day. By then, I should be healed anyway."

Sydney kept the triumph off her face with difficulty. With studied indifference, she stacked the plates and yawned. "Good. I'm going to get some sleep." She curled up on the carpet facing him, ready to grab him if he made a move toward the window.

Sydney had just nodded off when Fawzi came through the door. "Good news! I've decided to contact the Americans directly."

Elian stared at him. "Which Americans would those be, Fawzi?"

The man shrugged. "We have opened several lines of communication over the years. I left messages with all of them. We'll see who barks first, eh? You'd better get some sleep." He cackled. "I mean *real* sleep. You'll need to be rested." He left before Sydney could respond.

Elian crouched near her ear. "Most likely someone at the embassy. As far as I know, Fawzi has no contacts with either the military or the CIA."

Sydney waited a minute for the effect of his warm breath on her libido to recede. "What do you think their response will be?"

"Not sure. We should plan for any contingency. If they refuse to cough up, we'll have to make a break for it."

Sydney lay back. As she closed her eyes, she felt something moist brush her forehead. "Sleep tight. I'll take the first watch," he whispered. Too tired to argue, she slept.

****

Shouting in the compound woke them as the morning sun seeped in through the shuttered window. Elian stood by the door. He held a finger to his lips. "It sounds as though the whole camp is on the move. I'm betting Fawzi's heard from the Americans."

Sydney sat up and ran her fingers through her hair, wishing she'd brought a clip to hold it back. The long blonde strands were tangled from two days of strenuous activity.

Leila came in with a tray. She set it down with shaking hands. She said in Arabic, her eyes wide with fear, "The Americans are coming."

Sydney tried to be gentle. "Which ones, do you know, Leila? Diplomats? Or soldiers?"

Before the woman could answer, Fawzi shouldered his way into the room, behind him several young men toting rifles. He jerked his head at Leila, who scuttled out. "Get ready."

"Why?"

Sydney couldn't believe the arrogant tone Elian used. From his expression, neither could his captor. He raised his arm and shook it at Elian. "Now!" He left.

Sydney glared at Elian. "What were you trying to do?"

"An experiment. Sometimes these guys respond to bullying."

"Well, it didn't work. He looked ready to hit you."

Elian laughed. "So now we know. I say we follow orders."

They finished off the breakfast Leila had left and sat down to await events. The noise outside continued unabated. Sydney listened for the sound of a helicopter or jeep but only heard shouts. Half an hour later, Fawzi threw open the door and grabbed Sydney roughly. "Come." He stuck his chin out to Elian. "You too."

The two Americans followed him to a cart. An ancient horse stood blowing and stamping its hooves. Despite his age and sway back, Sydney could make out the graceful, delicate lines of a pure Arabian. Al-Hurriyeh threw their packs onto the cart and indicated they were to get in as well. A young man with an Israeli-made Tavor assault rifle jumped in next to them, and another man threw a tarp over them. They heard a whistle, and the cart started to move.

"What's going on?" she whispered.

Elian tried to raise the tarp, but the guard pushed it back. "*Là.*" Sydney started to translate.

"I know, it means *no*. I'm thinking Fawzi wants us out of the way until he knows what the Americans are planning."

They jolted over a rocky path, the pull on her body telling her they were ascending a hill. The scent of cedar wafted under the tarp. "We must be in the woods again."

The cart stopped. The guard hopped out and extended his hand to Sydney. A small shed stood in a clearing surrounded by beautiful cedar trees. The youth pushed them inside. They heard a match strike and soon smelled cheap tobacco. Sydney looked at Elian. "Now what?"

"It's the old *hurry up and wait* routine. Get used to it. Fawzi's probably negotiating with whatever Americans have shown up. It could be a while." He sat down on his haunches and pulled a piece of pita bread out of his pocket. "Want some?"

She shook her head, setting off a wave of dizziness. Elian caught her before she fell, and regarded her with concern. "Too many interrupted REM cycles I think. Better try to sleep."

Sydney didn't argue.

She woke to a whirring sound. It went over their heads and faded away. *Helicopter.* Elian lay with his head on her lap. She resisted the urge to stroke his soft russet hair. One lock had fallen across his forehead. The vision of a young man with a long ponytail and tie-dyed shirt rose before her. *Elian.* In a flash, a snotty apprentice journalist, a drink in Paris, a sex dream, and the real thing in Cairo hove onto her memory screen. A reluctant smile played across her lips.

She must have twitched, because he raised his head. "Did the chopper leave?"

"I think so."

He reached a hand around her neck and drew her lips to his. "Might as well enjoy ourselves."

"You're such a romantic."

He chuckled and squeezed her nipple through the safari shirt. "I know."

"Now, Elian…"

But he didn't have time to put his plan into execution. They heard a loud crack, and the door flew open. Their guard lay face down in the clearing. A large form stepped over him and crossed the threshold. He was almost as tall as Elian, but broad-shouldered and thick-armed. She caught a glimpse of something shiny on his chest. *Dog tags.* "Ma'am? Sydney Bellek?"

She opened her mouth, but nothing came out. Elian's arm snaked around her middle from behind. His hot breath seared her ear. "Who are you?"

"Lieutenant Bailey Forbes, SEAL Team Nine, at your service, Mr. Davies. Are you ready to go?"

Neither captive saw any reason to procrastinate. They followed the soldier through the trees and over a small bluff. A chopper sat in a small field, its propellers spinning slowly. Another Navy SEAL stood by the cab. "Stay low," ordered their rescuer. They crouched and ran toward the helicopter.

Suddenly, all hell broke loose. Shouts and gunshots rose behind them. Sydney could hear Fawzi yelling, "Get them!" in Arabic. She paused to look over her shoulder. The trees bent and swayed in the gusts from the rotors. Smoke rose in little puffs between the trunks. Lieutenant Forbes put a hand on the small of her back and shoved her into the aircraft. Someone inside grabbed her and pushed her head down. The pilot revved the engine. The bird strained, aching to rise. Sydney couldn't see anything but the floor. She screamed. "Elian! Where's Elian?"

The soldier let her go, and she bobbed up, staring out the window. Elian stood uncertainly, staring up at her, and she realized that the copter was in fact taking off. He took a step toward her, and she heard a barrage of gunfire. As she watched in horror, he fell forward into the grass. "*No!*"

Her rescuer patted her awkwardly. "I'm sorry, ma'am. I think he'd been hit in the leg—that's why he stopped. Looks like that last volley got him." He signaled to the pilot. "I'm afraid we have to get out of here." The chopper banked right and headed north.

Chapter Nine

Alexandria, Present Day

Olivia gaped at her mother, eyes wide. Her sandwich fell from her nerveless fingers onto the tablecloth. "Oh my God, Mother. How devastating. What did you do? How could you have gone on?"

Sydney picked up the sandwich and laid it on Olivia's paper plate. She dabbed a napkin to her lips. "Oh, it wasn't hard," she said lightly.

"Mother!"

Sydney slowly poured champagne into her glass and tossed a piece of bread at the mallards waiting patiently by the picnic table. "Of course I was upset, but at the loss of a colleague. A friend. A—"

"I know—a friend with benefits. Seriously, Mother"—Olivia took Sydney's hand in hers—"were you honest with yourself about your feelings? Are you being honest with me now?"

"Honest? Of course I am—why shouldn't I be? Again, we'd been together so few times. We'd never talked about feelings. If I'd thought about love at all, I would have shrugged it off as a useless, ill-timed dream." She threw another piece of bread at the ducks. "Oh, I was upset at first, but I expected the weird empty feeling to go away eventually. It took me a long time to figure out that it planned to stay, eating a hole in my heart. I wonder…" A puzzled expression flitted over her features, as though a brand new thought had just struck her. "I wonder…maybe, if we hadn't lost each other on that field in Lebanon, we would never have found each other." She looked at her empty hand and then at the waiting drake.

Olivia, busy shoveling leftovers into a paper bag, didn't notice her mother's sudden silence. "I begin to see that this was not a case of love at first sight."

Sydney wiped the crumbs off her palms. "True, at least not for me. Elian—as I learned much, much later—knew we were meant for each other from the age of seven. Precocious brat."

Olivia kissed her cheek. "Now, now. How could you have been so blind?"

"I'm not sure exactly. I had such a full life—so many adventures—that I never felt ready to commit to anyone. It just didn't fit my plans or my world view."

"That sounds so selfish."

Sydney huffed at her daughter. "Not selfish at all—rather the opposite. Call it absorbed by things other than myself. So much out there fascinated me—I wanted to see and experience and learn everything I could. Love, romance, marriage—were not a priority. The way I saw it, if I stopped to smell the roses I'd miss out on the next adventure. Life seemed too short and love too…too all-consuming."

"Weren't you ever lonely?"

"Oh sure. But a friend once explained to me that I'm an introvert. That doesn't mean I don't love people, I do—especially relatives—" She held her hands up to ward off the threatened blow. "But they tire me after a while. Entertaining them is exhausting. I'm most at ease and content in my own company."

Olivia rose and stared out at the Potomac River. Sunbeams danced in her rich, brown hair, reminding Sydney of Elian. Beyond her, a pair of kayaks raced each other in the calm water. The warm Washington air smelled of wisteria and narcissus. "I'm sorry, Mother."

"Sorry? Why? That I enjoy my own company? It's simply my nature. Yours is a much more gregarious one—I don't think you're happy unless you have a crowd around you."

"I suppose. The presence of people comforts me."

"Just like your father."

"And now? Are you sorry you settled down?"

"Have I?"

"Well, you've been around for me for twenty-six years."

"Why, Olivia, you sound worried. Silly girl—I've told you *ad nauseum* that having you put everything else in perspective. I'd lost Elian, but I had his eyes"—she touched her daughter's face gently—"and his chin and…"

"All right, all right, that's enough." Her daughter backed away hastily. She checked her watch. "It's still early. If you're not too tired, I think we have time for one more act." She sat down and picked up her pen. "What happened next?"

****

Turkey, 1983

An hour later, the helicopter set down on a desert plain. Desiccated bushes and huge broken boulders littered the arid landscape. The pilot and the other SEAL stayed in the ship while Lieutenant Forbes led Sydney to a small encampment, where another soldier stood waiting for them. A lone gnarled pistachio tree lent a modicum of shade to the area, and in the distance something gleamed blue. *A mirage? Or water?* "Where are we?"

"Need to know basis, ma'am. Let's just say we're still in the Middle East."

"That's helpful. Lieutenant Forbes, will you go back for Mr. Davies?"

"I had orders to rescue you without causing an incident. We'll see what the commander says when we report."

Sydney glared at him. "You don't call a shootout with an armed militia an *incident*?" When he didn't answer she added, "He's an American citizen."

The SEAL regarded her with grave eyes. "We sure know that, ma'am. Now, will you come with me?"

He led her to a folding camp chair by a tent the color of sand, poured a mug of muddy coffee from a pot on a tiny camp stove, and handed it to her. "Sit tight, ma'am. We'll be back in a jiffy." He crooked a finger at the other man, and they moved off toward a jeep parked near the chopper.

Sydney took a sip of the coffee and spit it out but not before it burned the tip of her tongue. A strange noise distracted her from the pain. She looked up to find a mourning dove perched on a lower limb of the pistachio tree. It cooed softly. Tears welled up in her eyes, and she began to rock back and forth, moaning in time with the dove. "Where are you, Elian? Are you alive? Oh, my dear."

Misery expanded in her chest, threatening to explode. She missed him with an agony she'd never known before. His absence filled the air like a scent.

Anise, that's what he smelled like. She lifted her nose and sniffed. Nothing but burned coffee and musty blankets. She kept rocking.

When the soldiers came back, she took a deep breath and gave them a tentative, if damp, smile. Lieutenant Forbes set down a canteen and three cardboard boxes. The other man, introduced only as Stan, handed her a plate and a foil zip bag marked MRE. She read the label. "So this is the famous Meal Ready to Eat us civilians hear about."

Stan nodded. He opened his box. "Hey, we lucked out! Beef stew. That's the best of 'em. Hard to come by."

Forbes took a swig from the canteen and handed it to Sydney. "And peaches. I say they're better n' fresh."

"Aw, you've been out here too long, Lieutenant."

Sydney let them debate the gastronomic niceties of dehydrated food while she wolfed down her stew. The sun set in a glorious chromatic display of hues, the rainbow of colors reminding her of Elian. She coughed to cover the sob. Darkness descended abruptly, and she shivered.

"Best hit the sack, ma'am. There's a blanket and cot in the tent. We'll wake you in the morning."

Sydney didn't argue. The thin Navy-issue blanket could have been a mink coat for all she cared. Her head hit the sliver of pillow and she slept.

****

"Are you ready, ma'am?" Sydney woke with a jerk. As the soldiers knocked down the tent and packed the jeep, she watched the sun peek over the horizon like Kilroy checking her out. Lieutenant Forbes led her back to the helicopter.

At cruising altitude, the glint of blue she'd seen the day before turned out to be a vast sea sparkling in the distance. Below her lay a dry plain interspersed with small villages. "Are we still in Lebanon?"

"No, ma'am."

They flew west along a shoreline for a while, then turned north. A few minutes later, a large city spread out below them and beyond it an enormous military complex. She pointed out the window and shouted, "What city is that?"

"Adana."

"We're in Turkey? Oh, that must be the U.S. Air Force base then."

"İncirlik. Yes. You'll be safe here."

She almost snapped, *I'm not worried about me, mister*, but there didn't seem much point. The chopper landed, and she bent over and ran out from under the spinning blades. An officer in an Air Force uniform stood on the tarmac.

"Miss Bellek? I'm Captain Walker Adams, Mission Support. I'll be your guide and liaison while you're visiting with us. Will you come with me please?"

Visiting? Sydney stifled a snort at his euphemism and followed him. As they entered a long, low terminal she noticed a restroom. Laying a hand on the captain's arm, she whispered urgently, "Listen, I haven't had a bath in ages. It would be nice to…er, freshen up. May I?"

The officer smiled a tight-lipped smile. "No problem. I'll wait." He surveyed her less than pristine attire. "You *would* look…better with a little soap."

She almost laughed.

Sydney spent the next three days briefing the base commander, Colonel Barrett, and assorted military types, plus a few unidentified plainclothes men, on the confrontation between Fawzi and the Israelis. She didn't see Lieutenant Forbes again, but Captain Adams squired her around Adana and listened attentively to her woes.

"More wine?"

"Sure." She held out her glass. "Thanks, Captain Adams."

"Please, call me Walker."

Sydney hesitated. This was not the time to get better acquainted. On the other hand, antagonizing her escort didn't seem diplomatic. "Er…Walker. This Kavaklidere Yakut is excellent. I'd forgotten how good Turkish wines are."

"Yes, the fruit is quite intense and complex. Did you know it's blended solely from local grapes?"

"I read somewhere that Kavaklidere is the oldest vintner in Turkey."

"The oldest *modern* winemaker, maybe. I believe Ataturk established it in 1929 as part of his modernization program, but they've been making wine in Anatolia for almost six thousand years." He took a long pull on the glass. "It's too bad we can't get it at the PX."

"Only American products?"

"Pretty much. Supply and demand, you know. Unfortunately, many of the families stationed here never leave the base. It's a shame."

"Yes. What's the point of 'Join the military, see the world' if you never venture off American soil?"

They clinked glasses. Sydney watched Adams as

he perused the menu. His swarthy complexion and black hair and eyes belied his name. He'd said it helped him blend in with the Turkish populace, which, as communications officer, came in handy. They'd discovered they both had one Turkish parent, and laughed at the clash of cultures they'd endured growing up. It helped to talk with him.

"Have you heard any more about Mr. Davies?"

He shook his head. "An inquiry can't go through diplomatic channels, considering how we got you out, so I'm relying on informants. A rumor is circulating that Phalangist troops picked up an American in the mountains—no word on his condition."

She thought she'd kept the sniffle to herself, but he laid a friendly hand on hers. "I wish I could be more help. How well did you know him?"

Sydney had decided to keep the intimate part of the relationship a secret. It could only make Elian more vulnerable if he were alive and a hostage. "Not well. We worked for competing newspapers. In fact, he was trying to scoop my story when al-Hurriyeh captured him."

Walker kept his hand on hers and squeezed. "That's…that's good. I mean," he said hastily, "I…er…"

His helpless gurgle endeared him to her. "Don't worry about it." She picked up her menu. "What shall we order?"

"Let's get some *mezze*, shall we? How about lamb's liver and some squid?"

"Appetizers sound lovely. I do want the Circassian chicken dip as well—that's the one with mashed walnuts and yogurt, right? I haven't had that since I was in college. My aunt lived in Istanbul and she had a huge walnut tree. When I came to visit, we picked our own."

He pointed at her hand and laughed. "That explains why your fingertips are black. Walnuts stain permanently. I know." He held up a hand. A white scar ran across the palm. "My brother did that to me when I was ten. He rubbed my hands with walnut juice while I slept and by the time I woke up the only way to remove it was to scrape the skin off." He waited for the expected laugh, but none came. At the sight of his hand, the image of another scar, a white line scratched across Elian's hand, displaced the view. She choked on her wine. Walker jumped out of his chair and hovered over her anxiously. "Are you all right?"

"Yes, yes." She touched her lips with the napkin to hide her distress. "Tell me more about your childhood. Did you grow up in Turkey?"

"I spent the first twelve years of my life here." Adams launched into a colorful description of his life as the child of a professor at Robert College, now Boğaziçi University, in Istanbul.

Sydney lapsed into reverie, letting his warm voice spread soothing syllables over her. Would she ever see Elian again? Did he die back there on the field? Would the pain ever fade? *Of course it will. It's not like you loved him.* She hoped someday soon to believe that.

The waiter brought several small bowls, and they spooned bits of each dish on to their plates. As they finished the wine, Walker called for the check. "We'd better get back to the base. The commander of HQ in İzmir is coming in and wants to hear the latest news."

When he let her off at her quarters, Walker leaned out of the Jeep. "I'll see you tomorrow?"

"Um, sure. My editor is expecting the column, and it's easier to send from here. Can I count on you to put it in the pouch?"

"Absolutely. You know it'll have to be approved before it goes out."

"I know." She waved him off and lay down on her bunk. The room was quite large and even had its own bathroom. Walker had implied that, the Master Sergeant Command Chief being a woman, she had insisted upon the unusually comfortable facilities for females. She stared at the ceiling.

Are you alive, Elian? Can you feel me reaching out? She saw again the look of surprise on his face as he fell forward, gunshots screaming around him. *He's dead. There's no way he'd survive that fusillade.*

Walker tried to sound positive, but she knew he, too, assumed Elian was dead. The U.S. military would hardly pull ground forces out of Beirut to retrieve the body of one insignificant journalist. On the other hand, they seemed to consider her important—the Navy SEALs had intimated her rescue took precedence, and she'd been wined and dined since arriving at İncirlik. They seemed to be expecting something from her. *Or expecting something to happen.* But what?

She'd had no access to news since she'd come to the base. Whether the Christian militia had suffered at the hands of either the Israelis or the Americans she didn't know. If Elian were alive and they held him…but no. Fawzi tried it once and failed. He'd be more likely to kill Elian. Or let him go.

Someone knocked. "Sydney? Are you decent?"

"Yes, Walker."

Walker stuck his head around the door. "Oh good.

Sorry to bother you so late, but Lieutenant General Hogue would like to see you."

****

"We understand you speak fluent Arabic, Miss Bellek."

"Yes." Sydney surveyed the group of officers.

A lieutenant commander leaned across the table, his eyes bright. "And you have briefed Colonel Barrett on the exchange between the Israeli spies and al-Hurriyeh in the Christian militia camp?"

"Yes."

He sat back beaming as though he'd picked the winning lottery number.

Sydney felt bewildered. What did they want? Why were they so pleased? "Can you tell me what is going on?"

"Do you recognize this, Miss Bellek?" The stiff-shouldered man introduced to her as General Hogue held out a tiny camera. His bald head was unnaturally elongated, reminding her unpleasantly of a pork sausage.

"That's Elian's! Er, I mean, Mr. Davies's."

"So it doesn't belong to you?" He opened up the back to show her. "Any idea where the film might be?"

"Davies took it out before we escaped. He hid it."

"Where?"

"In his...in his sock." Her voice trembled with misery. "They'll have destroyed it by now."

"Probably." The general put the camera down. "Do you have any idea what it contained?"

"I don't know what else was on it, but he'd taken pictures of the Israelis and Fawzi at their confab. Where did you find the camera?"

"In al-Hurriyeh's compound. He's abandoned the place."

"No sign of…" Sydney held her breath.

He shook his head. "I'm sorry, Miss Bellek. We found no trace of Mr. Davies or the film. It's too bad, because it could help corroborate your story. Still, what you've given us may be enough."

"Enough for what?"

The sausage head bobbed, and the general's little piggy eyes closed to slits. "I'm afraid that information is highly classified. Suffice it to say, you've helped the U.S. military to clarify the…er…lay of the land. Based on your information, our operation has a much greater expectation of success."

Sydney was too polite to say, *huh*, but her eyes showed her irritation. *Patience, Syd. You'll weasel it out of Walker later.*

"Now, as soon as we finish debriefing you, Captain Adams will arrange transport for you back to Washington. I hope they've taken good care of you here?"

Sydney surveyed her one frock, a little on the dilapidated side now. Her only other outfit consisted of sweatpants and a T-shirt emblazoned with "İncirlik Air Base—We Do Planes." "I rather think I could use a trip to the PX."

****

Alexandria, Present Day

"Did you get the scoop from Uncle Walker?"

Sydney pursed her lips. "Only more military gobbledygook. I gathered that the U.S. needed proof of Israeli involvement in gun running before they could intervene. In any event, a couple of months later, the

Americans cancelled all operations and withdrew."

"So here you are with the entire U.S. military at your disposal, and you still had no idea of Pop's whereabouts? When did they declare him officially dead? Or did they?"

Sydney's gaze strayed to the river. Up to her left lay the Wilson Bridge. A tour boat chugged under it, headed toward Mount Vernon. Olivia knew her mother's thoughts had faded into the past.

"Mother?"

Sydney started. "Sorry, dear." She looked at the cooler. "Is there any more champagne?"

Olivia poured some into her mother's glass. "Another sandwich?"

"Please—you make such lovely cucumber sandwiches, dear."

"It's the Miracle Whip. I know it sounds odd, but the sweetness complements the slight bitterness of the cucumber."

"You're right. Did you learn that from the church basement ladies?"

"I did. They also taught me how to make the deviled eggs you love."

Sydney sighed. "Alas, they both go so well with wine. Why can't these Methodists accept that Jesus drank wine, so—"

"Mother, can we get back to the story?"

"Yes, dear. May I have a cookie?"

Olivia opened the white box and handed her mother a cookie. Sydney squinted at the sky. "I do want to stop by the Torpedo Factory on the way home."

"There's plenty of time. Answer the question."

"You mean about declaring him dead? They didn't.

He remained a missing person. I think they just forgot to close the books."

"How awful for you. You never had closure and—"

"Don't you dare spew that psycho-babble drivel at me, Olivia."

Her daughter tossed her head. "Okay, then. How…or when…did you learn for sure Father hadn't died in Lebanon?"

"For sure? Not for another four years. Unless you count the episode in Beirut. Once I got back to the States, I gave up looking for him."

"Gave up looking for the love of your life?"

"Olivia, for the last time, I didn't know that. I know it sounds terribly unromantic—not like your books at all—but that's the way it was. We'd spent so little time together, and—"

"What about the sex? Surely the passion must have told you something?"

"Not really." Sydney blushed before her daughter's accusing eyes. "Every…er, coupling…occurred in what you'd call the heat of the moment. Danger and gunfire tend to focus the loins."

"Very funny. So you're saying you were too self-absorbed to recognize how you felt about Pop."

"In my defense, dear, for all intents and purposes he was dead. It wouldn't have been healthy for me to dwell on an irretrievable love. I'm not Jane Eyre."

"Jane Eyre had a happy ending. You're thinking of Wuthering Heights."

"Whatever."

Olivia packed up the remains of their picnic. As she closed the basket's lid, she stopped. "Wait a minute.

Did you say something about an episode in Beirut? What are you talking about?"

Sydney checked her watch ostentatiously. "We must be getting on. Let's save that for the next installment, shall we?"

Her daughter sighed. "All right, as usual you leave 'em hankering for more. Did you get the dress altered?"

"Yes—it will look lovely, won't it?"

"The ivory is perfect for your complexion."

"Yes, it is." Sydney's lips turned up in a blissful smile. "It will be very nice. April in Paris." She shook herself. "What are your plans vis-à-vis the looming males?"

"What can I do?" Olivia's shoulders sagged. "Ben decided for me."

Sydney gave her a keen glance. "He did? I thought he said it was up to you."

"Same thing. He obviously feels no pressing need to fight for me."

"Really." Sydney raised her brows. "You don't think he's fighting for you the only way he knows how?"

"What's that supposed to mean?"

"He's treating you like an adult by respecting you enough to let you choose freely. You told me Rémy just talks over any objections you offer. Which approach do you prefer?"

Olivia picked up the picnic basket. "It's not a question of approach, Mother."

Sydney folded the tablecloth haphazardly and tried to force the untidy bundle into her tote bag. Olivia gently took it from her and refolded it, taking care to make each corner perfectly square. Sydney regarded her with an enigmatic smile. "Then let me ask you this. Which one made you cry?"

****

"That's that. I'm all set for the trip." Sydney lay back in the armchair. "Nothing to do but while away the days."

"Maybe we could continue. We've got all evening. I'm not leaving till the morning."

"Have you heard from him?"

Olivia shook her head. "I don't expect to."

Sydney gazed at her daughter. "He does know you're coming, right?"

"Of course. I'll spend the night and drive back the next day. I…I only need to ask him one question, but I want to be facing him when he answers."

Her mother pursed her lips. "Take my advice, dear girl. Don't let a lifetime's happiness hinge on an ill-considered choice of syntax."

"You know Ben always picks his words carefully. That's why he's so good at his job."

"Yes, I know. The newspapers call him 'Mr. Gaffeless.' But giving a speech is not as difficult as reciting a love poem." She laughed. "Maybe Benjamin should draft the words and have Rémy deliver it…à la Cyrano de Bergerac?"

Olivia's glance was withering. "Can we get back to your story now? Aren't we close to the end?"

"Hardly, dear. You weren't born yet, remember? In fact, I didn't even know I was pregnant."

"When did you figure that out? When you went into labor?"

"No need to be sarcastic. Let me see—I stayed at İncirlik another couple of weeks. Walker was so attentive and sweet. I just let him heal me."

"Didn't your editor want you home?"

"Malcolm? Once he learned the Air Force would pay my airfare, he was just as happy that I stay. I could send dispatches easily enough through the military pouch. Plus he could swagger around the press club talking about his 'correspondent in the field.' He loved it. Good thing I was on site too, what with the bombing."

"Bombing? Wait a minute—you mean the embassy bombing in Beirut? My God, you covered that too? It's one thing after another over there."

"The meeting with al-Hurriyeh and the Israelis took place in March, right after Sharon had been reprimanded for the Israeli involvement in the refugee camp massacres. Hezbollah bombed the U.S. Embassy in April." Sydney closed her eyes. "I'd never seen such devastation. Scores of people were killed and the building flattened."

"It still makes me angry." Olivia rapped the table. "It's not like the Americans were the bad guys. Why does everyone hate us?"

"People always hate the white knight. Americans are the poster child for success and liberty and violence-free elections. It's human nature to want the worst for someone better than you."

Olivia drew in a deep breath. "So you covered that as well—and the Marine barracks bombing six months later?"

"No, no, I went back to Washington a few days after the embassy bombing. I felt way too sick to stay."

"Sick! Did you pick up something in Lebanon? Or on the base? A worm?"

Sydney gave her daughter a look heavy with meaning. Olivia's confusion vanished as the truth hit her.

"Oh, right. Me."

"Yes, you. I gained forty pounds with you. By the time you arrived, I would have killed for a parasite."

"So what happened with Uncle Walker? You've hinted that he had a thing for you. How come you never told me?"

"It hardly seemed appropriate." Sydney rang the bell. "Let's get some tea. I'd best back up the story a bit."

****

Turkey, 1983

"You are the most amazing kisser, Sydney."

Sydney unleashed her arms from Walker's neck. "Why, thank you."

He tickled her chin. "I wonder what else you're good at."

She felt for the doorknob behind her. "Not much else. Really."

He moved closer, and she opened the door. "I'd like to investigate further, if I may. For instance"—his finger went to her blouse—"if I unbuttoned this, what would I discover?" He peered under her collar. "Two perfect breasts encased in delicate purple lace? And what would happen if I—"

Sydney stepped inside. "Walker, that's enough."

His fingers held on to her nipples through the thin silk, and he followed her. The nipples hardened and her bosom heaved, longing to allow him to suckle. He let go and sent his arms around her, pulling her close. He ground his hips against hers, the thick rod pulsing next to her groin, rousing the sleeping sex.

She felt her insides quicken and warm at the thought of his hands touching her, opening her to take his cock. Her thighs reflexively spread a little wider.

Walker must have sensed her heat, for he pressed against her, his hands dropping to her buttocks. He sent a finger under her panties and down her ass crack. Then it moved around and inserted itself. She jumped, which only sent it further inside. He wiggled it, and adding his thumb to the mix, squeezed her clitoris. She bucked against him, longing to feel stuffed, feel whole, feel satisfied. But a vague form, snowy with static, floated into view over Walker's head. She could make out two orbs of blue staring through the mist at her. "No, Walker. I told you, I can't."

He let go, his fingers making wet slurping sounds as he pulled them out. He rocked back on his heels. "Don't tell me you don't want it. Your eyes are glazed."

She grabbed the door to steady herself. "I can't deny that, but Walker, it's too soon."

"You mean, we don't know each other well enough? We've spent every waking minute of the last three weeks together. What else do you need to know? Except what I look like naked?"

She laughed in spite of herself. "It's not you, Walker. It's me. I…I…need some time." She couldn't tell him that she missed a dead man, one she didn't love or even know as well as she knew Walker. It made no sense, even to her. She patted his shoulder awkwardly, her eyes sympathetic. "I'm sorry."

"Yeah, well…me too." He turned to go but paused. "Look, I'm guessing that Davies meant more to you than you'll admit, maybe even to yourself. I wish the circumstances were different. If you could stay here a bit longer…" He gave her a lopsided smile. "I feel certain my natural charm would win you over. As it is, you're leaving in a couple of days, and our paths may never cross again. It sounds hokey I know, but I'll be here, waiting, if you change your mind. At least until they transfer me. Say, I could put in for Bali. How does that sound?"

Sydney pecked his cheek. "Good night, Walker."

****

Sirens woke her about midnight. Someone banged on her door. "Miss Bellek? The captain asked me to escort you to the bunker."

"I'll be out in a jiffy." Sydney rose quickly and threw on her jeans and a denim shirt, ran her fingers through her hair and splashed water on her face. She opened the door to find a young man in camouflage. "Are we under attack, Airman?"

"No, ma'am. We're scrambling whatever planes we have on base. There's been an incident in Beirut."

"Incident?" *Another one?* "What kind of incident?"

"Captain Adams can tell you more."

She entered the mission operations building and took an elevator down to the basement. Several officers, including Walker, stood before large screens. Walker turned. "Oh good. Lieutenant General Hogue ordered you here for your own safety."

"What's happened?"

"A suicide bomber detonated a huge device on the American embassy grounds in Beirut tonight. We have very few details at this point."

"Casualties?"

"No idea yet."

"Do you know who did it?"

"The Islamic Jihad has claimed responsibility, but we're hearing rumors that Hezbollah or even the Syrians are to blame."

Sydney gulped down the suspicion that threatened to close off her throat. "Could it be Phalangists?"

One of the other officers shook his head. "We don't think so. The PLO is distancing itself as well. We'll know more tomorrow."

Sydney's fingers tingled the way they always did when a news story beckoned. She turned to Walker as the likeliest man in the room to understand. "How soon can I get there?"

His eyes widened. Another captain leaned in. "Ma'am, the Air Force is not a shuttle service for journalists."

She started to bluster, but Walker put a soothing hand on her arm. "Every plane we could spare has already taken off, Sydney. Maybe we can requisition a jeep tomorrow, but I doubt it."

She shook him off and glared at the assembled soldiers. "I'll find my way there myself then." She stormed out of the room.

****

"I only have twenty lira. Will you take dollars?"

"*Hayır*. No. Twenty lira good." The fellow took her cash and gestured at the back seat of the shared taxi known as a *dolmuş*, already inhabited by two dark-haired women who could have been twins and a chicken in a cage. "We stop in İskenderun, then Antakya. You take bus from there."

Sydney squeezed in, holding her backpack on her lap. She smiled tentatively at the women. They bobbed their heads in unison with the hen. The ancient Buick took off, rattling and groaning, down the highway. No one said a word for over eighty miles. The driver let the women off at İskenderun, and took on a male passenger at a small village just beyond the town. The man smoked nonstop to Antakya, where Sydney gratefully took her leave and her first deep breath in forty miles.

She found a fleet of buses in the central square and chose one marked Tripoli/Beirut. Painted in Day-Glo colors in a spirited paisley pattern, with festoons of beads and trinkets hanging from the ceiling, it could have been a carbon copy of Tom Wolfe's vehicle in *The Electric Kool-aid Acid Test*. She grabbed the last seat and settled down into a field of corpulent women in voluminous skirts and colorful wool stockings, and men chain-smoking homemade cigarettes, their faces as gray as their shirts.

At the border crossing into Lebanon, she worried that her presence would create difficulties. The atmosphere on the bus sparked with tension, but the border guards made only a halfhearted effort to act tough, then accepted a hen and a curse from one of the women and waved them on. The driver turned his radio up to ear-shattering decibels, so no one felt the need to talk.

They reached the outskirts of Beirut at midnight. Sydney left the bus in a Christian section and found her way to a hotel, being careful to speak only Arabic. No one answered at the *Observer* news bureau, so she begged some coffee from the hotel clerk and went to bed.

****

"What the hell are you doing here, Sydney? Don't

you know the place is going bonkers?"

"I'm sorry, Ted, did I forget to mention that I'm a reporter? For the same paper you work for?"

"But Sydney…"

"What's the best way to get to your office?"

"Okay, okay, I'll send a car." Rising enthusiasm tempered Ted's unease. "I admit I'm glad you're here, Sydney—we could use another Arabic speaker. Elie went out to Baalbeck to check on his family, and Bruce is in the hospital with a shrapnel wound."

"See you in a bit then. Oh, I'll need a tape recorder."

As they drove through the crumbled streets, Sydney felt more and more depressed. Eight years of civil war had left a debris-strewn city and a battered populace. People's faces dripped exhaustion. Too many factions, too many militias, all trying to keep the peace and carve out a bit of someone else's territory for themselves. Add to that too many foreign countries dabbling in Lebanon's affairs, and voilà! Chaos.

The *Observer*'s offices were still intact, although most of the windows had been blown out.

"Do you suppose if all the international groups left, the Lebanese could work it out for themselves, Ted?"

"Nah. It goes too far back. The Ottomans were the last overlords to impose a workable system for keeping everyone out of each other's faces."

"You mean the millet system?"

"Yeah—you can still see the remnants of the neighborhoods. Every religious sect or ethnic group— Maronite, Jew, Shi'ite, Sunni, Druze, Orthodox—had its own little area in which it could practice its religion, run its own courts and schools, even build roads and buildings. The boundaries were clear. Then the Allies screwed it all up."

"I know, I know, they secretly partitioned the region into spheres of influence in the midst of the First World War. The English got Iraq and Jordan, and the French got Syria and Lebanon."

"And insisted the Christian minority run the new government—guaranteeing friction with the Muslim majority."

"Fascinating historical perspective, Ted—but I'm a breaking-news kind of girl. I'm off." Sydney grabbed her shoulder bag. "How do I get down to the embassy?"

"Walk."

"Okey doke. Did you get that recorder for me?"

He tossed a tiny box to her. "You still have the necklace camera?"

"Yup, and this time I hope I get to use it."

"Me too. It cost the paper a bundle."

Sydney headed down to the Raouché section of the city, where the ruins of the embassy lay. Three days after the tragedy, wisps of smoke still spiraled up from the twisted pipes and concrete rubble. A few beggars and policemen poked around in the mess, looking for justification. Sydney found a Marine guard and showed him her press pass. "What can you tell me, Sergeant?"

"Not much, ma'am. Temporary quarters have been set up in the British Embassy. Try there."

It seemed every available clerk and undersecretary had been shanghaied into moving boxes and setting up telephones, and Sydney found no one to help her. One heavily perspiring man shouted in broken English that perhaps tomorrow someone would be available. She checked her watch. Almost six o'clock. No sense in hanging around.

She headed toward the shore and the huge arch known as the Pigeon Rock. She found a bench and sat gazing out at the choppy Mediterranean. It reminded her of the evening she spent there with Elian. Could it have only been a few weeks? It seemed like years and a lifetime ago. His face, its hooked nose, its cobalt eyes, its stray lock of roan hair, rose before her. Without thinking, she held out a hand toward the image, longing to touch him. The ache came again, the one that hit below the belt right in her gut. She stood up to go back to the boulevard and—her eyes blurred with tears—stumbled on the uneven surface. Her knees came in painful contact with a boulder, and she let her body fall onto it. *I miss him. I can't help it. Why did he have to die?*

She found a tissue and wiped her eyes. A few pedestrians stopped to peer at her from the other side of the street. At her wave, they moved on, all except one, wrapped in a long, hooded cloak. She studied the fellow. *Something familiar about him.* She stood and took a step into the road, but at that moment, a horn sounded loudly and a taxi roared past. When she looked again, the man had disappeared.

The following day she made her way to the embassy's temporary quarters and managed to find a Foreign Service officer willing to give her a report on the status quo. Two hours later, she sat in a small bar with Ted.

"That's it. Now, can I have another *arak*?"

"Sure." Ted signaled the bartender. "Excellent work. I think Malcolm will be interested in your impressions of the atmosphere outside the city as well.

Why don't you take the rest of the day off? I'll have your plane ticket by tomorrow."

"Thanks, Ted. I may just head to the hotel and hit the sack. I'm feeling really beat for some reason." She looked at the milky glass of anise-flavored liquor and put it down.

Ted gave her a shocked look. "What, you're not finishing your drink?"

"I guess alcohol doesn't have the appeal it used to."

"Well, that's a new one. I'll have to tell your drinking buddies over at the Front Page." He inspected her pale face. "I sure hope you're not coming down with something."

"Just tired. It's not exactly been a restful few weeks."

"Well, save it for the American medical system, will you?"

"Will do. Can you give me a ride back to my hotel? It's in Ashrafiyah."

"Why did you pick a hotel there? That's over four kilometers from here."

Sydney didn't have the energy to explain that she had chosen the main Christian section of town in hopes of hearing news of Elian or al-Hurriyeh. "Closest I could get."

Ted shook his head. "All right, but let Pierre drop me off first."

Luckily, the bureau driver was a Christian and lived near Sydney's hotel. He made sure the hotel manager knew she must be protected. "Andros, if she has any complaints, the entire press corps will make sure you never get another American guest." The manager shrugged the threat off but escorted Sydney to her room himself and brought her fresh towels.

She let the day's stress dissolve in the hot bath and pulled on the *jellaba* that served as her nightgown. Despite the sign warning her to keep her window closed at night, she pulled the curtains aside and sniffed. The balmy night air smelled of blossoming henna and gun smoke. She looked out at the dark street. At first it appeared deserted, but as her eyes adjusted to the gloom, she made out a huddled shape sitting on a garbage can across the road. As she watched, the creature looked up and straight into her eyes. Its vacant stare did not obscure the vivid blue of the irises. *Elian.* She grabbed her coat and took the stairs to the lobby two at a time. Ignoring the concierge's protestations, she ran out the door to an empty street. "Elian! Elian! Where are you?"

Stepping into the road, she looked around wildly. No one. As she turned to go back to the hotel, something pierced her heel. Blood dripped from her bare foot onto the sidewalk. Ignoring the pain, she took one last sweep of the neighborhood, then hobbled back into the hotel.

The concierge made her sit down and insisted he clean the cut. "Mademoiselle, you shouldn't go out alone at night. There is so much rubble and broken glass around nowadays. Even if you don't find a robber to mug you, you can injure yourself. Just look at this!" He fussed over her, bandaging the wound with several strips of gauze.

Sydney let him work as she mulled over what she'd seen. It couldn't have been Elian—he'd have recognized her. The ragged thing had looked right through her. *I wanted to see him so badly, I conjured him out of thin air, that's all.* Heart sagging, she accepted a glass of mint tea and trudged back upstairs. Her stomach still felt iffy after the *arak*. She drank her tea and soon fell asleep.

****

She'd paid her hotel bill and stood waiting for the taxi to take her to the airport when she saw him again. A man taller than his hunched shoulders suggested limped down an alley across from the hotel. His hooded cloak covered him down to his shabby sandals. "Elian!" She ran after him.

The man turned into another alley. She followed him. He stopped at a pastry vendor. As he fumbled in his pocket, the hood fell back on his shoulders. Before he pulled it back up, she'd taken note of filthy, matted chestnut hair, one shaft spiking straight up. *His cowlick.* "Elian!" He straightened, a piece of baklava at his lips, and looked around as though he heard her voice but didn't recognize it. She started toward him. He threw her a terrified stare and took off. She ran after him. "Elian! It's me!"

She stopped short when the alley disgorged onto a major boulevard. Her quarry disappeared in the crowds. Turning, she retraced her steps to the hotel. Her taxi beeped at the curb. As she got in, she whispered, "If it's you, Elian, I'll find you. I promise. I may not have recognized you each time we met, but I will now. I'll know you in whatever disguise you adopt, whatever persona you take on, wherever you hide." She leaned forward to speak to the driver, but paused. *Of course, if it's not you, but only my imagination running amok...*

Chapter Ten

Alexandria, Present Day

"Mother, your cup!"

"What—oh. I must have dozed off."

"I'm tiring you out. I'm sorry."

"No, Olivia, I'm fine. I'll take a nap tomorrow while you're gone."

"Good girl."

Sydney frowned. "I hate hanging around here while you get to travel."

"What are you talking about? You'll be in a first class seat on a luxury airliner in a week. I'll be stuck on Ninety-Five for eight hours."

"Still…" Sydney fidgeted. "It's been way too long since I've gone anywhere. The trip can't come soon enough."

"Well, you know what air travel's like nowadays. A lot of hurry up and wait."

"Oh…" Sydney smiled. "It's always been like that. Of course, passenger comfort levels have changed. In the early years, you got more than an in-flight catalogue and half a glass of apple juice."

"That's right, the Stratocruiser. That must have been fun."

"Yes, what little I remember of it."

"I looked them up after you told me you'd been

one of the first children to fly in it. The Pan Am Boeing 377 Stratocruiser had a full-size bar lounge in the lower level."

Sydney closed her eyes. "And they had berths where the overhead bins are nowadays, all made up like on a train."

"That's right." Olivia nodded. "Even the regular seats reclined to a nearly horizontal position. I saw a picture of the buffet for first class on the flight you probably took. Whooey. Whole sides of ham and prime rib."

"Not to mention the desserts—peach Melba and Baked Alaska. Yum. The serving dishes were silver, and the martini glasses embossed." She grimaced. "Not like today, when you're lucky if a short-tempered stewardess tosses you a handful of peanuts in a plastic bag. Why, even when I was twenty-one—flying to Paris on my way to Cairo—they offered a choice of meals on a printed menu and wine was complimentary." She shook her head sadly. "It's just not the same."

"That was what, 1974? What kind of plane did you take then?"

"Let's see…oh, yes, the Seven Seas. A DC-7. It had a lounge as well—very retro, a perfect venue for a belly dancer as I recall. What a tank that was! The last of the piston-engine planes, but so comfortable. By the time I flew on it, the jets had already taken over the transatlantic routes." She looked at the ceiling. "Come to think of it, I've managed to fly quite a few of the new designs as they came into service—from the 707 on. I think my favorites were the 747s—huge, yes, but they still managed to seem intimate."

"Because you were always with Father, that's

why."

"Maybe. But the Queen of the Skies—that was a lovely ship. Why don't they name airplanes anymore?"

"They do. You're flying the Dreamliner to Paris, or didn't you know?"

"What is it? A Boeing, right? Seven...what?"

"787."

"From zero to eighty in one lifetime, huh?"

"Cute. Speaking of flying, before you nodded off, you were on a plane leaving Beirut. Going where?"

"I had a layover in Paris, before going on to Washington." She sighed. "For the first time—or so it seemed, Elian wouldn't be there. It turned out to be a particularly unpleasant stay anyway."

"Me?"

"You."

****

Boeing 747-200B Jumbo Jet and Airbus 310, 1983

"April in Paris. Magical."

Sydney pretended she hadn't heard. Her seatmate, a portly Lebanese businessman, had talked nonstop from Beirut in what he obviously considered a mesmerizing display of macho charm. He was only slightly less objectionable than the constant sales pitches for Johnny Walker Red from the stewardesses. Evidently Middle East Airlines depended on duty-free whiskey for a significant portion of its profits.

If only she could have napped during the flight, but the enormous 747 was packed with passengers escaping the tumult of Beirut. By dint of well-placed bribes, Ted had wangled the last seat on the plane for Sydney— unfortunately, the middle seat of the four-seat section in the center of the plane. Adding to her blessings, her row apparently constituted the border between feuding factions of an extended Druze family.

The stewardess tapped the intercom and blew into it. "Please make sure your tray tables are in the locked and upright position. We'll be landing in Paris momentarily."

Sydney looked out over the rows of heads as they circled the city and headed north to Charles De Gaulle Airport. Feeble sunlight pinged off the mud-colored Seine. A Bateau Mouche chugged past the Île de la Cité in the shadow of Notre Dame, tourists hanging off the railings. On the riverbank, booksellers would soon be opening their kiosks and setting out the leather-bound products of a disappearing industry. Shopkeepers would be pulling up their metal accordion doors and dragging out carts filled with spring vegetables. Asparagus, artichokes, baby greens, endive. Young boys in aprons would be sweeping the sidewalks and bakers rising up to the street from their basement ovens like latter-day Vulcans, loaded down with warm baguettes. She could almost hear the squeals of schoolgirls chasing each other through the convent gates while the church bells pealed for Mass.

She sniffed, pretending she could smell Paris from the confines of the airplane cabin. Instead she caught another whiff of the Egyptian cigarette her companion smoked. Trying not to gag, she rose and headed to the bathroom. The stewardess stopped her. "Mademoiselle, we're about to land. You'll have to stay in your seat."

For answer, Sydney held a hand to her mouth and goggled at the stewardess. It had the desired effect, and she made it to the restroom in time to vomit in the proper receptacle.

Lapses of Memory

****

Paris had never looked worse. Sydney stared out at the smoke-darkened rooftops, crumbling brick chimneys spewing coal ash into the sky. A light rain had superseded the morning sun, and the city drooped in the mist. She lay on her side, waiting for the next alarm bell to send her to the toilet. This was not how she'd pictured her layover in the city she loved. At least she'd booked into a boutique hotel in Montmartre rather than the Orly Hilton this time. The sleek but cold airport hotel would have been even bleaker without Elian there. She thought back to their meeting, the drinks, the brush with sex. She saw again his eyes boring into hers, willing her to remember him.

But I didn't. He had remembered her though. Every time they met—why did Paris always enter the picture?—he could plunge into conversation as though the hiatus of years since they last talked didn't exist. For her, every encounter with him seemed new and fresh and original. She wondered which she preferred.

She shook her head—a mistake, since it reminded her that she had a horrendous headache. She scooched across the bed and dialed the concierge desk. "Could I have some hot tea brought up please?"

When the young maid appeared with her tray, she recited an obviously memorized speech. "Mademoiselle? You have a phone call. From America. Can you come down to the lobby?"

Sydney trailed after her. The manager handed her the old-fashioned telephone. "Hello?"

"Sydney? This is Walker. Walker Adams."

"Walker? Where are you?"

"I'm in Washington. Your editor told me you were

in Paris. Will you be coming home soon?"

"Tomorrow." The grumbling in her stomach grew louder. "How long will you be in DC?"

"A couple of weeks. Why don't you call me when you're home and rested?"

"Sure." She took down the number and handed the receiver back to the manager. "*Merci*, monsieur."

"*De rien*, mademoiselle." He checked his watch. "There is a nice, quiet bistro around the corner I can recommend if you care for some supper." He tapped his chest. "My brother-in-law runs it—he cooks excellent omelettes."

The thought of eggs did not appeal any more than the arak had, but a *croque-monsieur* might quell those horrible noises coming from her nether regions. "Thank you, I will try it."

She made her way past the graceful white basilica of Sacré Cœur, its tiered ranks of domes forming a stairway to heaven, to a bright pink stucco house aptly named La Maison Rose. The proprietor led her to a window seat and hovered over her, rubbing his hands like some erstwhile Uriah Heep. She ordered the grilled ham and cheese sandwich known as a *croque-monsieur* and a bottle of Evian and waved him off with a weak smile.

She felt better after dinner and decided to take a walk before retiring. Strolling the narrow, ancient streets of Montmartre for an hour, she admired the paintings by aspiring Cézannes and Seurats lined up along the iron churchyard fences and pretended to ignore the ubiquitous mimes. She loved Paris. Especially in April. "Magical." She laughed at herself and found her way back to the hotel.

****

Sydney watched the sun drop down in orange flames as the plane took off. The Airbus 310 seemed a bit more bourgeois than the Boeings of her earlier flights. The one she'd flown on with Elian to Beirut—that was a doozy. What was its nickname? The Big Top—that was it, so-called because of its stretched upper deck. Fast, luxurious—Pan Am had even revived the reclining Sleeperettes from the old Boeing 377 design.

She sniffed the back of the seat. *It's got that brand new car smell. This must be hot off the assembly line.* She flipped through the magazine. Sure enough, the Airbus 310 first went into service in 1982. *Good.* With her still queasy stomach, Sydney felt grateful she didn't have to spend five hours breathing other people's DNA.

She reflected on the speed with which airplanes had developed over her lifetime, from the old Stratocruiser, in which a privileged few could while away the long puddle-jumping flight in luxury, to this lumpish freighter. She'd have to try the new supersonic one—the Concorde. *Maybe next time I go to Paris.*

An ominous gurgle distracted her. She lay back in her seat and closed her eyes. At least Walker would be in Washington. It would be nice to have company. For a slow instant, the memory of a dirty creature with wild red-brown hair and cerulean eyes drifted across her consciousness. *Let it go, Sydney.*

****

Alexandria, Present Day

"Let's stop there, shall we? I need to get some rest before the drive."

Sydney was grateful Olivia did not point out the

real reason for halting—that she'd dropped off again. *Am I getting old?* She surveyed her slim body and blonde curls. *Nah.* "Yes, you'd better. I hate to think of you driving up Ninety-Five all by yourself."

"I'll take the Baltimore-Washington Parkway. It's not unpleasant."

"And you'll stay at Benjamin's with his mother?"

"No. I didn't want to make this meeting any more awkward than it already is. His mother doesn't need to know all the sordid details."

"I see." Sydney reflected that the old lady had probably already wheedled the sordid details out of her son, but it didn't seem helpful to mention that. She kissed her daughter. "Take care and good night. I love you."

"I love you too, Mother."

****

"So you're back." Sydney put the cracker down and indicated a chair.

Olivia dropped into it, but not before pouring herself a glass of sherry and drinking it down in one gulp. "That's better."

Her mother regarded her with sympathy. "I hear the traffic was horrendous."

"Yes."

"From the look on your face, I'm guessing you'd rate that the best part of the trip."

Olivia's shaking hand went to her temple. She squeezed her eyes shut—to keep the pain at bay? Or hide it? Sydney watched her, giving her time. Her daughter hated scenes, hated not being in control of her emotions. She and Benjamin were so much alike— *perhaps that's why she enjoys the ever-ebullient Rémy?*

She sipped her sherry.

"He...Ben...wished me well."

Sydney could see him in her mind's eye. An expressionless face, his eyes the color of teardrops, his lips clamped tightly together. Hiding his emotions. Letting the scene play out. Letting her go. He'd never pressured Olivia, even at the beginning of their courtship. Sydney had often wondered if it was lack of confidence that made him so aloof. Olivia—brilliant, beautiful, a successful author, talk of the talk shows—she could have anyone she wanted. Or so Sydney suspected he believed. *Yet Benjamin comes from a distinguished family—Plymouth colonists, governors, Revolutionary War heroes, Supreme Court justices.* He had served with distinction in the Navy and zoomed up the ranks of Senator McNichol's professional staff. He wasn't the handsomest of men, true, but his manner was kind and his handshake strong. And he loved Olivia. Sydney knew that. She just didn't know whether Olivia returned the sentiment.

"And?"

"And that's it."

Sydney rose. "I'm going to find Alice and see what's keeping dinner."

Her daughter nodded without looking up. As Sydney left, she pulled a pad of paper out and clicked her pen. Whenever Olivia had a problem to solve or obstacle to overcome she would write randomly, letting the thoughts bounce around, forming and reforming into solutions. Once, years ago, Sydney had come across a file folder labeled "Bits and Pieces." In it she read hundreds of paragraphs, each one like a snippet from the middle of a story, detailing fears, affections, and indeterminate plotlines, each one petering out at the bottom of the page. She made a mental note to read this one when she could get her hands on it.

A few minutes later, she emerged from the kitchen to find Olivia shrugging on her jacket. "You're not hungry? Alice made your favorite—sausages over mashed potatoes and fresh peas."

"Tell her thanks and to please save any leftovers. I'm going home, Mother. I'm dog tired."

"Why don't you stay here tonight?"

Olivia shook her head. "I need my things around me. I'll see you tomorrow."

Sydney waited until she heard the door slam and sprinted to the drawing room. Taking a wary look around, she slipped the notebook out of what Olivia mistakenly believed to be a hiding place. *Ha.* She turned to the last page and read.

She got in the cab. "I'll write when I get home."

He nodded. "Sure."

She blew him a kiss. He caught it and blew it back. She gazed into his eyes, his English eyes, cold as the whiskey and warm as the dew. They shimmered. He waved but turned away before she could lift an unsteady hand.

She gave her instructions to the driver. No point in looking back. She looked. Nothing but the back of his head, cocoa brown waves of hair, thinning slightly. Moving away.

It was over.

Sydney closed the notebook and put it away. Over? *Except that, unless I fix this, every night in the shower for the next twenty years, she'll think of him.*

****

Sydney checked her watch. "When is Rémy coming to pick you up?"

"Not until one."

"Aren't you going shopping?" Her mother surveyed her daughter with barely disguised distress. "You need travel clothes!"

"I can order everything online now. It's easier to find what I need on the travel websites."

Sydney rolled her eyes. "I suppose in addition to the French oven on board, Rémy has full laundry facilities."

Olivia laughed. "Of course."

"What kind of aircraft is it, anyway?" Sydney considered herself quite an aficionado after so many years.

"A Gulfstream Aerospace G-IV. Very comfortable."

"I read about those—not huge, and they fly about as fast as my old Stratocruiser."

"You're such a snob, Mother. For your information, Rémy's plane is a lot faster than your 'ocean liner of the air,' if not quite as luxurious. In fact, he told me it set a record in 1987."

"What, for number of baguettes baked at thirty thousand feet?"

"Ha, ha. No, for flying west around the world in forty-five and a half hours. So there."

Sydney put down her coffee cup. She didn't like the detour the conversation had taken. *Better get it back on track.* "Olivia, are you sure you want to go through with this?"

"What—travel around the world in a beautiful jet with a handsome, rich man who pampers me mercilessly?"

Her mother clucked her tongue, looking for a weak spot. "Still, it seems awfully precipitate. You've only just returned."

"You mean from the debacle in Connecticut, don't you? Mother, he showed no emotion at all. I don't think he cared."

Her mother eyed her. "You don't believe that."

"I've got to, Mother. What choice do I have? I took the ball to his court, and he left it lying on the grass. Rémy loves me. We'll have great fun. Now, can we get back to my first nine months of life?"

****

Alexandria, 1983

A week of misery following her return to Washington left Sydney limp and ragged.

"Go to the doctor, Sydney."

"You know, I think I will, Malcolm. I must have picked up something nasty in Lebanon."

"That wouldn't surprise me. You did say you rode with chickens, right?"

"You're suggesting avian flu?"

"No, I'm suggesting you shouldn't hang out with rogue poultry. It will only lead to a life of crime."

"Hens—the gateway animal. Okay, okay. I'll make an appointment."

****

"Excuse me? What did you say?"

"I said, Miss Bellek"—the doctor kept an even tone, but Sydney could see his eyes spark with exasperation—"that you do not have a parasite. It could simply be the flu."

Sydney shook her head vigorously. "Impossible.

I'm never sick. Thanks to the alcohol."

The doctor lent her a cold smile. "Well then, there's one more possibility we can test for. Now, we'll be taking…"

The technical words flowed over Sydney and moved on. She found her attention frequently wandering off since she had returned, usually in the direction of Lebanon and a memory. She deliberately camouflaged his face, but couldn't avoid flashes on a white scar, a jawline, a deep, gruff voice. When she asked Ted to keep an eye out for Elian, he pointed out that her description—a tall man with blue eyes wearing a hooded cloak—was hardly definitive.

She'd called Elian's editor at the *News-Register* in Baltimore, but Craddock had heard nothing from his reporter.

"He'd better show up soon. He owes me a fin from that last poker game."

"What about the Navy? The SEALS rescued us—they must know something."

"Their spokesman claims they have no information on a civilian named Elian Davies. He *suggested* that, given the state of affairs in Lebanon, the person could be missing in action, and I was welcome to presume him dead. If I hear anything, I'll let you know."

"Thanks. Same here."

"Miss Bellek?"

"Oh, sorry, doctor. You were saying?"

"If you'll wait, we'll have the results of the test in a few minutes."

"Fine."

Chapter Eleven

Alexandria, Present Day

"And that's when you found out about me."
"What an awful day that was!"
"Thanks a lot, Mother."
"Oh, you know what I mean, Olivia. Here I was, alone, grieving over your father, unable to work—"
"You didn't lose your job, did you?"
"No, but after I told him the news, Malcolm put me on desk duty. He kept eyeing my tummy over the months and dropping hints about priorities. I knew he'd never send me overseas again. My career came to an abrupt standstill. Thank God for Walker."
"Uncle Walker is still my favorite courtesy uncle."
"He's a dear."
"So how did you hook up with him again?"
"He'd never left Washington."
"Oh, that's right. He called you in Paris, but didn't he tell you he'd be in Washington only a couple of weeks? What did the Air Force have to say about him hanging around?"
"Plenty, but we're getting ahead of ourselves. That's the doorbell. It must be Rémy." Sydney made no move to rise.

They heard Alice open the door and then Rémy's footsteps and his voice calling from below. "Darling?

Are you ready?"

Olivia gave her mother a meaningful look. "You'll be polite, won't you?"

"Me?" Sydney put a hand to her throat and played with an imaginary string of pearls. "I adore Rémy, you know that."

Skepticism painted Olivia's face a light green. "I'm not so sure any more."

"Just because he can be a bit domineering and…and French, doesn't mean I don't like him."

"French?"

"You know, rather emotive…histrionic even. When he doesn't get his own way. That sort of thing." Sydney fastened her eyes on the ceiling. Rémy walked in on a silent scene. He kissed Sydney's cheek.

"*Bonjour*, Madame Davies. *Ça va bien, j'espère?*"

"*Oui, oui, ça va. Merci*, Rémy." Sydney crossed her ankles gracefully and sat forward on the edge of the delicate Queen Anne settee. "I hear you are taking my daughter shopping."

Rémy's mouth opened in a brilliant smile, a tribute to Gallic orthodontia. "So she has told you. *Ma chère* Olivia has agreed to come with me around the world. Isn't it *merveilleux*?"

Sydney didn't respond. Olivia picked up her purse. "I won't be late. We can continue this evening, if you're up to it."

Rémy started. "We're not having dinner together?"

She put a gentle hand on his arm, soothing him. "Not tonight, Rémy. I have too much to do, and Mother and I must finish the project before either of us leaves town."

He started to protest, but caught Sydney's eye. She

could swear he shivered. *Good.* "You two run along. I'll see you about six, Olivia?"

They left. Sydney watched the Ferrari pull away from the curb. Then she went to the telephone and picked it up.

****

"Well, finally! I'd begun to think you weren't coming."

"Sorry—I had to wait for Rémy to pick me up. Is that a gimlet? I want one."

Sydney poured vodka into a cocktail shaker filled with ice and gave it a couple of jiggles. She filled a stemmed martini glass with the vodka, dropped in a teaspoon of Rose's Lime Juice, and, swirling it gently, handed it to Olivia. "What did you buy?"

Olivia displayed her purchases. "Travel toilet paper, foldable binoculars, disposable underwear—"

"Olivia!"

Her daughter giggled. "Not *edible*, Mother, disposable. After a couple of rinse-outs, I can toss them. They're very useful."

"Does Rémy know that?"

"Rémy left me at the store. He had some business to conduct at the wine conference."

"I'd forgotten. Is he here to sell his wines?"

Olivia nodded and sipped her gimlet. "He threw a lavish tasting at the Willard. Lots of politicians and lobbyists looking for free shrimp. A few representatives of Virginia wineries. The only important attendees were the big wine store buyers."

Sydney mused. "Rémy probably makes a swell salesman. He's so smooth. So enthusiastic."

"And so European, eh?"

"I'm sure the accent helps. Americans are pushovers for a sexy accent." She sighed. "Doesn't hurt that he's so handsome either." She sipped her drink and spoke to the wall. "I've never trusted salesmen. They're like trial lawyers—they'll say anything."

"Mother! You've known Rémy for years. Do you honestly think he's a charlatan?"

Sydney's eyebrows rose. "Your words, not mine, dear."

"Look, Mother, I don't feel like listening to your innuendos right now. Rémy is a good man, and…and…I'm going on this trip, and that's all there is to it." Olivia pulled out her notebook. "Uncle Walker. He's still in Washington. Go on."

****

Washington DC, 1983

Sydney watched glumly as the nurse drew the ultrasound pen over her abdomen. "Looking good, Sydney. You still don't want to know the sex?"

"My mother always said the best time to find out the sex of your baby is just after you've given birth. You're just glad to have it out and could care less whether it has two heads or three."

"Fine. You can get dressed."

Sydney walked into the now too familiar waiting room to find Walker sitting, rigid, both feet tapping. He stared directly ahead, studiously ignoring the grunts and groans of the pregnant women on either side of him trying to get comfortable on the unpadded chairs Sydney felt sure Dr. Obermeister ordered specially. "You made it. Thanks for picking me up."

His face dissolved into relief, and he stood. "My pleasure. You're looking…radiant."

She chuckled. "You wrote that on your sleeve, didn't you?"

"On my underwear."

"Don't make me blush."

He helped her into his car. "You still up for dinner at Luigi's?"

"Are you kidding? I'm famished. This second trimester is making up for everything I upchucked in the first."

"What a pretty picture. You've certainly become more graphic in your speech with this pregnancy, Sydney. It's a wonder you even *can* blush."

The maitre d' saw them coming and had bread and butter on the table before they even sat down.

"Thank you, Luigi. How thoughtful of you."

Luigi winked at Walker. "After this, your fourth visit to Luigi's, I know that *madame* needs sustenance right away. The veal piccata as usual?"

"Yes, please."

Walker ordered a salad. Finishing it quickly, he sat back to watch Sydney eat, an affectionate smile teetering on his lips. An hour later, she scraped the last droplet of chocolate icing from her plate and patted her bulging stomach. "That was delicious. Thank you, Walker."

"I'm glad I can be here for you."

Sydney fought her heavy eyelids back to the open position. "Speaking of, when do you have to go back to Turkey? You've been here over four months—I thought you were only assigned here temporarily."

"Oh," he said carelessly, "you know the military. Everything takes longer than they expect. Which brings me to tonight's topic."

"*Hmm*? I didn't see an agenda. Don't we have to approve the minutes first?"

"Waived." He pushed the candle aside and bent toward her. "Sydney? I've asked for a permanent transfer to the Pentagon."

"Oh?"

"They've tentatively agreed but require proof that the grounds I gave are justified."

Sydney stifled a yawn. *It's after eight o'clock, for heaven's sake. I wish he'd get on with this.* She thought of the hot bath waiting at home and forced a smile. "And what's that?"

"That…that…" He pushed something toward her. Her eyes dropped to a small velvet box. "…that I'm getting married."

Without thinking, she opened it. Long seconds clicked by. Sydney stared at the ring. Walker stared at her. The couple at the next table stared at them both. The waiter passed by their table and stopped to stare. Finally Sydney took a sip of water and whispered, "Oh, my."

No one seemed particularly impressed with this response. The waiter raised his hand as if to suggest a more appropriate reply, and the woman at the next table whispered loudly to her companion. Sydney caught the words "milk" and "cow."

As she opened her mouth again, praying that something sensible would issue from it, Walker as usual let her off the hook. "Look, take your time. I just thought…" He raised his hand to signal for the check and almost took the waiter's eye out.

"I…I…" She couldn't do it. She couldn't answer him. *Not yet.*

They left a small crowd glaring at their retreating backs and muttering disgruntled objections. Walker drove her to her house in silence and left her at the door.

Sydney stumbled inside and collapsed on the couch. Something hard gouged into her hip. She pulled out the box. The diamond was quite large, the setting very simple. *It is a beautiful ring.* A long-lost memory rose like Venus from the sea, a memory of a plastic ring with a large pink crystal. Elian had found it on the beach in Tangier. He'd tried to give it to her, but she'd run off laughing. When he caught up with her, she had puffed, "I'll wait for a real diamond," and pushed his hand away.

Elian had tossed the child's ring down and mumbled, "Okay."

Should I have taken the toy? Something told her she'd still be wearing it. *And I'd never be able to move on.* No. She picked up Walker's offering and slipped it on. Mrs. Walker Adams. The Adams family. Party of three. It just might work.

****

Alexandria, Present Day

"Mother, you never told me you actually considered his proposal!"

"Well, I did. I wanted you to have a father. Yin and yang—that sort of thing. Every child needs exposure to both estrogen and testosterone in order to be well-adjusted. Anyway, I was terrified at the prospect of raising you alone."

Olivia regarded the older woman. "Did you…did you ever consider…*not* having me?"

A flip answer on her lips, the look in her daughter's

eyes made Sydney pause. "Never."

Olivia let out a tiny sigh. "Now, about Uncle Walker. What did Father say when he found out about the proposal?"

"Oh, he was perfectly reasonable, as usual. You know that scar Uncle Walker has on his cheek?"

Olivia put a hand to her mouth. "No. He didn't. Did they fight?"

"Don't be ridiculous, dear. Would you pass me the cheese? I'd like another drink too, as long as you're up."

"I'm not up…" The eloquent silence emanating from her mother forced her to stand. "Oh, all right. So what did Pop do to him?"

"I think we're getting a little ahead of ourselves, don't you?" Sydney settled back and took a large bite of bread and Camembert.

"You're going to tell me the story of my birthday, aren't you?"

"My God, child, you should know it by heart by now—you've asked me to tell it at least once a year since the day you could produce a full sentence." She shook her head. "Why are children so fascinated by the gory details of their rough and brutish entry into the world?"

"I can't answer that, but you do tell it so funny." Olivia slathered some cheese on her cracker. "Go on."

"No." At Olivia's growl, she softened. "Suffice it to say, Christmas preparations were totally disrupted. I missed the fruitcake, but at least I got to have champagne on New Year's."

"All you think about is your stomach."

"When you're pregnant, you think of nothing else.

What you can eat, what you can't drink, how far will that T-shirt stretch over it, why is that woman staring at it, oh my God, has the baby actually poked a hole and squeezed out through my belly button…things like that."

"Thank you for the indelible picture. Remind me never to have children."

"Oh, you will, my love, you will," replied Sydney comfortably.

"Did Uncle Sergei make it back from Botswana in time?"

"Yes, and his amiable wife made my life a living hell."

"Aunt Tina? How?"

"Oh, she fussed over me and you and made special meals and cleaned the house twice a day and bought treats and made cheeping sounds and generally acted the part of doting grandmother, so that I didn't have a chance to miss my own mother."

Olivia sighed happily. "She is the most nurturing woman."

"Yes, I love her dearly. But then she left, and you were still here, apparently still expecting to be fed and clothed and changed. And brought up."

"Amazing I turned out so well, isn't it?"

"Only because I had a mere four years to ruin you before fate stepped in."

"Mr. *Deus Ex Machina* himself."

"My sweet lollipop."

Olivia pursed her lips at the endearment. "That nickname just doesn't fit him, Mother."

Sydney smirked. "Oh, yes it does."

Her daughter made a show of fanning her face.

"Okay, let's move on, shall we? It's 1987. I'm a perfect cherub of four. Continue."

"No, no, we haven't finished with Walker. You're still a mute bowling ball with sharp knees."

"Oh my God, I forgot you had decided to accept his offer. I know how it turned out, but not the details." Olivia sipped her drink. "I'm amazed I've never heard this before."

"You were never interested before—that's old age for you." She ducked the hurled cracker and picked up the bread basket. "Let me just get you another cracker."

****

Washington, DC, 1983

"I see."

None of the usual platitudes would do, given the abject misery on Walker's face. "I'm sorry. I wish so much I could say yes, Walker. You're a wonderful man"—*here I go*—"I mean, I don't deserve…I—" Her voice faded to a mumble. She couldn't tell him her answer had never been in doubt. She'd worn Walker's ring to bed the night of his proposal, prepared to accept him the next day. About midnight, she rose, pulled it off, and placed it back in the box.

He touched her hand. "I understand. Such is life. Just because you don't deserve me doesn't mean someone else does…or is it doesn't?" She looked up quickly to see his black eyes twinkle. "I'll be okay. Friends?"

She smiled mistily. "Forever."

"Now—" He stood up. "I've got to get back to the Pentagon."

"How long will you be in town?"

He shrugged. "Not sure. We're preparing for the

NATO summit this fall. It will be in Ankara this year, and they're all aquiver. I'll probably be shuttling back and forth for months before I go back to İncirlik for good."

Sydney kept her distress at the news to herself. *He wouldn't understand.* Even though he didn't set her heart on fire, Walker made her feel safe and indulged. *Just like Sergei.* She missed her brother. He'd been such a strong presence in her life after their parents died in a car crash. When he joined the Peace Corps and toddled off to Botswana, she experienced her one and only panic attack. Then when he wrote to say he'd met a woman there and planned to marry and settle down, the void widened into a chasm. It had taken her six months to gather her wits and her ambition and head out on assignments again. "You'll come by and visit often, won't you?"

"You can't keep me away." He picked up his cap. "You'll be needing rides to the doctor anyway. Consider it my baby shower gift."

After he left, Sydney sat, chin in hand. She hadn't thought about Sergei in a while. She should probably let him know about the baby. She went off to find paper and pen.

****

"Yes, I'll get some rest, Malcolm…Yes, I'm fully aware that the baby is overdue…Yes, I'm doing the breathing exercises…Look, thanks for your advice, Malcolm. Yes. I'll…Wait a sec!" Holding the receiver to her ear, Sydney flipped back to the last channel and stared intently at the television. "What? Oh…it's nothing. I just thought I saw someone I knew on the CMB news. Never mind. Look, I'll see you tomorrow, okay? Bye."

She turned up the volume. The cable anchor, his hair permanently glued on and his lips shiny with gel, loomed into view. "That breaking news report came from our local affiliate in Boston, WXZZ. Thanks for the update, George. We'll get back to Massachusetts and the crash of a medivac helicopter after these messages."

Three news cycles later, they still hadn't returned to it. Disgusted, she finally muted the sound, only to see the Breaking News banner and the anchor, his glistening lips flapping silently. By the time she found the remote, she'd missed the introduction, and to add insult to her injury, for the first time in modern history the station neglected to give the reporter a tag line. Luckily, despite the anchor calling him George, Sydney didn't require confirmation of his identity. Elian stood before the camera in dapper suit and hyacinth tie, his brilliant eyes boring into the camera.

"...unfortunately, there were no survivors. The police have not released the names of the victims yet. We'll bring you more information when we have it."

Sydney picked up the telephone. "Malcolm? Yes, I'm awake. Yes, I'll get some rest, but only if you help me. I need the name of a reporter for WXZZ in Boston ASAP. It's the CMB affiliate. I think he's on the disaster beat. Can you find it for me?"

Malcolm indicated that he considered Sydney's request a suitable teaching moment for his high school intern, known around the newsroom to the boy's utter bafflement as Do-Right. "I'll get Dudley right on it."

Sydney hung up, depressed. Having met and quailed before said Dudley, a brawny young man with a promising career in football but, alas, not in investigative journalism, she didn't hold out much hope. She checked her watch. Ten-thirty. Every bone ached from the task of holding up those forty extra pounds, only seven of which could be blamed on the baby. *I'll just lie down for a minute. Then I'll make a few calls.* The yawn took the remainder of her strength. *Tomorrow.*

****

Sydney woke with a start. She put her hand out to turn on the light but thought better of it. What a dream!

She'd found herself standing in the ruins of a dank and hoary castle. Walls of enormous gray stone blocks rose up to a roofless sky. Cannons boomed in the distance. A woman in a long mud-covered cloak went hurrying by. She stopped when she saw Sydney. "Get out! They're coming! You'll be killed!" Sydney tried to follow her but couldn't move. Someone had bound her ankles and wrists. She teetered precariously, trying not to fall. Suddenly silence fell. In the quiet, she heard a strange tinkling. She looked down.

She was clad only in semi-transparent harem pants. Ropes of beads circled her waist. When she moved, they jingled and sang.

"Are you ready to do as I say?" A gruff voice came from behind her. She craned her neck, but the man kept out of her line of sight. Two gloved hands snaked around to her chest and grabbed her bare breasts, massaging the nipples. They tightened, as did her stomach muscles. Bolts of lust shot from there to her extremities, setting her skin on fire. She couldn't speak.

"Answer me!" The hands withdrew but soon returned, gloveless now. They rubbed her belly, making the beads jump, and trailed down her skin to her mound. Still she stayed mute. His fingers spread out, pressing and searching. They found an opening and inserted themselves. Sydney bucked against them.

"Who...who are you?"

"You know who I am."

"No, no I don't."

In reply, she heard cloth rustling and felt something soft touch her ankles. "Bend over!" commanded the voice. She obeyed. A rigid object, wet and rough, touched her. His tongue. She fought to escape, but the man's arms held her close to him. Something sharp insinuated itself along with his tongue. A finger? She pushed back at it. *Mmm*. Not bad. Then tongue and fingers were gone. She waited. She knew what the next sensation would be. A long time ago a man had done this to her, a man she loved.

Sure enough, a thick penis touched the lips and pushed in. She felt stuffed, but it entered easily. Soon it began to move, in and out. His hands walked around her hips and began to rub her belly. She held still, loving his girdling embrace. The phrase "between a rock and a hard place" ran through her head, and she giggled. The voice said, "Ah, you like this, little one. You want it harder?"

She nodded, but instead of increasing his efforts, the man spun her around, pushing her back to the ground. A knife flashed, and her bonds were cut. She couldn't see the man's face in the gloom, only a hard cock bobbing. He lifted her thighs and placed them around his middle, then plunged into her, pounding her insides. The tender yielding flesh sucked on his rod, drawing him in. She felt her body scraping along the stone floor, grinding into the dust and rubble. She rose to meet him, partly to get away from the pain, partly because she'd seen his face. *Elian*. He stared into her eyes, his own blue ones bright with desire but without recognition. She opened her mouth but instead of his name, said only, "More! More."

He obliged, rubbing his hands over her breasts as he entered her. She felt a snap as her orgasm ignited, rose to a peak, then erupted. Elian collapsed on her.

They lay a minute, then he rose. Staring hard at her, he began to retie her hands.

"No, Elian, no! Please, let me go with you."

"It is dangerous."

"I don't care. I must be with you."

He studied her, then lifted her with one huge paw. She saw a jagged white line cutting across the back of his hand. "Be prepared."

They walked out of the castle. A mob awaited them. As Sydney and Elian passed, the crowd began to throw objects at them. Something oozed down her naked back. She brought her fingers around and sniffed. Eggs.

Sydney sat up. *Whew*! The dream dredged up so many memories, all converging. She touched the sheets. They were damp. She ran a palm over them, bringing the scent of sex to her nose. How she missed Elian! It had been so long—eight…no, nine months, since that last fleeting glimpse in Lebanon. Where was he? Did he still roam the streets of Beirut, a beggar? No, he couldn't be. She'd seen him on the television, reporting from Boston, of that she was positive. *Maybe*.

Her hand crept down automatically to her belly. Would he never know his child? What if the fellow on the news weren't Elian, but merely her longing made flesh? A stranger? She felt the baby kick. It kicked harder. *Oh my sweet baby—will you never have a father?* She touched the wet sheet again. Her hand sank into a substantial puddle. *Oh my God, it isn't from the dream—my water's broken!*

She groped for the phone. "Hello? Hello, Sergei. Can you come? Yes, it's time."

Chapter Twelve

Alexandria, Present Day

"Thus spake Zarathustra."

"Pardon me?"

"I was going to add," said Olivia patiently, "and so I was born."

Sydney shot her daughter a look. "Yes. It was quite an occasion. Good time had by all. Et cetera, et cetera. I told you I didn't intend to go over that ground again."

"I agree. This is about you."

"Oh goody, because I'm hungry, and I'm sure I heard Alice call. Shall we head down?"

Olivia stood and helped her mother up. "Did you ever find the elusive Boston reporter?"

"Long story. No. What with your birth and learning how to open a folding stroller without embarrassing myself and breast-feeding every two hours because you had jaundice, and Sergei and Auntie Tina underfoot, I didn't get a chance. By the time I'd emerged from the whirlwind, your father had left the television station."

"But he stayed in journalism. Why couldn't you find him?"

"Look, I'll tell you later. I believe Alice is ready for us."

Together, they descended the ornate mahogany staircase to the front hall. Sydney called in a loud voice,

"Alice, we're all here! Alice!"

Olivia glanced at her mother. "There's no need to shout."

"Uh, no. You're right. Very unladylike." Sydney scratched the crown of her head, a habit she had when she was nervous. She dropped her hand lest her daughter suspect.

Olivia opened the door to the dining room and stopped. A tall, thin man stood awkwardly by the table, his long, patrician fingers nervously tapping the back of the chair. He stared at Olivia, mouth twitching in what could have been a rare attempt at a smile. Olivia spat out, "Benjamin!" Hands on hips, elbows out, she swung around, barely skimming her mother's solar plexus. "Mother!"

Alice appeared from the kitchen door with a tray. "Dinner is served."

The meal couldn't have been jollier. Olivia spent most of the time scowling at her mother whenever she thought Benjamin wasn't looking, and Benjamin spent most of the time examining his plate. Sydney gave up on small talk after the first ten minutes. As Alice cleared the dishes, she poured coffee into her grandmother's delicate Wedgewood cups.

"Shall we take our coffee into the living room?" The other two diners nodded mutely. Sydney reflected that perhaps she had miscalculated the teeniest bit. She preceded them and surreptitiously poured a thimbleful of brandy into her coffee before turning to face them. "Well, it's so good to see you, Benjamin. How's the senator?"

Benjamin sat on a spindly chair as far from Olivia as possible. "Look, Mrs. Davies—"

"Sydney, please."

"Uh, Sydney. I appreciate your invitation, and I'm ready to talk, but I think"—he glanced at Olivia—"she feels differently."

Olivia's eyes grew wide. "Me? It's you who told me, and I quote, 'I guess there's nothing more to be said.'"

Benjamin stood and began to pace. His light gray eyes glinted in the lamplight. He dug under his mop of rich brown hair with a finger. "But you said—no, you *announced*—that you intended to go with Rémy."

Olivia flounced onto the sofa, spilling her coffee. "I did no such thing. I asked you what you thought, and you—"

"You could care less what I felt, Olivia. You'd made your decision. I know only too well that there's no changing your mind once you've settled on a course of action."

"Well, I—"

At this point, Sydney slipped backwards out of the room, taking care to grab the brandy bottle. Her work was done. With luck, not temporarily.

****

She heard the door slam, and her heart sank. All seemed still below, and just as Sydney gave in to the unlikely hope that the combatants had left together, her bedroom doorknob turned. "Olivia?"

"Yes. Are you awake?"

"How could I not be?"

Olivia sat on the bed next to her mother. She twiddled her thumbs for a bit. "Mother, I'm not going to berate you for meddling. I know you're trying to help, but the situation is hopeless."

"But not serious?" her mother asked, her tone upbeat.

Olivia shook her head. "He can't or won't tell me how he feels. Without any positive feedback from him, I have to protect myself."

Sydney threw her book across the room. "Damned feminism!"

Startled, Olivia picked up the book. "What are you talking about?"

"It's because of so-called women's liberation that a man is no longer allowed to throw a woman over his shoulder and carry her off. Men today are required to *listen* and *feel*, not act and fix, which is their nature. Benjamin is acting the way he's supposed to act in today's anti-male world. Mark my words, if he could, he would."

"Would what?"

"Throw you over his shoulder. Carry you off."

"Nonsense, he doesn't have it in him. He'll always be Clark Kent, never Superman."

"Well, Clark Kent had a steady job…*and* lived in a comfortable house with a picket fence…and…and…air conditioning." Sydney laid a gentle hand on her daughter's. "That's why you can trust him, Olivia. Rémy is so…mercurial. You never know who he'll be next."

"I like that. Every day's an adventure."

Her mother regarded her. "I know you, Olivia. You talk a good game, but you're happiest cultivating your own garden."

"You're quoting Voltaire now?"

"Whatever works." She kissed her daughter's forehead. "I fear you're making a mistake."

"Aren't you perhaps visiting your own mistakes upon me? Could all this interference stem from your guilt at leaving my father on the battlefield?"

Sydney froze. "You go too far, Olivia."

"I'm sorry, Mother. Am I wrong?"

Her mother's taut cheekbones relaxed. "Yes, you are, but of course we haven't finished the story."

"That's exactly my point. We need to focus on your story. Time is running short." Olivia stood. "I'm going home. I'll be back in the morning."

Sydney lay back on the pillows. "Not too early, dear. I need my beauty sleep for Paris."

Olivia grinned. "Good. You'll leave me and mine alone now?"

"What do you think?"

****

"All right, here's the deal."

"Yes, dear. More coffee?"

"No thanks, Mother. We only have four more days to finish this. I'm leaving the same day you are."

"You are? That's wonderful. We can sit together in the terminal—you know that's the part of traveling I hate the most."

"I know, the waiting."

Sydney closed her eyes. "I've often wondered how many hours I've wasted sitting on hard plastic chairs with my suitcase wedged between my knees, juggling coffee and newspaper and making up ungenerous stories about the other poor saps wasting their time sitting—"

"Yes, yes, days, years of your life. I won't be able to while away my remaining hours with you, though. Rémy's plane is at the general aviation airfield.

Different building."

"Oh, that's too bad. Is it near the international terminal?"

"Yes. I may hitch a ride with you."

"Rémy isn't picking you up?"

"No, he has to head over early to do the paperwork and go through customs."

"I see. You're sure you won't have another cup of coffee?"

"I'm sure." She waved a hand over the pile of notebooks and pads of paper. "I'll have to scan these notes and get them in some sort of order before I go. So I propose that we set the discussion of my love life aside for the nonce and get some work done." She raised an expectant pen.

"Well, if time is of the essence, let's skip ahead."

"How far?"

"About four years. That's when the dance to denouement really began."

"Did nothing happen in the interim?"

"Other than raising a precocious child?"

"I mean with the search for Pop?"

Sydney shook her head. "I told you, he'd left WXZZ by the time I reactivated my search. The dreadful Dudley Do-Right had utterly failed, possibly because he couldn't locate Boston on a map, let alone find its area code. No Elian Davies turned up in any news directory. The truth didn't occur to me, so I concluded it had all been my pre-birth hormones stirring the pot and told myself to set my quest on the back burner."

"So you left the kitchen." Olivia tittered.

"What?"

"You moved on."
"Not at all."

****

Alexandria, 1987

"Yes, I understand. Thank you." Sydney put the phone back in its bed and checked her watch. She had another hour before she had to pick Olivia up from her play date. She pulled the list toward her. Covered in cross-outs, erasures, and careted additions, it looked like the first attempt at a poem. *Let's see. I called the embassy last week. Of course, I only talked to Phil that time. I need to wangle the name of the CIA guy out of him. When did I last grill the Navy attaché—what's his name? Michael? I haven't heard from Monsieur Atlas at the hotel yet either.* She wished the telephone system in Lebanon worked better. She'd given up after the fifth attempt to complete a call and wrote him a letter asking if he'd seen Elian.

Leaning back in her chair, she frowned at the framed photograph of Walker by her typewriter. Why couldn't she accept the utter futility of her project? The reporter she'd caught a fleeting glimpse of the day she went into labor had disappeared into some black hole. She felt sure now she'd only imagined his resemblance to Elian. No, her Elian, the real Elian, had died on that Lebanese field, murdered by al-Hurriyeh's troops.

Or by friendly fire. The suspicion had haunted her for four years. It would explain why she met a brick wall whenever she asked questions of the military. Walker Adams couldn't help—as the communications officer for Mission Support at İncirlik Air Base he had no access to Navy SEAL files, files that would give statistics on the mission that rescued Sydney back in

1983. Even if there were evidence that he'd survived, the U.S. government could hardly be expected to track an obscure Elian look-alike, a private citizen, wandering the sidewalks of Beirut.

I know it was he. I know it. I'd know those eyes anywhere. And that cowlick. But he hadn't acknowledged her. Why not? Amnesia? Or perhaps to shield her from some danger? Or maybe to keep her from horning in on a scoop…that idea always cheered her up. She could indulge in random hostile thoughts directed at the father of her child, and the pain diminished a little. Before it started up again. It never seemed far away, even after four long years.

She heard the mailman drop the post in her mailbox. As she sorted through the bills and flyers, the telephone rang. "Sydney? Malcolm here. Can you come into the office today?"

Her mind half on the letters, half on the approaching hour of Olivia's reclamation, she had no brain cells left to listen to her editor. "I'm sorry, Malcolm. What did you say?"

"I said…oh, never mind. Call me back. I've a job for you."

Sydney let the phone fall. She stared at the envelope in her hand. Official mail from İncirlik Air Base? She opened the thick manila mailer only to find another envelope inside. She recognized Walker's handwriting.

Dear Sydney,

I hope you and Olivia are doing well and that you received the package. She's probably outgrown the dress already, but Jeannie thought it would go so well with her blue eyes. She saw the photo I have on my desk and insisted on buying it for Olivia. I think I've mentioned Jeannie—she's the librarian I met at the officer's club in İzmir? Anyway, she's been a true friend while I nurse my broken heart—just joking! And, well, might as well spit it out. We've decided to get married. I know you can't make the wedding, nor would I expect you to want to come. But I—we—would like your blessing. I'll call when I can.

All my love, Walker

The telephone rang. She picked it up from the floor.

"Sydney? This is Allison…Allison Teague, Jody's mom? I'm here at the Tate's, and Beatrice wondered if I could drop Olivia at your house? It's getting a bit late, and Beatrice has a doctor's appointment."

Sydney ripped her mind back to the present. She knew how to respond, but the words stuck in her throat. Mutely nodding at the phone didn't seem to have the desired effect, so she pinched the back of her hand. "Ouch! I'm sorry, Allison. I've just had some…jolting news. Yes, it would be wonderful if you could bring Olivia home for me—please apologize to Beatrice. Thank you so much." She gave her the address.

After a suitable display of gratitude and lengthy acknowledgement of her infringement of the cardinal rule of play dates—never, ever be late picking up your child—she waved Allison and little Laura off and took her charge up for a nap.

"Mama, where were you?"

Sydney tucked her in. "I had a letter from Uncle Walker. He asked if you liked your new blue dress."

The little girl clutched the dress to her breast. She refused to wear it, but liked to snuggle with it. As a result, it had become stained and torn without ever seeing the outside world. "I do, I do, Mama. Mama? Is Unca Walka coming to visit soon?"

Without warning Sydney's tears began to fall. "No, I'm afraid he's very busy, dear. Very busy."

****

Alexandria, Present Day

"That must have been so devastating, Mother. It's hard to give up an old lover, even one you dumped."

"Olivia, what a callous thing to say!"

"Well, you yourself admitted you cried. Anyway, it meant that your bond with him was forever altered. His marriage created a barrier between you."

"Not really. We'd never been more than friends. He wanted to marry me so you would have a father. Once he realized he could be an uncle and avoid all the financial and emotional hazards, he jumped at the chance."

"You're kidding. Say you're kidding."

"I'm kidding. Absolutely. Is it lunch time yet?"

"Not until you finish the story."

"Not much left to tell."

"Well, then you'll eat soon."

Sydney tapped her fingers on the table. "Do we have all day? Just in case this takes longer than expected?"

"If you're asking whether I'm going to see Rémy today, the answer is no. I told him I needed a little time off."

"Did you tell him about your trip to Connecticut? About…last night?"

Olivia dropped her eyes. "No." She rose and began to pace. "It's not important anyway, is it? Just more of the same. Nothing has changed. In either relationship."

"I see. Olivia?" Sydney regarded her daughter with new concern. "Have you considered the possibility that you're being unfair to Rémy?"

Olivia stopped, one foot in midair. "To *Rémy*?"

"Yes. After all, your heart is not entirely his. Using this trip to take your mind off Benjamin is rather self-serving. One could almost say manipulative."

The flush rose hotly in Olivia's cheeks, and her eyes glittered. "I resent that, Mother. I'm doing no such thing. I've always been honest with Rémy about Ben."

"But he thinks…" Sydney paused. "What *does* he think? Do you know?"

Putting a hand to her forehead, Olivia sat heavily. "I guess I don't know, do I? He hasn't asked about Ben since I mentioned him on our first date. Like the trip, he doesn't really discuss anything."

"I know." Sydney nodded. "He changes the subject, talks over your objections, goes on and on about what a wonderful time you'll have together, that sort of thing. Has he told you how he feels about you?"

"N…no. But why would he ask me on a round-the-world trip if he didn't love me?"

"For company?"

Olivia didn't answer. After a minute, Sydney indicated the notebook. "Why don't we continue with my story. We can talk more at lunch."

****

Washington, DC, 1987

"Malcolm, I can't just up and leave for London on a moment's notice."

"Why not?"

"You perhaps remember a little thing called

Olivia? I thought we'd agreed I could pick and choose assignments now."

"And you'll choose this one, trust me. I want you to cover the SST controversy."

"You mean the issue of landing rights for the Concorde?"

"No, that's been resolved. Once Washington decided that prestige and revenues trumped the apocryphal health dangers of the sonic boom, New Yorkers jumped on the bandwagon too. Issue solved. No, right now the big debate is fuel costs and customers. Air France and British Airways are dropping routes right and left—"

"At the same time that they're breaking all kinds of speed records. Yeah, I read about it. It sounds like the supersonic jet may be a brilliant idea ahead of its time."

"If they could only come up with a different, cheaper fuel."

"Not gonna happen."

"Look, we're getting into the weeds, here, Sydney. Why don't you pull all the details together when you get to London?" Malcolm's voice faded. "What's that, Busby?" He came back to the receiver. "Busby tells me that Sarah—Sarah Paisley, over in Lifestyle? She's looking for a puff piece on women pilots—you know, Amelia Earhart, Sally Ride, that sort of thing."

Sydney frowned. "That's not really in my portfolio, Malcolm. I'm a professional—"

"Yeah, yeah, okay. How about this? Something on the growth of commercial air transportation—you know, how fast it's evolved from the open cockpit mail planes that carried a couple of passengers, to the SST. But make it…er…puffy. Say, didn't you fly on one of those early behemoths when you were a little girl?"

Despite her misgivings, the project began to intrigue Sydney. "I did—the Boeing Stratocruiser. Of course, we couldn't fly nonstop across the Atlantic back then. Pan Am hopped from New York to Canada to Greenland to Iceland before landing in Europe."

"Still, I remember you saying how luxurious it was—sleeping births, caviar, champagne, a lavish buffet catered by Maxim's. You showed me those photos of silver dishes and white-gloved waiters."

She laughed. "Yes, but it only accommodated a hundred souls, and they had to cough up a lot of money for the ride. Just like the SST."

"Wow, excellent. You could bring the story full-circle. We may be talking above the fold here."

"Of the Style section, Malcolm. Not my dream placement."

"The only place it fits, Syd. Come on, be a sport. Sarah's been giving me a hard time—she wants to be taken more seriously…I mean, wants her section to be taken more seriously."

"And she won't go out with you until you give in?"

"Sydney! You know I don't approve of office romances."

"Unless you're involved, I know." An idea struck her. "Full circle…wait a minute, maybe I could do something even more attention-grabbing, Malcolm. I could bring Olivia with me—we could fly on the SST."

The editor paused. "I don't know, Sydney. She's really too young to be useful."

"Useful? That's a nice way to refer to my daughter."

"All right, all right." He sounded flustered. "I don't

have time to argue. She can go."

She blew him a loud kiss. "Great. When do you want us in Paris?"

"I want you in London. Not Paris."

Sydney scrabbled around and pulled up the day's newspaper. "The Paris Air Show begins in two weeks. Guess what? They're exhibiting an SST. Oh, and all the British airline industry people will be there."

"*Sheesh*, Sydney."

She counted silently. *One, two…*

"Have Nancy cut the tickets."

****

"Mama, I'm tired. An' I'm hungry. What's that big thing over there? Why is that boy staring at me? Mama, make him stop. *Ewww*, he stuck his tongue out at me. Mama…"

"*Shh*, Olivia. We'll get a snack soon. I want you to look at something. Come along."

The little girl whined as loudly as she dared but followed her mother. Sydney stopped before an enormous silver airplane suspended from the museum's ceiling. Painted in large red letters across its side, she read Pan American.

Olivia pointed a chubby finger. "What's that, Mama?"

"It's an airplane."

"It's fat."

"That's because it had to hold a lot of passengers—up to a hundred—plus seats and food and fuel and baggage."

"That plane over there is much skinnier."

"It is, isn't it? It's much newer." Sydney gently turned her daughter's face back to the old airplane.

"This is the one I flew on when I was about your age. I went to Paris on it, just like you're going to."

"I'm going to fly on that plane? Will the mus…museum let me?"

"No." Her mother laughed. "We'll take a different plane. A much skinnier one."

Sydney stood before the silver monster, imagining it as a great lumbering beast. She drew on her sketchy memories of her first flight, bolstered by the reminiscences of her brother Sergei. The two of them, running up and down the aisle in their pajamas, and the lollipop her father had given her. And something else. Someone else. She closed her eyes, but when the mist parted, she saw only her father, his bushy black moustache tickling her nose, and then her mother, in heels and pearls, one hand furtively tugging at her girdle. Another woman, dressed in a neat, blue uniform, helping Sydney into her bunk. There stood Sergei in the aisle, proudly displaying the wings the captain had given him, and the First Flight certificate. No, someone else held the certificate. A boy, younger than Sergei, with reddish brown hair curling over his collar and searing blue eyes.

Elian.

Olivia put a tiny hand on her mother's. "Mama? Are you okay?"

Lost in astonished revelation, Sydney didn't answer. *That's what he meant in Cairo…or was it Beirut?* Every time they met, Elian had asked her if she remembered him. Most of the time, she shrugged it off as his usual line with women. *I was wrong. He wanted me to recognize him, to recall even our first meeting…how many years ago? Thirty?* And she had disappointed him every time. A cold fist squeezed her heart. She leaned forward, hand to her breast, pushing the pain back inside.

"Mama?"

A beam of light shot through the tall museum windows. Dust motes picked it up and formed a rainbow that passed over their heads. She followed it with her eyes. It came to rest on a man who stood at the other end of the exhibit. *A rainbow crossed the space between Elian and me that morning as we left the plane in Paris. The first time we parted.*

There had been another rainbow, one that sparkled in the Moroccan sun. It mantled…who? A boy with the same sharp chin, the russet hair, eyes the color of a cloudless tropical sky. Elian. *He called himself Eddie.* No wonder she hadn't made the connection. The eight years that had passed since their first meeting didn't help. Sydney couldn't be expected to remember. Wait—that meant Elian had been on board the flight to Paris when she was thirteen as well. It also meant that the second rainbow in her young life also tied her to Elian—the day he left her for the second time.

She'd written reams and reams of adolescent poetry after Eddie, or rather Elian, left that time and made much of the rainbow link in her daydreams of true love. As the years passed, though, the idea became only a silly fantasy, a flash of imagined understanding. It meant nothing. She'd forgotten. Or had she?

"Excuse me, did I hear you telling your daughter you'd flown on this plane?"

She turned to find herself face to face with Elian. Somehow, it didn't surprise her. Olivia held her hand tightly, and she squeezed it. "Yes. Elian. Elian Davies, isn't it?"

He checked, and the tentative smile of a stranger making idle conversation evaporated. "No, I'm sorry. I'm afraid you have me confused with someone else."

She peered into his azure eyes. They held no recognition, even hidden, of her. "You don't know me?"

He shook his head. Her elation receded like an ebbing wave. The irony of her belated awareness and his obvious lack thereof failed to amuse. Olivia tugged at her skirt. "Mama, can we go now?"

Sydney ignored her. "Did you fly on this plane too?"

He followed her gaze. "Yes, in 1958. I was about seven. My parents took me to live in Berlin."

"I know…er…I mean, yes, that route continued on to Berlin after stopping in Paris. I was five. Perhaps we took the same flight." She studied his face, wondering which memories remained and which were lost. "Do you remember much about it?"

"The flight? A little. More than I do about my recent past."

Aha. "Why is that?"

He took a step back, as though he had revealed too much. "It's not important." He began to move away.

She didn't have much time. She put a hand out, touching his sleeve. "I'd like to hear your memories—the ones you have. I'm…uh…doing a story about the growth of commercial air transport for my newspaper, the *Observer*." At his blank look, she hastily added, "It's really more about how rapidly the airplane designs changed to accommodate more people and more distance at greater efficiency. You know, from the white glove service and sleeping berths that came with long flights to the three-hour SST trip with hardly enough time to pee."

She peered at him, searching for a sign. He'd perked up, even cracked a smile at her little joke. *But will he bite?* She gave him an inviting look. "So you see, I'm collecting anecdotes from people who flew on any of the early transatlantic crossings—you know, the Boeing 377"—she gestured at the plane in front of them—"and the 707, the DC-7C, all those." She paused to catch her breath and held out her hand. "My name is Sydney Bellek, and this is my daughter Olivia. Would you…would you care to have a cup of tea with us?"

He hesitated. Something gleamed in his eyes as he stared at her, then disappeared. "George. George Khouri. A cup of tea sounds delightful. Shall we go down to the café?"

Chapter Thirteen

Alexandria, Present Day

"It shouldn't have taken him that long to recognize you. I mean, the love of his life and all."

"Oh, I wouldn't blame him too much. It took me almost thirty years to put it together after all. At least he had the excuse of a blow to the head."

"A blow—oh, you mean in Lebanon? So they *did* shoot him?"

"I'm getting to that. Hold your horses."

Olivia tapped an impatient finger on the table. "Okay, after four years Pop turns up, only he doesn't recognize you and he thinks he's some guy named George Khouri. How long did it take to bring him around?"

"Long enough for me to fear it would never happen. I only had two weeks before we were due to leave for Paris. In the interim, I had to corral his attention, gain his trust, and hit him with the awful truth—"

"Me?"

"You. Plus I had to find out what had happened to him back in Lebanon. Like I said, he wasn't a spill-the-beans-on-the-first-date kind of guy. Thank God his girlfriend had just dumped him. If I'd had to get rid of her as well, I don't think I'd have had a chance."

"Girlfriend?"

Sydney pulled another pair of underwear from her drawer and stuffed it into the carry-on. She held up a nearly transparent bit of underwired ivory silk, a pink satin ribbon laced through the cups. "Shall I take this?"

"Mother!"

"What? I'm not dead yet."

Olivia rolled her eyes. "You were saying? Father's girlfriend?"

"Apparently she'd left him for another man just the week before—one who had authentic identification instead of the manufactured one Elian used. That made Elian fair game and open to new…er…ideas. I capitalized on that."

"You vixen."

"Yes." Her mother folded her hands demurely. "Quite the wicked maid." When Olivia didn't rise to the bait, Sydney looked at her more closely. "Something's wrong."

"Wrong?"

"You know I can't continue until you confess. Something's happened. Is it Benjamin?"

"No!" Olivia took a deep breath. "Look, I've got an errand to run. I'll be back for lunch."

"Don't take your time. You know I need periodic nourishment."

****

"There you are. I'm starved. Come into the kitchen." Sydney sat down and set a plate before her daughter. "Now, tell me what upset you."

Olivia picked up her sandwich and put it down. "It's just…it's just your mention of old girlfriends hit a nerve."

Sydney put down her fork and poured wine into each of their glasses. "I always say a nice Gavi di Gavi will soothe the savage beast," she remarked. "It's Rémy then?"

"Oh, Mother…" The words rushed from Olivia's mouth, tumbling over each other in a desperate attempt to crush the abomination.

Like a witch doctor blowing the demons away.

"Yesterday evening, on my way home? I…I saw Rémy with…with…another woman. I'm not sure who she is, but I'm pretty sure I saw her photograph in one of his wine magazines. Standing next to Rémy."

"Ah." Sydney wondered if she'd been wrong about the man. Perhaps her worry that Olivia would break his heart was premature. The alternative theory—that he merely wanted a companion for his travels—might hit closer to the mark. She took a peep at Olivia's stricken face. *Don't pile on.* "I wouldn't make too much of it. She's likely an associate of his."

"I think she's more than that. They were in Brabo's. I saw them through the window. They were…they were nuzzling."

Uh oh. "Are you sure?"

Olivia took a swallow of the wine. "Well, they were sitting close together, and he was whispering in her ear."

"How do you know? You were on the sidewalk."

"Okay, okay, he was speaking into her ear. Whatever."

Sydney pursed her lips. "What's her name? We can at least find out if she's in the wine business. It's probably perfectly innocent—they were discussing a sale or something."

"I...don't know. Maybe." Olivia's chin wobbled. "I can't lose him too, Mother."

"There, there—you haven't lost either one, you know."

Olivia blew her nose. "I asked a...friend to check her out. He didn't think it would take long."

"Good." Sydney eyed her laptop.

"Mother, stay out of it." Olivia put her plate in the sink. "Are you finished with lunch?"

Sydney wolfed down the last bite of sandwich and tossed off the wine. "Yes."

"Good. Let's get back to Pop's other woman."

"Later, if you don't mind. The old lady needs a nap. Now shoo. I'll call you in half an hour or so."

Olivia left, grumbling. Sydney reached her laptop in two strides.

****

"Olivia? Where are you?"

"Downstairs, Mother. Are you ready to go back to work?"

"Absolutely. Do come up."

Olivia sat down at the desk and took out the recorder and her notebook. "We were discussing the problem of Pop's ex-girlfriend."

"Cleo wasn't the problem. George himself constituted the greatest obstacle to my reunion with Elian."

"George?"

"Elian insisted that he was George Khouri. It didn't matter that he'd made up his identity. He'd settled on it and couldn't be budged. I couldn't even get him to *pretend* he was Elian Davies."

"Typical man."

Sydney nodded. "A safe, secure identity takes precedence over the truth. In this case, I could understand, though. He knew he'd been through hell, and he didn't want to relive it."

****

Washington, DC, 1987

"More wine?" Elian held the bottle out.

"Yes, thank you. This dry Riesling is exceptional, don't you think?"

"Very nice."

"It's perfect with the lobster."

"I guess."

Sydney pressed on. "Of course, I miss the Middle Eastern wines, Turkish…and Lebanese. They're not available here. Did you…did you taste them while you were in Beirut?"

"No, but then I'm more of a beer man." He grinned at her. "Still trying to resurrect this Elian fellow?"

"You agreed that I might probe a bit. Even if you're not who I think you are."

"I don't mind." He took her hand. "It keeps you focused on me."

Sydney hadn't decided whether she wanted him with or without his proper name yet, so she gently withdrew her hand. "Tell me what you remember of those first days."

"You mean, after I woke up in the hospital?"

"Yes."

Elian sat back and ran a hand over his face. Sydney noticed it had a slight tremor. "The nurses said a jeep dumped me on the steps of the St. Theodore Hospital in the middle of the night. Someone had patched me up pretty haphazardly, and the night staff had to clean all the wounds out and redo the bandages. Apparently I was delirious and gabbled on and on about seals and whirlwinds and harpoons." His fingers went to the scar still visible at his temple. "I imagine because I felt like a speared fish. They said at least two bullets had grazed my head, and one determined little fellow lodged himself in my thigh."

"Did they patch up your…er…*other* injury?" Sydney kept her face straight with some difficulty.

"Other—" He stared at her. "Wait, how did you—"

"I told you. I was there. I did the initial…er…triage." She couldn't help it. The giggle leaked out.

He glowered at her and drank the last of the wine without offering her any. Once she'd subsided, he continued with dignity. "The *earlier* wound had healed nicely. In fact, the nurse spoke admiringly of the repair."

Sydney blew on her fingers and polished an imaginary medal. "I knew the years of surgery on my Barbies would stand me in good stead."

"More likely I benefited from the skills of a Lebanese matron."

Sydney wanted to continue the argument, but the forbidding look on his face gave her pause. She still had time. No use pushing him so hard he withdrew. "When you regained consciousness, were you aware of who you were or what had happened to you?"

He shook his head. "No, and whoever dropped me off had removed any identification I'd had on me."

"Al-Hurriyeh's people must have picked you up after the helicopter took off. They couldn't afford a dead American on their hands, so they brought you in.

They also wouldn't stick around to take credit."

"I've pieced that much together since then. As I said, I had no clue who I was, so the head nurse…" He paused, smiling reminiscently. "Dora, what a handful she was—"

"Could we move on with the story, please?"

Elian grinned at her. "I like to dwell on that part—it always makes your eyes flash." He turned wistful. "I sure wish I remembered why you're jealous."

"I'm *not* jealous." She tamped down her vexation along with the burgeoning desire to kiss him. "Dora?"

"She named me after her grandson, George. A good Maronite name, she said. Her little way of skewering the Orthodox nurses, who wanted to call me Sarkis. So I became George Khouri. If anyone asked, they attributed my lack of Arabic and ease with English to being brought up in the States."

"When did they release you?"

"Let's see." He buttered the last roll. Sydney snatched it from him and took a large bite before finishing off her water with a belligerent glare. "Yes, it was the day of the U.S. Embassy bombing. The whole city was in an uproar. They needed all the available hospital beds so they discharged me. Dora gave me a little money, and I wandered the streets, not sure where I belonged or where I should be headed."

"That's when I saw you."

"So you say. That period passed pretty much in a blur. If you'd called me, I wouldn't have answered to the name."

"I know." The misery of that night clutched at her, still painful after so many years. "How did you make your way back to America?"

"Eventually, I found a job at AUB—American University of Beirut—in the press office. I soon graduated to editor-in-chief of their alumni magazine. A visiting trustee, a Peter Khouri, met me at a party. He insisted we were related, and I saw no reason to disagree. Within a month, he'd found me a job at the Boston *Crier*."

"From there you moved on to television, correct?"

He finished the last bite of steak from her plate. She tried to cuff him and missed. "Yes, the CMB affiliate in Boston."

"I know. I told you I saw you. You were reporting on a helicopter crash."

"Wow, that was four years ago." He squinted at her. "So how come you didn't try to find me then?"

Sydney patted her flat stomach. "Events kind of interfered with my quest."

"Oh, of course. Olivia. Not that it mattered." He signaled to the waiter. "I left WXZZ less than a month later to work at the *World*. I didn't get back into television until this year."

"That explains why Do-Right couldn't find you."

"Do right?" He stared at her.

"Never mind. It's all moot now. So you went back to CMB?"

He nodded. "Yup. They loved me so much they booted me upstairs to the Washington bureau. Luckily, they let me take a few weeks off to settle in and meet this wonderful woman. Did I mention her?"

"Cleo? I thought she dumped you?" *Can he understand my words through these gritted teeth?*

"No, this one has glorious waves of honey gold hair, Betty Grable's legs, warm brown eyes with little flecks of butterscotch—"

Sydney, her heart rattling in its cage, interrupted before she lost it and jumped in his lap. "*Hmm*, that reminds me. Shall we get dessert?"

He rolled his eyes. "She thinks of nothing but her stomach."

Nine months of ventral obsession came back like a blow to the belly. *Story of my life.* "All right then, let's take a walk along the waterfront."

"Better idea." He gestured to the waiter.

They left Landini Brothers and wandered down past the Torpedo Factory to the pier. The late spring weather had brought out both the ducks and the humans. Other people's laughter and conversations filled the silence that lay between them. A man set up a table with wine glasses and began to run his finger around the rims, creating an eerie, silvery tintinnabulation. Sydney, lost in her thoughts, tossed bits of the roll she'd brought from the restaurant into the water. A wedge of American coots scooted over, their white bills pumping back and forth as if they believed the movement would help them go faster. Elian hung over the railing.

"Sydney? Can I ask you something?"

"Uh huh."

"Would you have picked me up that day at the Smithsonian if you didn't think I was this Elian of yours?"

She started to say something flippant but noticed his eyes glimmering in the feeble yellow light. "I…"

He continued to stare at the water. "Sydney, these last two weeks have been…special. I never thought…I mean, I know it's strange. And me with no real background—nothing to offer you, no...*me* as it were. I—"

She stopped his meandering with her lips. His arms went tentatively around her. For a minute, they floated in a cocoon of mist, the voices and music fading into the background. She drowned in a mixture of new feelings and old memories, of hope and despair, of the past and the possibility, hitherto unanticipated, of a future. He stepped back, holding her at arm's length. His voice steady, he whispered, "The moment. Let's live for that tonight."

Resolved to accept his wish, at least for now, she followed him.

****

Alexandria, Present Day

"You made love that night, didn't you?"

"Glorious, wondrous, fabulous love. I don't mind admitting it."

"And yet you had no intention of staying with him unless he accepted his true identity."

"That's not entirely true. Yes, my main goal was to make him remember me, but I didn't have time to assess my feelings for George Khouri. I only had a week left."

"What about me? When were you going to explain my relationship to him? Or rather to Elian? Or did you intend to keep that a secret?"

Sydney opened the window a little wider. She picked up a book and put it down. Olivia waited. "You know, I could never seem to find the right moment. Every day things grew more complicated. You tell me. How do I explain to a man who refuses to believe he is who I say he is that he's also the father of my child?"

"I see what you mean. He's not going to accept his…progeny if he doesn't accept his identity." Olivia chuckled. "You probably should have married Uncle Walker after all. You could have let Pop believe he was my father. Ease into the truth of my heritage."

"Ha, ha. That would sure have cleared things up. And what, may I ask, should I have done about his current wife, Jeannie?"

"Lessee…you'd have to have annulled the marriage to Walker, or…"

Sydney threw up her hands. "So you see why I couldn't just come out and tell him."

"You had to be the most frustrating creature. Here Pop had fallen in love with you again, and you were quibbling over his name."

"The story isn't over yet. Wait and see who you accuse of quibbling."

Alice knocked and stuck her head around the door. "Olivia? There's a Mr. Sunderland to see you."

"I'll be right down." Olivia turned to her mother. "He may have some information for me on…on…"

"On Rémy's new pet?"

Her daughter grimaced. "Let's hope you're right about it being merely business. I'll be right back."

Sydney spent the next ten minutes drumming her fingers on her bureau. Just when she'd decided to change not only her dress but her hairdo, Olivia returned.

"Well?"

Her daughter sighed. "Her name is Celeste Roussin. She used to manage one of Rémy's estates. Rumor had it they were involved."

"And now?"

"Sunderland couldn't find much on her love life. She left Rémy's employ voluntarily, and she's got her own business now, doing international investigations of some sort."

"You mean, she's a private investigator?"

Olivia nodded. "He found a couple of articles about her online. She cracked a big fraud scheme in the wine-export business a couple of years ago."

"Wow, interesting." Sydney paused. "I wonder what she's doing in the States?"

"Rémy's here for the French wine-importers conference. Maybe it has something to do with that."

"Let me ask you this. When you saw this Celeste and Rémy canoodling, did he look happy, angry, or shifty?"

"Mother, how would I know? It's not like I stood there on the street for hours trying to read their lips."

"Facial expressions, dear. Not words. I wonder—"

"Don't you dare, Mother. You've got enough on your plate."

"It's the journalist in me, dear. I can't help but speculate. It could be Rémy rekindling an old romance." At Olivia's expression, she patted her hand. "It's more likely something much more mundane. Look, I promise to intrude only minimally if you promise to confront…er, ask Rémy what's going on."

"I will. I have to know. I'm not going anywhere with him until this is resolved."

"Good. Now, do you want to hear about my night with your father? Or more precisely, with George?"

Olivia reddened. "Depends. Were your activities really…um…spicy? Lusty? Raunchy? What's the heat level?"

"Heat level?" Sydney pretended to look puzzled. "Is that a term of art in romance writing?"

"Yes. I can probably endure two flames without blushing, but if it goes to three I may have to leave the room."

Her mother grinned. "As I recall, your novels are rated four flames, but I understand. I think…yes… we're talking three flames." She assumed a gratified air. "Definitely three."

Her daughter rose hastily. "How about if I turn the recorder on and you talk to the mike? I'll be in the next room."

Sydney pursed her lips to hide the smirk. "That should work. I'll call for help if the recorder starts to smoke. It was a wild night."

Olivia skipped out of the room. Her mother picked up the machine and tapped it. "Testing, testing."

****

Washington, DC, 1987

The night clerk at the boutique hotel on King Street didn't raise an eyebrow. "Mr. Khouri, good evening. No messages. Will you be needing anything else this evening?"

Elian mumbled, "Er…no. No thanks." He took Sydney's arm. His hand trembled slightly, and he squeezed a little too hard, making her jump. "Shall we have a nightcap in the bar?"

Sydney, knowing what would happen in a few minutes, responded tranquilly, "No, I don't think so."

"Oh. Okay." Elian stumbled twice on the carpet and dropped the room key.

They took the elevator to the top floor and walked into a luxuriously furnished suite. A Chinese carpet covered the floor, and gauzy white drapes billowed softly in the breeze from the open French windows. Sydney laughed. "It looks like something out of a Fred Astaire movie." She plumped a satin-covered pillow and checked her face in the enormous rococo mirror.

"I'll…I'll go get some ice." Elian backed out of the room. She heard his feet pounding down the hall. Sydney wandered around, turning lamps off and closing the curtains. She checked the minibar and took out a bag of M&Ms. When Elian returned, he found her lying on the bed, popping candy bits into her mouth, letting her tongue peep out between her lips and sucking delicately.

Elian heaved a deep breath. He moved toward the bed, leaned down, brushed her lips with his, took a handful of her blouse, and ripped it open. She held very still. He rubbed the nipple through the thin lace of her bra, then trailed his finger down to her belly. When she didn't respond he took a step back and stood, his foot lightly tapping the floor. She'd begun to wonder what he was waiting for when he bent toward her. "May I?" She lifted her hips and he pulled the skirt off. He paused again, as though relishing the building tension. She reached up and grabbed his jeans, squeezing his cock. His breath came out with a whoosh. Before he could move, she pulled his belt out and unzipped his pants, allowing his penis to spring out.

After that things progressed quickly. They wasted no time removing any more clothes but simply rolled down whatever impeded progress. His cock found its way inside her, and he closed with her, vacuuming out the space between their bodies. They moved together as though they'd performed the same dance many times, instantly familiar with each other's tempo and pulse. At one point, Elian paused to touch her cheek wonderingly, and she said softly, "You know me. You know my skin and my bones and my veins. You know my very cells. You are mine."

"I am yours."

They rocked, wave on wave of murmurs echoing around them. "Come to me, come to me, come."

She came.

An hour later, she woke him up. This time she straddled him, guiding his hardening cock inside. Leaning back, she pressed her hips toward his chest and rolled her ass over his balls, riding them like a hobo on the rails. When she straightened, he arched his back, grabbed her hips, and pulled her into him. Their eyes locked, they reached into each other and found the bubble of desire, pricked it to release the lust, and shuddered.

He came.

An hour later, a rough tongue lapped at the moist and tender lips of her vagina. It tickled and sucked, waking her and driving her on a fast track toward orgasm. She yelped as his tongue speared inside, probing the hungry clitoris. "Oh my God, Elian!"

Oh no, I called him Elian! She brought a fist to her mouth, afraid he would stop, afraid he'd be furious. Or hurt. If she could only take back the name. Would he jump up, sneer at the woman with the strange fantasy? Shake his fist at her and hurl himself out of the room? She waited, unable to breathe.

Without a word, he withdrew his fingers and tongue, but instead of backing off, his lips steamrolled up over her belly and breasts to alight on her mouth.

Male and female met and held.

They came.

More than an hour later, she cracked an eye open to see what warmed her face. *I couldn't be blushing.* The sun peeped through the curtains, bright and hot. Her watch read ten o'clock. Thank God Olivia had had a sleepover at her friend's, or she'd be in deep trouble.

She put a hand under her neck and reflected on the night's activities. It didn't take long before shame crept into the pool of contentment, muddying the clear water. The word strumpet sprang to mind. *How could I have been so…so easy? What will he think of me?* She looked for Elian but found only his feet. She pinched a toe.

The foot jerked, and the covers thrashed. "What the hell?" He fought the blankets off and found her crouched at the head of the bed, the sheet pulled up to her chin. "Sydney? Are you okay?"

She couldn't look at him. It might not be so bad if he recalled their earlier trysts, but as far as he was concerned, they'd known each other less than two weeks. And she had a child. His child. But he didn't know that. She wondered if that would make it better or worse. The mattress bounced, and footsteps padded toward the bathroom. "Coming?"

Well, he doesn't appear to hate me. Yet. She shut off the thinking part of her brain and went directly to feeling. "Okay." As she slipped into the stall behind him, he lathered himself, humming a tune. She closed her eyes and let the hot water rinse off the odor of unbridled sex. Plucking the soap from his hands, she began to wash her front.

She heard an intake of breath. "Here, let me." He

took the soap back and began to rub in slow, sensual circles over her body. Just before she let out a scream of repressed desire, he dropped the bar on the tile floor, "That'll do it."

Elian backed to the wall, bringing her with him. With one heave, he pulled her legs around him and lifted her onto his penis. She let gravity draw her down, settling in a very gratifying way over the thick, pulsing rod. He lifted her again and again she sank back down on him. They fell into a rhythm, the soap lubricating their route. "It feels fantastic. Don't stop," she cried.

At that moment, he gave one great thrust and stiffened. She almost fell to the floor, her thighs shaking. He held her up and kissed her deeply, rolling his tongue in her mouth. "Good morning."

Sydney gazed at him, wishing she knew what to do. Or how she felt. Everything that she wanted to happen had just happened. Except with the wrong man. Well, not the wrong man. But…*I give up.* She stepped out of the shower, found a terry cloth robe hanging on the door, and stumbled back to the bed, pulling the pillow over her head. She didn't hear him leave. She didn't hear anything until the phone rang, waking her.

"Room 405? I have a call from an Alice Hafer for a Miss Bellek. Will you accept it?"

Sydney sat up. Her head ached, and every orifice in her body felt rough and drawn. She pulled the robe together over her naked breasts. "Yes, please put her through."

"Miss Bellek? This is Alice. Mrs. Teague called and said it's time to pick Olivia up. She said the girls partied all night and are exhausted but behaved very well. Shall I go?"

"Yes, yes, thanks. I'll be home soon. The...the meeting went so late, I decided to stay in the hotel. Where the meeting was. Did you get my message?" She waited anxiously through the pause.

"That's how I had this number. I'll see you when you get home."

Brrr. Alice could be withering. She'd have to start looking for another nanny for Olivia. Alice seemed to understand her mother a little too well.

Chapter Fourteen

Alexandria, Present Day

"Are you finished?"

"Yes, dear, you may enter."

Olivia peeked around the door. "It must have been a long night."

Her mother smiled serenely. "Not long enough."

"You still hadn't told him he was my father, had you?"

"No, and you needn't look at me like that. It didn't seem right to spring an instant family on him. Not before he recollected the occasion of your siring."

"To be fair"—Olivia spoke thoughtfully—"at that point you hadn't told me much about my father either. As I recall, you skipped the part about his demise."

"Well, technically, he hadn't died, but you're right. For the first four years of your life, you believed your father had disappeared into the jungle to live with the chimpanzees. It seemed simpler than explaining that, even though he'd been declared missing, presumed dead, I felt in my bones he was alive. It would only have confused you."

"Confused me? Why?"

"Well, you wouldn't know whether to be sad that he'd been killed or happy that he existed somewhere. Or sad that he lived but not with us…or…er…are you laughing at me, Olivia?"

"No, sir, not me."

"Good. That would be very rude." Sydney directed a hard look at Olivia. "Anyway, I had to make up a story to explain why he didn't come see his daughter, when in fact he didn't know about you."

"Hence the chimpanzees."

Sydney hesitated. "Er…yes. And then when we found him again, I thought if I could revive his memories, it would all come out in the wash. And he'd tell you. So I didn't have to. See?" Her imploring face failed to work on her daughter.

"Shut up and drink your gin."

"Okay. Now there's only a little bit more. Do you want to hear it tonight?"

"Yes, please." Olivia poured herself a drink and sat down.

As Sydney opened her mouth, the telephone rang. She snatched the receiver up before her daughter could reach it. "Hello? Yes. Wait, let me get a pen." She crooked a finger at Olivia, who obediently handed her a pad and pencil. "Okay, shoot….Really? *Hmm*. What about in 2001…Interpol? No idea who ordered it? All right, get back to me when you've tracked it down. Thanks, Joe."

Sydney could feel her daughter's angry eyes boring into the back of her head and deliberately returned the phone to its cradle before turning around.

Olivia rasped, "You've been snooping, haven't you?"

She took a peep at her daughter. "What can I say? It's a habit. And my duty to protect my daughter from charlatans."

"Are you saying Rémy is a crook?"

"No, no." Sydney picked up the notebook and read her notes. "He seems to have had several brushes with the law, however. Nothing ever stuck."

"What kind of brushes?"

"Oh, minor things. He's been linked to some shady characters over the years. Back in the nineties, Interpol pulled him in a few times for consorting with a bootleg operation. Then in 2001, they officially arrested him."

"For what?"

"A large shipment of passion fruit was sent from his beach house in St. Maarten to an address in Florida."

"Passion fruit?" Olivia stared at her, baffled. "That doesn't sound particularly malignant."

"The Florida agriculture department would sooner people smuggled Uzis into Miami than fruit. If the cargo harbored any nasty foreign fungi or beetles, it would have devastated Florida's economy."

"So what happened?"

"According to Joe, the FBI, the Florida State Police, and Interpol reached some kind of agreement. All very hush hush, but they let Rémy go."

"Did he bribe someone?"

Sydney shook her head. "No evidence of that. Whatever the reason for his release, the orders came from very high up in the French government."

"Interesting. I wonder…will Joe call if he learns anything more specific?"

"He's on another assignment. He only had time to do the preliminary legwork. Your job is to weasel the rest of the story out of Rémy tomorrow."

"If I can." Olivia's mouth sagged. "I was sure of

his affection up until a day ago. Now I don't know where I stand."

Her mother patted her shoulder awkwardly. "I know I meddled, but isn't it best to get these little mysteries out in the open?"

"I suppose." Olivia lips trembled and her face puckered. "Do you want to go on tonight?"

Sydney pretended to yawn. "How about if we take it up tomorrow afternoon? Maybe we'll know more about Rémy's little escapades then and can put it behind us."

"All right."

****

"Well?"

"I'm not going to talk about it yet. You have to give me the next installment, or we'll never finish before you leave."

Sydney took a stab at pouting, which had absolutely no effect on her daughter. She sat down and folded her hands in her lap. "So…where was I?"

"You'd enjoyed a night of enthusiastic sex—or so I presume from the sated look on your face when you finished narrating it. You'd ditched your poor, neglected daughter with appalling indifference, and—as proof that justice will prevail—your lover had bailed on you."

"Oh yes, that's where."

****

Washington, DC, 1987

Why did she expect to hear from him? Why not? *Maybe he thinks I'm a slut. Gee, ya think?* She'd shared a wild ride with him, showing no signs of maidenly virtue or modesty. As far as he was concerned, they'd known each other for maybe a fortnight. Not once during their night together had she mentioned—or to be honest, thought about—Olivia. Sydney stuck her head under the kitchen faucet again. Towels lay in wet lumps all over the floor. She felt around for the last dry one and pressed it against her eyes to ease the stinging. Cold drops trickled down her back from her sopping hair, soaking through the thin T-shirt. The discomfort helped. *Now I understand what motivated the flagellants. Whipping themselves was a perfect distraction from a life of wanton sin.*

"Mama? Are you okay?" Sydney wrapped the towel turban-like around her head and turned to her daughter. Olivia's eyes grew round, and she backed away a step. "Mama? Are you cwying?"

Sydney gathered the child into her arms. "Yes, Olivia. Mama's a little sad right now. But it's okay. We'll be okay."

"Dat's good, because we're goin' onna trip." She patted her chest with pride. "Onna airpwane."

"We are indeed. Now go on upstairs. We have some packing to do."

She watched the little girl's sturdy legs climb the stairs. Her red-brown hair had been plaited into two braids, yet still a tuft of hair stood straight up from the crown. A cowlick. Just like her father's. Sydney turned back to the sink.

****

Concorde SST, 1987

The moment. That's what he'd said. "Let's live for the moment." He never intended to come back. It was all a big game to him. This deranged woman believed him to be her long-lost lover, so why not take advantage of it? Seize the opportunity for a quick tumble, a free piece of ass. Which she gave willingly. All for a vague memory...or was it simply more of her wishful thinking? She wanted a father for her child, and she wanted that father to be Elian. She wanted it so badly she'd believe anything, even that Elian was alive and in love with her.

"Mrs. Bellek? Would you like a pillow?"

"No, thank you, but my daughter would."

The stewardess gently tucked a pillow behind Olivia's head. The little girl opened her eyes. "This is a pwane, right, Mama? Not a building? Will we be here a long time? It has really big wings, doesn't it? It's a lot bigger than my friend Tommy's airpwane. I bet it's not a toy, eever, is it, Mama?"

"No, it's not a toy. It's a real airplane, Olivia. A Concorde. A very fast jet. Did you hear what the captain said?"

"Yes, Mama."

The stewardess laughed. "Can I get you anything else, ma'am?"

"Yes, I'd like a whiskey. Bourbon, please."

"I'll be right back."

Sydney leaned back against the deeply cushioned seat. She was glad Malcolm had sprung for the Concorde. Since it only held a hundred passengers and the entire plane was first class, she didn't have to worry about Olivia being a nuisance. Of course, the child had been royally pampered by the staff from the moment they boarded. The co-pilot had taken her to see the cockpit, and the pilot gave her a pair of plastic wings and a First Flight certificate suitable for framing.

"Look, Mama, they're just like the ones you have!

Pin them on me, pwease?"

"Yes, they are." Sydney explained to the captain that she'd been given the same items on her first flight so long ago. "Only this plane is significantly larger and faster than that old Boeing 377."

The captain had been impressed. "You flew on the Stratocruiser? Wow." His reaction made Sydney feel old, even though the pilot obviously had a few years on her. He showed a bewildered Olivia and a fascinated Sydney the instrument panel. "The Concorde makes the flight between New York and Heathrow in three and a half hours, twice as fast as a regular jet. Just last year, she flew round the world in less than thirty-two hours."

Sydney sipped her drink. Working hard to ignore the ache in her heart, she read her notes on the controversy surrounding the Concorde. Environmental concerns dogged it from its earliest days. People were convinced the sonic boom produced when it broke the sound barrier at speeds of 1,350 miles per hour would wreak all kinds of havoc—baby mutations, cancer, insanity. At first, Congress passed legislation to prohibit the SST—short for Supersonic Transport—from touching down on U.S. soil, but it soon lifted the ban. New York tried to deny landing rights on its own, but public outcry forced them to back down. Other objections related to the enormous government subsidies required to make it commercially viable. Lately, British Airways and Air France had begun dropping routes, which was why Sydney and Olivia could only get to London and would have to take a connecting flight to Paris.

Paris. How often had she met Elian on the way to Paris! At five, then again at thirteen. They'd had that one drink when she was—how old? Twenty? No, twenty-one. She'd been drawn to him then, but too young to understand that she'd met her one and only. The episode in Cairo made it no clearer. She savored the memory of an awkward first mating, one she'd considered at the time merely a resume builder.

Then came Iran. A gurney slick with sweat slipped onto her mind's stage. Two sapphirine eyes boring into her, desire—and something else—flickering in them. She concentrated on those eyes—what had they shown? Surely not love. He didn't know her well enough to love her…or did he? He hadn't said anything about love, even during those encounters in Lebanon. Yes, they'd had sex. He'd held her close. But he hadn't spoken of love. In fact, she reflected, he'd never mentioned feelings at all. Each time they met, he claimed to remember her. Each time she'd disappointed him by not recognizing him. *Is that what he was waiting for? For me to acknowledge our past? Our rainbow link? Would he have said he loved me then?*

Her lip trembled, and a tear dropped on the notebook, the wet circle widening, blurring the ink. *This must be God's cynical little joke. I know him now. I love him now. And now* he *doesn't remember* me.

The stewardess handed her a menu, printed in elegant script on heavy stock. Sydney looked it over. "I'll have the selection of foie gras and caviar canapés to start, please. Olivia, would you like *entrecôte Henri IV* or…" She read from the menu. "…crayfish tails gently poached in white wine and finished with cream and Dolcelatta cheese?"

As Olivia stared at her mother in disbelief, the stewardess whispered, "I think we can rustle up something…er…simpler for your daughter. How about a grilled cheese sandwich?"

Sydney smiled. "That would be perfect. I'll have the *entrecôte* then. Thank you." She got out a coloring book and crayons for Olivia and settled back into her thoughts.

She'd heard nothing from Elian for two days following their lovemaking, days of agonized self-recrimination. If it weren't for travel preparations and frantic meetings with Malcolm, she probably would have spent the whole time in bed. The day before she left for Paris the telephone rang.

"Sydney?"

Deep breath. *Try to swallow that big lump of whatever. Let the pulse slow.* "Yes?"

"It's George. Look, I'm sorry I haven't been in touch. I've been…out of town. Are you free tonight?"

Blink twice and whatever you do, don't let those knees buckle. "I…"

"Please? I know you're leaving for Paris soon. I just need a few minutes."

"Okay." She couldn't have gotten more words out if she wanted to.

"Wonderful. I'll pick you up at six-thirty." She heard a click and the phone went dead.

****

Alexandria, Present Day

"Why are you stopping, Mother?"

"I'm a little tired, dear. And to be honest, I'm not looking forward to this part of the story."

"I see."

"Plus I want to know what happened with Rémy. You saw him this morning."

"Yes."

"And?"

"After he'd calmed down, he confessed."

"Whoa, back up. 'Calmed down'? What upset him?"

Olivia mumbled something.

"I didn't catch that."

"He flew off the handle when I told him I'd seen him with Celeste. I've never seen him so angry. Mother, I swear he almost slapped me."

Sydney's face hardened, and her eyes closed to slits. "Where is he now?" she said in a tightly controlled voice.

"It's all right, Mother. We resolved it. If you sit down, I'll explain."

Sydney reluctantly settled on the edge of a chair. Anger burned her throat. No one…no one threatened her daughter. There would be consequences. She pretended to listen.

Olivia paced the room. "At first, Rémy tried to pass his anger off as outrage that I would suspect him of being unfaithful."

"Twisted it around to make it your fault, eh?"

"Mother…"

"Sorry. You did say 'confessed,' didn't you?"

"Perhaps that's not the appropriate word. When I told him I knew about Celeste and her current business, he feared their plan had been compromised. Once I convinced him I would keep his secret, he told me the whole story."

An odd look passed over Sydney's features, one of skepticism mixed with curiosity. "Go on."

"Over the past year, there's been a rash of

mislabeled French wines appearing in the U.S. market—"

"You mean, as in jug wine labeled as *premier cru*?"

Olivia nodded. "Yes. The American wholesalers at the conference wanted to know what, if anything, was being done to secure the imports and catch the perpetrators. There'd been no problem with Rémy's wines at his tasting, and he assumed the debate didn't concern him. Until the day of the banquet."

"Let me guess. One of his wines was on the menu and turned out to be schlock."

"Right. When the president of the Eastern Seaboard Wine Merchant's Society spit out his 1985 Chambertin-Clos de Beaumec and declared it vinegar, all hell broke loose. In the midst of the ruckus, Celeste Roussin came up to Rémy and offered her services."

Sydney kept a straight face with some difficulty. "How convenient. Or is it fortuitous? I'm not sure…Gratuitous?" She stared up at the ceiling.

"Anyhoo…he and his savior toddled off to Brabo, where I happened to pass by and see them."

Sydney brought her gaze back to her daughter. "*Hmm.*"

Olivia crossed her arms and hunched down on the chair. "Really."

"So what did she propose?"

"She told him she was investigating a Basque gang suspected of being the conduit for the cheap wine. They would make the switch in transit, the good wine siphoned off to the Azores and the bad sent on to the U.S. in its place. She and her partner had so far been unable to identify the person supplying the good wine."

"Why? The cheap wine would be labeled, wouldn't it? Why not trace the label back to the vineyard?"

"It's not that simple. In the beginning of the scam, most of the wines were only second tier, so the wine merchants didn't pay much attention. A certain percentage of bad wine is always factored into any shipment. The thieves cleverly used a variety of labels from several wine regions. It would have been impossible to follow all the leads."

"And the vineyards wouldn't know until too late that their wine had disappeared and been replaced by jug stuff."

"Correct, but this time, Rémy had brought the wines himself."

"Direct from the source. So if they were switched, either he did it…or—"

"Or someone in his organization did. Celeste wanted to use Remy's wine to trace the supplier."

"Like following the pebbles back to the pond scum."

"Exactly. It didn't take long. Last night, she called to tell him the police had arrested the manager of one of his estates, a Monsieur Bel Ami."

"Did our Mister Bel Ami happen to be the manager who had replaced Ms. Roussin?"

Olivia gawked at her. "How did you know?"

Sydney shrugged. "Journalist's intuition again. Interesting names, don't you think? Bel Ami? 'Good friend'? And Roussin…yes, that's slang for a copper, a policeman." She cupped her chin in her hand. "Yes…interesting. Olivia, the whole affair seems a bit contrived to me. Have you given any thought to the notion that she might have set him up?"

"To discredit him? Or embarrass him?"

"Or to bag him. That reminds me, I heard from Joe today. He had more news about the passion fruit scam."

"Did he discover why they released Rémy?"

"He could only track down one witness—a former Florida agriculture official. Once Joe explained that the statute of limitations had expired—"

"Huh?"

"Hey, the guy had no clue what Joe was talking about, and Joe can be very persuasive."

"He learned from the best."

Sydney had the grace to blush. "Thank you, dear. So anyway, according to the official, rumor had it that Rémy worked for the French government, that he was an undercover investigator."

"So," said Olivia slowly, "he's a good guy."

Sydney tried to hide her disappointment. "Sort of. He's still a bit of a sneak."

"Mother!"

Sydney shrugged. "Roussin may not know his true profession and thought she could trap him. Or use him as bait to catch Bel Ami. Either way, she might have doctored the one bottle herself. How did your little *tête-à-tête* with him end?"

Olivia wouldn't look at her. "He…uh…got a call. She…uh…wanted to celebrate." The rest came out in a rush. "He knew I'd be here with you, that we were trying to finish the book. It really doesn't bother me. At all."

"I see."

"Look, Mother. Rémy may have a rakish side, but he's serious about his business, and he's serious about me. It's not healthy to distrust him."

"Maybe yes, maybe no. Promise me you'll keep a wary eye on him."

Alice knocked. "Your tickets have arrived, madame."

"Oh good. I have the window seat, as requested?"

"Yes, ma'am."

Sydney mentally thumbed her nose at her brother. She still got a kick out of sitting wherever she wanted.

"Mother? Are you too tired to continue?"

"No, no, not now. I only wanted to hear the latest about Rémy. Once I get into my story, I lose track of other narratives. Where did we stop?"

"You were on the plane to Paris."

"Oh, yes…" Sydney paused. "No…I mean yes, but I'd backtracked a little to the day before I left for France. To the penultimate battle with Elian."

****

Washington, DC, 1987

Elian tried unsuccessfully to take Sydney's hand. "You probably think I'm a monster, walking out like that."

"You've done it before."

"I have?" His puzzled look changed swiftly to understanding. "Oh, Elian did. But, Sydney, I'm not Elian."

Sydney shrugged and took a large swig of her gin and tonic. The combination of juniper berry and lime soothed her throat. The alcohol soothed her mind. "What did you want to tell me?" She kept her voice deliberately cool.

"Well, that's part of it. I wanted to reiterate. I'm not your Elian. I think you still harbor some hope that I am. Sydney, it's not realistic. And more important—at least to me—as long as you see me as him, you don't see me as me."

That got her attention. "Huh?"

"You see, my dear…" He made a grab for her hand again, but she curled it around the highball glass. "I think I'm falling in love with you. The short time I've spent with you has changed my mind about settling down." Sydney said nothing, and after a minute Elian continued. "I admit that, in the beginning, I went along with your project because I knew you'd dump me in a New York minute if I didn't. So I pretended to seriously consider your theory and reexamine my life. Sydney, I didn't expect it to evolve into…I didn't expect to end up doing it in order to make *you* happy."

She stood. "That's the most insulting speech I think I've ever heard. You're admitting that you lied to me for a…for a roll in the hay. Worse, that you're sorry to discover you have feelings for me!"

"Wait!" He grabbed her elbow and drew her back down. "Don't go. Yes, I fudged a little, but only as an excuse to keep seeing you. The…sex…came naturally, a natural extension of our attraction to each other." He hung his head so Sydney couldn't see his face. "After our night together, things changed. I haven't been able to get you out of my mind. Sydney, I want an honest relationship. I want you to care for me—George Khouri—not for some ephemeral person you knew years ago."

She stared at him, unable to process this new idea. *Love him? Love George Khouri? Do I? Could I?*

Elian continued. "Until that night, we were strangers, unfettered, separate and free. You had your agenda; I had mine. From what you've told me about

Davies, that's pretty much the extent of your commitment to him as well. Sydney, that's not enough for me now."

She opened her mouth to protest, but no words came out. She knew he was right about Elian. To her, he had always been the perfect lover, unrivaled by mere mortals, but he'd never actually been around long enough to prove it. She closed her eyes and attempted to conjure up his image without reference to the man before her. Sea-blue eyes blazed in a chiseled face, the sharp chin thrust out, a model of determination. A ringlet of russet hair tumbled down his forehead. When she opened them, she saw…Elian. "Elian…George. You are Elian. I don't know how to convince you. You're the boy I knew in Morocco, the man in Paris, in Tehran, in Beirut. I can't help it—you can't convince me otherwise."

His face set in a grim line. "Sydney, I can't play this charade any more. I want to marry you. I want to be Olivia's father, but I want to do it as George Khouri, not Elian Davies."

"Oh my God, El…George. You *are* her father. Don't you see? Elian Davies is Olivia's father." She gulped for air, her heart banging against its cell walls. There, it was out in the open. What would he do now?

Elian stood. Slowly, he raised a palm and signaled to the waiter. "Sydney, my offer stands. I would love to be Olivia's stepfather and your husband. But only on my terms."

Sydney's jaw dropped. Could he be in total denial? Did the revelation that he had sired Olivia not affect him? "You don't believe me?"

Elian took the check, signed it, and gave it back to

the waiter. Finally, he faced her. "No, I don't. When we first met, you might have intended to use my paternity as a hook to reel me in, but that stratagem doesn't work now. I want to be her father. Can't you just drop the act and accept reality for the marvelous thing it is?"

For an instant, she considered acquiescing. He didn't have to believe her. He didn't have to remember, did he? She could pretend she accepted his new identity. They could be happy. Olivia would have a father. *A father is a father, right?* So what if he didn't acknowledge his genetic tie? She, Sydney, could take the fact to her grave, and no one would be the wiser. Her head went down in the beginning of a nod, but she paused. "It's no use…George. I can't live a lie, either. You want me to leave my daughter in perpetual ignorance of her real father. No."

He stared at her in silence. Finally he picked up his jacket. "I guess that's it, then."

"Yes."

Chapter Fifteen

Alexandria, Present Day

"Ladies, come quick!" Alice's excited voice floated up from the living room.

The two women hurried down the stairs. "What is it?"

"There, on the television." The nanny pointed at the screen.

Olivia and Sydney followed her finger to see Benjamin, speaking before a bank of microphones. Sydney turned up the volume.

"Senator McNichol has returned to Washington, yes. The Senate is back in session and the majority leader has indicated there will be votes this week. The senator has a duty to his constituents to be here, at work, at his job."

A voice in the crowd shouted, "Where is Mrs. McNichol? Has she been heard from? What about Senator Lawrence? How can he show his face on the Senate floor after this?"

Benjamin's face closed down in a stolid expression Olivia knew well. He said stiffly, "You'll have to direct your questions concerning Senator Lawrence to his press secretary. As to Mrs. McNichol, she is a private citizen and entitled to her...er...privacy." He stalked away, waving an angry hand at the raucous mob. The three women stood staring at the empty podium. A reporter poked his head in front of the camera.

"We just heard from Benjamin Knox, McNichol's chief of staff, on the breaking news. The senator himself has yet to make a formal statement. Back to you, Cornell."

The screen switched to a flashy neon set and an anchor upholstered in Armani, perfect hair revealing just a hint of dignified gray at the temples. "Well, there you have it. Our current information is that Senator McNichol hastily returned to Washington upon the news that his wife"—here the anchor permitted himself a tiny snigger—"decamped with the junior senator from Connecticut, Senator Charles Lawrence. For further enlightenment, let's go to Bill Rickey, standing by at the Lawrence press conference. Bill?"

"Cornell? Yes, the presser is just wrapping up. Felicia Coates, Senator Lawrence's press secretary, claims…are you ready for this?" The reporter could hardly keep his face straight. "She *says* that the senator is 'indisposed' and will likely miss the first few days of the session."

"Did you ask her where the senator is at present?"

This time the reporter definitely snickered. "She said…she said…Pardon me…that he is, and I quote, 'taking the waters.' "

"You mean their story is he's at a *spa*?"

"I have the statement here in my formerly nicotine-stained fingers."

The anchor turned to camera two. "Well, folks, this should certainly be an interesting session. Stay tuned."

Alice turned the television off. "Oh my."

"Oh my indeed."

"My, my." Sydney touched Olivia's elbow. "You'd better call Benjamin."

"Me? Why?"

"Because, dear one, he needs you."

****

"Poor Senator McNichol is a basket case. I'd forgotten what an avaricious creature his second wife is. She took the silver and the Ming vase and walked out of their Chevy Chase mansion while he was up in Connecticut."

"What will happen to Lawrence?"

"Ben says the ethics committee and the leadership are conferring. Most expect him to be censured."

"Can't they impeach him?"

"What? No. I suppose they could expel him, but it's more likely they'll leave it to the voters to recall him. That may happen, but it will take time."

Sydney chuckled. "First they'll have to find him. I hear he's been sighted at upwards of fifteen health resorts so far. Sales of mineral water and mud packs are booming."

"If he's smart," Alice sniffed, "he'll ask for sanctuary on an Indian reservation."

"Why?"

"Indian reservations are sovereign territory. The law couldn't touch him."

"I don't know about that. Anyway, don't Indians have horrible methods of torture?"

"Not currently. Unless you count gambling."

Sydney turned to Olivia. "So how is Benjamin doing?"

"He's all right. He was glad to see me."

"And you?"

Olivia riffled through the magazines on the coffee table, picking one up and then another. Finally she mumbled, "What about me?"

"How was it, seeing him?"

"Like old times, Mother." Olivia threw the magazine down. "What do you think? He's focused on damage control. He has his hands full. I can't expect him to make another halfhearted attempt to win me back."

"Well, send him my condolences, poor thing. Will you see him tonight?"

"We're meeting for coffee this afternoon. I have a date with Rémy tonight."

"Oh."

Alice went to the door, but paused.

"What is it, Alice?"

"Pardon, ma'am, but you will be packed in time, won't you?"

"Of course. I'll check the bags at the airport."

"All right, but time is running very short."

"We still have a couple of days, Alice. We'll all be out of your hair soon enough."

"*Hmmph.*"

Sydney turned to her daughter. "Now, where were we?"

Olivia checked her notebook. "Penultimate battle over. 'Penultimate'—that sounds promising. You're on your way to Paris."

****

Washington, DC, 1987

"Hurry, Olivia. We only have thirty minutes to make the connection."

"Yes, Mama. We're going on anuvver plane,

Mama? Will it be as big as the uvver one?"

"No, dear, but it's only a short trip. We'll be in Paris in an hour."

A short time later, Sydney gazed out over the familiar spires and domes of her favorite city. The Eiffel Tower reared like an iron giraffe high above the Invalides. The sun sparkled on the Seine as it wound among the feudal buildings and crisp, glass-enclosed modern structures. She looked at her daughter and sighed. Life had to get better. She couldn't let her heartache rule their lives. She had work to do.

They checked into the Georges V Hotel, a venerable old place on the Champs Élysées. Malcolm had provided a generous per diem—"This time I want you to be able to hobnob with the VIPs"—and she planned to take full advantage of it. She had appointments with Air France and the minister of transportation and tourism set for Monday. "But this weekend, Olivia, I shall show you Paris."

****

"So, what did you like best, little one?"

"Oh, the puppets, the puppets!"

"The Grand Guignol? What, you didn't prefer the Louvre? The haute couture shops on the Faubourg St. Honoré? The Opéra?" Sydney laughed at her daughter's face. "You're right, the puppets were the best part of the day. Now, I want you to get some sleep." She kissed her daughter and quietly left the room.

Alice stood by the window, arms crossed. "If you'd like to go down to the lounge and have something to drink, Miss Sydney, I'll take care of the babe."

"Thank you, Alice. I'm so glad you were able to accompany us. I can't take Olivia to my meetings, and I can't leave her alone in the hotel."

The tall, sere nurse almost smiled. "As I told you, my sister Geraldine lives in the sixth arrondissement. She will entertain us. Tomorrow we plan to go up the Eiffel Tower."

"Olivia will love that." Sydney stretched. "I'm really not ready to settle down yet. A drink might just do the trick. You don't have to wait up."

From the look on Alice's face, she realized she hadn't had to give her permission.

The lounge was empty but for Sydney and a man in the far corner who hid behind his newspaper. The bartender wiped the immaculate bar with a corner of his apron. "Perhaps a Pernod, madame?"

"That sounds perfect, thank you."

He took out an Old Fashioned glass, filled it with an inch of Pernod, and added ice and two drops of Peychaud's bitters, pushing it across the counter to Sydney. She flipped the pages of an old *Paris Match* and sipped her drink. The slight licorice flavor of the Pernod reminded her painfully of Elian's scent.

A commotion from the lobby disturbed the stillness. A familiar voice called out, "Yes, thanks, I see her. Thanks again. Yes, I can find my way."

She looked up into the Pacific Ocean. "Elian?"

He held his hand out. "Walk with me."

Together, they stepped out of the hotel onto the boulevard. At that hour, the crowds had thinned, and they walked down to the Place de la Concorde. A light mist surrounded them, the harbinger of the constant drizzle for which Paris springs were famous. He led her into the tree-lined allée by the Jeu de Paume and indicated a bench. She sat willingly but couldn't make out his face in the dim light of the street lamp. He hadn't said a word during their walk. After pacing a minute, he sat down next to her, then jumped up almost immediately. "Come."

Sydney's jet lag had begun to kick in, and she resisted. "I'm tired." She raised her face to the sky. Drops of rain dampened her cheeks.

"Only a little farther. To the river."

They reached the promenade by the Seine before he let her pause for breath. He took hold of her arms and turned her to face him. "Sydney?"

Too bewildered to respond, she eyed him. "What do you want...is it George or Elian?"

"Ah, that's the crux, isn't it?"

"We've been over this before. Again, what do you want?" Her throat constricted, trying to hold back the harsh words, but she couldn't go on much longer.

"I have a question. You said you wouldn't marry George. Would you marry Elian?"

Her head began to spin. *Is he going to pretend to be Elian? Do I care?* In the midst of her confusion and exhaustion, she began to giggle. "Depends. Do you know an Elian?"

"Why are you laughing?" He sat on the parapet and kicked his heels against the stone. "It isn't funny, Sydney."

"Yes, it is." She snorted, choking on mirth. "Look what we're arguing about. Is he or isn't he? Will she or won't she? It's like some kind of Rossini farce."

His lips twitched. "I refuse to be the old fart who's cuckolded by his young wife."

"What part do you want to play then?"

He put an arm under her shoulders and legs and

lifted her high. Then he let her fall onto his lap, folded her to his chest, and kissed her. A stiff wind propelled her into his embrace, one that didn't take no for an answer. She let it push her closer. When she opened her eyes, a flash from the streetlight glanced through the drizzle. It made a rainbow that circled over Elian's head and settled on hers.

"I want to play Figaro."

She laughed. "All right, if I can be Suzanne, his love."

"Done."

****

Alexandria, Present Day

"Now we're getting somewhere. He recognized himself? Or…that doesn't sound right."

"He didn't specify. I think we'd both had enough of second-guessing each other at that point and just wanted to neck."

"Mother!"

Sydney checked her watch. "Don't you have to meet Benjamin at the bagel place?"

Olivia rose. "Yes. Damn."

"What do you mean?"

Olivia frowned. "We're so close to the HEA, I hate to leave."

Sydney looked bewildered. "HEA?"

"Oops, sorry. Happily Ever After. The required conclusion of any romance. You've *almost* accepted him. And he's *almost* accepted your premise. It's very frustrating. I want to hear the end."

Sydney cocked her head. "It will come. You know how it all comes out anyway."

"Yes." Olivia closed her eyes, a tiny smile dancing

across her lips. "But I love that glorious moment when they rush into each other's arms, speaking over each other, splattering each other with kisses and tears, giving—"

"Yes, yes, that will have to wait until tomorrow." Sydney gave her daughter a mischievous grin. "Perhaps we'll be able to discuss two…er…HEAs, no?"

Olivia picked up her purse. "Not a chance, Ma. See you tomorrow."

Sydney watched her daughter's car pull away from the curb, then called, "Alice! Where are you? We have to finish packing!"

****

"Well?"

Olivia set her coffee cup down. "Can't we start with your story?"

"You're dodging my question. I've been up all night stewing over what happened with you yesterday. I'm guessing from your bloodshot eyes and"—she checked her daughter's outfit—"that misbuttoned blouse, you didn't get home last night. Who were you with?"

"I don't need the third degree, Mother. I'll tell you. It isn't pretty though."

At Olivia's forlorn face, Sydney decided to relent. "What happened?"

Her daughter moved to the window and stared out at the magnolia. "I met Ben for coffee, expecting a cold conversation about Senator McNichol's plight and nothing more. Instead…Mother, he…he…Benjamin asked…he asked me…"

Sydney heroically restrained her fingers from snapping. "Asked you what?"

"To marry him." Olivia dropped heavily into the wing-backed chair.

Her mother froze, wild thoughts racing through her head. "I see." *Please oh please let her accept him.* She knew Benjamin was perfect for her daughter, if only she could be convinced. His upright, affectionate, loyal nature—manna to a parent—wouldn't do the trick, but she had caught him looking at Olivia now and then with fire in his eyes. Sydney sensed an ember in him, deliberately kept on a slow burn, but ready to ignite given the right match. Rémy de Beaumec, on the other hand—the handsome, debonair, rich, unpredictable Rémy—would only cause her grief. Sydney knew that instinctively, but did Olivia? "And your reply?"

It came out in a rush. "Oh, Mother, I don't know. He's never opened up like this before. He's always been so…so controlled. I never really knew what he was thinking. I felt shut out so often. Intellectually, I knew he loved me, but not emotionally. I…I almost didn't believe him."

"But he meant it?"

"Oh yes."

Sydney waited. It didn't seem necessary to articulate the question.

Olivia's lip quivered. "I started to say I would think about it, that I might reconsider, but before I had a chance to elaborate…I told you we were in the Bagel Bakery? Anyway, I saw Rémy standing on the sidewalk looking in…"

"Is this going to be a recurring theme? Because if so—"

Olivia didn't crack a smile. "He came rushing in and confronted Ben. It felt like a scene out of a Greek myth—Rémy as Zeus, the angry god, jealous of a mortal, spewing lightning bolts and tossing spears around."

"And Benjamin?"

"I dunno. Hercules maybe. You could see a vein throbbing in his neck—that always happens when he's furious. Otherwise, he sat very still under the onslaught."

Sydney took a moment to indulge in the stimulating picture of two bare-chested giants, muscles flexing, huge hairy feet stamping, the steam from their flaring nostrils swirling around them. "Wow."

Olivia didn't notice her mother's heightened color. "I was mortified."

"Really?"

The young woman started at the astonishment in her mother's voice. "Of course I was. Two men acting positively medieval over me? In public? What would you have done?"

Sydney shook her head. "Oh, I don't know. Stuck a rose between my teeth? Lounged on the piano while my swains sparred for my hand? Tossed a token at the suitor of choice?"

"Oh, for heaven's sake, Mother. I asked them both to leave before the management had to."

"And then what happened?"

"They left."

"And?"

A tear welled up in Olivia's eye. She brushed it away irritably. "Benjamin walked away. Rémy came back."

Shit. "So you made your choice?"

"Yes, Mother. I'm leaving with Rémy tomorrow."

Sydney returned to the couch. She took a taste of her coffee and grimaced. "Cold. Alice!"

The old retainer appeared.

"Could we have some fresh coffee?"

Alice looked from one woman to the other. "I see it's resolved."

"Yes, Alice. Coffee, Alice."

She left, shaking her head. Sydney heard her mutter, "She'll regret it. She'll regret it."

My own little Professor Higgins.

Olivia pulled her notebook out. "So, you said 'penultimate battle' before you left for Paris—that implies you two have one more hurdle to jump before nirvana."

"Did I?" Sydney's tone was innocent.

"Mother, no more games. Let's hear it." Olivia's tone brooked no discussion.

****

Paris, 1987

"Mama, Mr. Khouri is here in Pawis? How did he get here? Did he take a pwane too?"

"Yes, he did."

"What does he want? Why do we have to wait for him? I wanna go wif Alice to the tower."

"Quiet, Olivia. Mr. Khouri says he has something to tell you. You'll just have to wait."

"When will he be here?"

"Any minute. Now shush."

The hotel phone buzzed. Sydney answered it. "Yes, please send him up."

Mother and child perched together on the edge of the settee. Alice stuck her head around the bedroom door. "When can I take Olivia out?"

"Soon. Mr. Khouri said he had some news."

The nanny faded back into the bedroom.

Sydney answered the knock.

Elian wore a well-cut suit and a rich teal tie that matched his eyes. He stood stiffly and held out a slightly damp hand to Sydney. "Er, good morning."

She took the hand, held it, and gazed into his eyes. "Good morning."

He looked over at Olivia. "Good morning, Olivia."

She bounced on the sofa. "Hi."

"Um. Olivia? I'm...um..." He turned to Sydney, his forehead creased and lips open as though he needed extra oxygen. "Help me out here?"

Sydney took pity. "Olivia, Mr. Khouri and I have decided to get married. He'll be your new father. Does that make you happy?"

"Oh, yes!" Olivia ran to them and hugged them both. "It's grand." She did a little pirouette but stopped suddenly. "Mama, does that mean my old daddy is staying with the chimpanzees forever?"

Sydney put a hand to her mouth as both child and man stared at her. "Chimp—er...yes. Yes, it does. So everyone will be happy." She blinked at Elian.

The news seemed to satisfy Olivia. "Now can I go wif Alice?" She put her tiny hands on her hips. "She's taking me to da Eyeful Tower."

Elian dragged his dumbfounded gaze from Sydney and knelt down before Olivia. "That's nice, but first there's something I need to clarify."

"What's that?" Sydney sat back down, hand over her stomach to calm the butterflies.

"Olivia, I very much want to marry your mother, but first I have a confession to make. I'm not Mr.

Khouri, and I won't be your new father."

Déjà vu all over again. Damn, damn, damn.

"My name is Elian Davies. And Olivia, I'm your old father. I mean, your real father. I mean…"

****

Olivia safely gone, the chimpanzee story having been successfully dealt with, and squeals of delight still echoing in the room, Elian sat on the couch, cowering before Sydney.

Hands on hips in imitation of her daughter, she glared at him. "You knew. Last night. You made me think…you made me concede…" With her newfound happiness constantly interrupting the flow of anger, she had to find something to keep up her side of the argument. *Aha.* "You let me lie to my daughter."

Elian peeked at her. "In my defense, Olivia dropped the chimpanzee thing on me before I had a chance to deliver my entire speech. How was I to know you'd concocted possibly the strangest reason for a father's absence I've ever heard?"

"*Hmmph.*" That being all Sydney could muster by way of explanation, she moved on. "When did it come back to you?"

Elian ignored her and continued to grumble. "And now I'm going to have to come up with bedtime stories about my life with—what was Tarzan's ape friend's name? Cheetah?"

"Elian…"

"Okay, okay. It didn't really hit me until the day you left for Paris. I'd never taken your assertion seriously, but I couldn't stand the thought of losing you, so I decided to take a leap of faith. I called the *News-Register* and did some other digging. I pulled up some old newsreels. The resemblance, together with what I recalled of the events in Beirut, couldn't be denied."

"Why didn't you do that before?"

"I don't...know. Sydney, I was comfortable in my new persona. The whole affair in Beirut had been so unsettling, so terrifying. You've no idea what it's like not to know who you are—"

"It's worse knowing the man you love is wandering the streets and you can't help him."

He shook his head. "I'd make it up to you if I could. All those years wondering if I was alive. I guess I'm lucky I didn't know you existed. At any rate, I think I'd buried the doubts about my identity so deeply I couldn't easily resurrect them."

"And didn't want to. I do understand." She touched his cheek. "Then I came along and your carefully constructed world began to disintegrate. Did it...did it hit you like a bolt of lightning?"

"More like being run over by a train. That night, I fell asleep at a table littered with pictures and notes. When I woke up my cheek was stuck to a photograph. I recognized Peter and Ivana's house in Tehran. And there you stood, next to me. Glaring at me, actually. It all came back." He peered at her, his lips curving in a tentative smile. "Everything—even the bad parts. Sydney, I owe you an apology. Several, in fact."

Sydney didn't see any reason to waste time on past sins. She put a hand to either side of his face and bent down.

He began to draw back, alarm in his eyes, until she licked his nose. "You're not...you're not pissed?"

She sat on his lap. After a long, satisfying kiss she snuggled under his arm. "You remember the good parts too, I take it?"

He tickled her chin and let his hand drop to her breast, cupping it. "Oh, yes."

"Why didn't you tell me last night then?"

"You didn't give me a chance. Besides, I figured if you were willing to marry me whatever name I used, why argue?"

After that, actions spoke louder than words.

Chapter Sixteen

Alexandria, Present Day

"That is *so* romantic, Mother." Olivia's voice cracked a little.

"Yes, terribly. Boy, was I glad Alice had taken you off for the day."

"Thanks a lot." Olivia closed the notebook and turned off the recorder. "I think that's the best way to end it, don't you? No long-winded description of the ceremony and honeymoon."

Sydney grimaced. "We didn't have much of either. A quick trip to the magistrate, champagne, and our first night of nuptial bliss with you sleeping between us. I had to work the next day, and Elian had to fly back to his new job. It went downhill from there."

"At least you were in Paris." Olivia rose. "Now, you need to get some sleep. You have a big day tomorrow."

"So do you. I wish we could go the airport together."

"I thought we'd be able to, but I have some errands to do before I head out to Dulles. We'll see you in Paris anyway."

Sydney sighed. "Yes, dear. It will be fun, won't it? Do get a nap this afternoon, my dear."

"I'll try, Mother. You have everything you need for

the plane, right?"

"Mints, embroidery…" Sydney grinned mischievously. "Whiskey miniatures."

Olivia rolled her eyes. "Just don't get caught."

Sydney listened to her steps on the stairs. She gave a little sigh and turned back the covers on her bed. *I wish…well, that's neither here nor there.* As she went to the bedroom door to close it, she heard Olivia's voice below.

"Thank you, Ben. Yes, Ben. I understand."

Sydney stuck her head out, but Benjamin spoke too softly for her to hear. Olivia said, "It couldn't be helped. You had to leave. I do understand, really." More whispers. "Enough. I've given you my answer. There's no more to be said. Goodbye, Benjamin. I…I wish you all the best."

The front door closed quietly. A minute later, it opened again. She hopped to the window in time to see Olivia get in her car. Down the block, half hidden by an enormous azalea, stood Benjamin. He watched the car out of sight, then turned on his heel and strode away.

****

"Passport? Driver's license? Lipstick? I know you don't need any tickets. Would you like Pickens to take you to the airport?"

"No, I told you—I've some shopping to do. I'll take a taxi—I don't have to be at the airport as early as you do."

Sydney inspected her daughter with a critical air. "I like that suit. The color intensifies your eyes."

"And it's so slimming." Olivia laughed. "I think I look very chic."

"Yes. But."

"But what?"

Sydney took her daughter's hand and squeezed it. "Are you sure you're doing the right thing?"

Olivia shook her off. "We've been over this. I sent Ben away. I think he was relieved. I really do."

Sydney recollected a man standing, shoulders slumped, as Olivia drove off the day before. "I'm not so sure." She picked up a small enamel box that lay on her bureau and opened it. "Here, I want you to have this." She held out a thin gold chain. A small teardrop pearl hung from it.

"What is it?"

"It's the first gift your father gave me. He bought it in the bazaar in Tangier. I want you to have it."

Olivia's voice broke. "Oh, Mother."

Sydney put it around her daughter's neck and closed the catch. "Olivia, true love is not to be discarded lightly. You could find yourself regretting your decision years from now."

"I know, every night in the shower for the rest of my life, wondering where he was and what he was doing. But that was you, not me. I know what I'm doing."

"Do you? How well do you really know Rémy?"

Olivia sat down and put her head in her hands. "I had a dream last night, Mother. A vivid dream. In it, I was a minor goddess, a daughter of Thor. As the day dawned, I found myself astride a gray donkey, climbing a mountain. When we reached the peak, my mount turned into a beautiful white unicorn. On his back, I rose in the air, but a few yards up, the unicorn turned back into an ass and we both fell to earth. We tried again. And again. Each time we only made it up a little way before the magic died and we found ourselves on rock hard earth again, the unicorn once again a plain old donkey." She gazed at her mother. "You always remember your dreams. This is the first time I have. What does it mean, Mother?"

Sydney made her voice clear and firm. "Olivia, you want Rémy to be a unicorn. You want him to be your hero, your lover, your companion through all life's tribulations. But no matter how much you try, Olivia, he will always and only be an ass."

****

Boeing 787 Dreamliner

Sydney put down the newspaper and checked her watch again. *We should be boarding by now. I wonder what the holdup is.* The intercom erupted over her head. "Attention, passengers on Air France flight 2345 to Paris. Flight 0033 from Chicago with passengers connecting to flight 2345 was delayed due to weather. It will be arriving shortly. Thank you for your patience. We shall begin boarding as soon as possible."

That explains it. She settled back on the hard, curved chair and wondered for the thousandth time why airports couldn't provide padded seats. She wiggled a little until she noticed an old man ogling her. *I might as well get up and walk a bit.* After all, she'd be sitting soon enough. She wandered over to the big plate-glass windows that looked out on the tarmac. Huge jets moved like dancers in a chorus line, weaving in and out of lanes and sidling up to gates, while tiny trucks and even tinier people buzzed around them, prodding them along. From where she stood, she could see the general aviation terminal. With a start, she realized Rémy's jet sat at the first gate.

As she watched, Rémy appeared at the open hatch and waved. Olivia, her arms full of packages, walked toward the plane. Suddenly, Rémy's hand fell to his side, and his body went rigid. He took a step down, then stopped. Sydney's eyes swiveled to her daughter. Olivia still advanced toward the plane, but Rémy wasn't looking at her. Sydney followed his gaze. A tall, thin man in jeans and sweatshirt ran toward her daughter. *Benjamin.* Rémy yelled something, but Sydney couldn't hear through the glass. Olivia halted and slowly turned. She dropped her packages on the tarmac and waited for her pursuer. Sydney held her breath.

Benjamin slowed and held his arms out. Sydney saw his mouth open and his lips move.

For the fond mother, waiting, hoping, time froze. Memories passed dimly—of Elian, of Olivia as a child, of the places she'd been, the wars she'd lived through. She knew that though her own story was in its final chapters, Olivia's was about to begin. She prayed silently.

Someone clicked the resume button. She saw Olivia nod, and in one swift movement, Benjamin took her in his arms. As they kissed, Sydney thought of Casablanca, a doomed triangle of lovers, a plane whirring in the background. *By rights it should be foggy.* She shook herself. She could almost hear Elian grouse, "Must you always be so irreverent?"

Poor Rémy. He raised one arm, then dropped it. Stiffly, he pivoted and disappeared into the airplane. The hatch closed behind him. Olivia and Benjamin, oblivious to the baggage carts and mechanics and marshals around them, stuck fast to each other.

"Attention, passengers en route to Paris on Air

France flight 2345, we are now boarding first class. First class only, please." Sydney gave her pass to the attendant and walked down the ramp. The stewardess greeted her.

"We have a full flight, ma'am. May I get you a cocktail while the other passengers board?"

"Yes, please. Champagne, I think. I'm celebrating."

"Oh?" The stewardess raised her eyebrows.

"I want to offer a toast to the winding path of true love as it finally fetches up at the little cottage in the glade."

The stewardess took her speech in stride and went off to the galley.

Sydney had just accepted the glass when a shock of chestnut hair accompanied by a pair of sky blue eyes filled her vision. "Made it."

"I would have gone without you, you know."

Elian kissed her forehead and sat down. "I know. That's why I bribed the pilot to hold the plane up."

Sydney patted her husband's hand. "Tell me you didn't forget your suit. Father Lapierre said he wouldn't perform the ceremony unless you wore a suit."

"Damned Episcopalians."

"Yes, dear. May I remind you that it was you who insisted we renew our vows before we could get to the good stuff."

"You mean our second honeymoon?"

"Second? I don't recall having a first."

"It was in that bunker…or was it the ammo shed? No! I think that lovely night we spent in the Paris sewer."

"Ah, salad days. Are you sorry we've retired from

the news business?"

Elian pulled up the chair divider and pulled his bride to him. "I only kept at it to please you."

"Bullshit. You would never have let go as long as I still had a job. Always looking to scoop me, even when we worked together."

They sat in companionable silence while the plane taxied. Sydney sipped her champagne. "Oh, by the way, Benjamin came to the airport."

"So it's finally settled?"

"Yes."

"About time. Silly girl."

"Takes after you."

"She does, doesn't she?"

Sydney cuffed him. "Yes, she always has to have the snot kicked out of her before she understands I'm right."

"Yes, Sydney. I love you, Sydney."

"I love you too, George."

A word about the author…

Although M. S. Spencer has lived or traveled in five of the seven continents, the last thirty years were spent in Washington, D.C., as a librarian, Congressional staff assistant, speechwriter, editor, birdwatcher, kayaker, policy wonk, non-profit director, and parent. She holds a bachelor's degree from Vassar College, a diploma in Arabic Studies from the American University in Cairo, and Masters in Anthropology and in Library Science from the University of Chicago.

In a mad attempt to escape academia, she worked for the U.S. Senate, the U.S. Department of the Interior, in both public and academic library systems, and at the Torpedo Factory Art Center in Alexandria, Virginia. All of this tends to insinuate itself into her works.

Ms. Spencer has two fabulous grown children and one incredible granddaughter. She currently divides her time between the Gulf coast of Florida and a tiny village in Maine.

http://mssspencertalespinner.blogspot.com
https://www.facebook.com/msspencerromance
www.twitter.com/msspencerauthor

~*~

Other M. S. Spencer titles
available from The Wild Rose Press, Inc.:
ARTFUL DODGING: The Torpedo Factory Murders
THE MASON'S MARK: Love and Death in the Tower
WHIRLWIND ROMANCE
THE PENHALLOW TRAIN INCIDENT

Thank you for purchasing
this publication of The Wild Rose Press, Inc.

If you enjoyed the story, we would appreciate your
letting others know by leaving a review.

For other wonderful stories,
please visit our on-line bookstore at
www.thewildrosepress.com.

For questions or more information
contact us at
info@thewildrosepress.com.

The Wild Rose Press, Inc.
www.thewildrosepress.com

Stay current with The Wild Rose Press, Inc.

Like us on Facebook

https://www.facebook.com/TheWildRosePress

And Follow us on Twitter
https://twitter.com/WildRosePress